# HARD FLIGHT

"If you cooperate, there might be a chance to survive. Or a bullet in the head from my friend finishes it for you here and now," Encizo told the captured pilot in Spanish.

McCarter caught the drift of the Cuban's speech. He added emphasis to the threat by pulling out his handgun, easing off the safety and edging to the side, so he was partially behind the pilot. He locked back the hammer, close enough to the man so that he couldn't fail to hear the metallic sound.

"I will take you to where you want to go," the pilot croaked.

McCarter kept the gun in plain sight. "Don't try anything stupid," he warned. "I'd as soon kill you now as later. Makes no bloody difference to me. If I figure out you're taking us into a trap, I'll spill your brains all over the canopy of this chopper and fly the damn thing myself."

He pushed the pilot toward the aircraft's hatch, the muzzle of the Beretta wedged snugly against the man's spine.

D0888199

*Other titles in this series:*

DON PENDLETON'S
# MACK BOLAN.

# STONY MAN

## FLASHBACK

A GOLD EAGLE BOOK FROM
# WORLDWIDE.

TORONTO • NEW YORK • LONDON
AMSTERDAM • PARIS • SYDNEY • HAMBURG
STOCKHOLM • ATHENS • TOKYO • MILAN
MADRID • WARSAW • BUDAPEST • AUCKLAND

First edition January 1997

ISBN 0-373-61910-3

Special thanks and acknowledgment to
Michael Linaker for his contribution to this work.

FLASHBACK

# FLASHBACK

# PROLOGUE

*Puerto Rico*

Twenty minutes after eating breakfast that morning, Paul Chavez had to kill a man.

It happened quickly, in the living room of the apartment Chavez had been renting. How the guy had got in without him hearing, he never found out. It was enough that the man emerged from the shadows, a thin wire garrote in his hands.

Chavez faced a simple choice: the stranger died or Chavez did. The decision wasn't hard to make. He knew why the man had come for him and what he had to do.

He fought off the silent stranger's attack with surprising ease. The training he had gone through at Quantico had armed him with the necessary skills to not only block his adversary's attack, but to deliver a killing blow that stopped the man in his tracks, dead before he collapsed on the floor of the apartment.

In the silence that followed, Chavez checked out the corridor. Empty. Returning to his apartment, he quickly finished the packing he had started earlier, locked the door behind him and made his way to the underground parking garage. He located his rental car, unlocked the driver's door and, after dumping his carryall on the rear seat, slid behind the wheel.

The incident had only served to strengthen his resolve to leave Puerto Rico on the flight he'd booked the previous night. The fact that someone had been sent to kill him made Chavez realize that leaving the island was the wisest thing he could do. He had information that needed to be passed on to his mainland FBI field contact. Staying on the island any longer than necessary would only invite further attempts on his life, and there was no guarantee he would survive the next one.

He cruised out of the underground lot and swung the car along the highway, heading for Isla Verde Airport. His flight would depart in just under an hour, which left plenty of time for him to check in. He considered telephoning his mainland contact, but immediately dismissed the idea. Chavez couldn't risk the chance of anyone listening in. The situation he was in had tinged his thoughts with paranoia, and he was starting to see conspiracy all around him. After the attack in the apartment, he knew he wasn't paranoid after all.

He reached the airport without incident, parked in one of the public lots and headed for the terminal building, where he checked in and went to wait for his boarding call.

Minutes later he was following the other passengers who were on his flight along the walkway. An attractive young flight attendant ushered him on board and guided him to his seat. Chavez stowed his bag and sank into the window seat. He clipped his seat belt in place and leaned back, eyes closed, ignoring the general noise around him as the plane filled up.

He asked for a double whiskey when the attendant rolled the drinks cart down the aisle. The fiery liquid, as always, made him drowsy. Chavez levered the seat back and drifted into a restless sleep, roused only as the plane began its descent to Fort Lauderdale.

In the terminal building, he headed for a pay phone and called his contact, whom he arranged to meet in Miami. After completing the call, he went to the nearest car-rental desk and rented a vehicle. Twenty minutes later Chavez took delivery of a three-month-old Chevrolet, placed his bag on the rear seat and drove away from the airport.

If the man hadn't been so preoccupied with the earlier attack on his life, he might have noticed the dark blue Dodge that pulled into the stream of traffic three cars behind him. It remained at a discreet distance, unobtrusively tailing him.

When Chavez coasted to the curb across the street from a downtown bus station, the driver of the Dodge and his passenger followed him.

Chavez entered the bus station and made his way through to a line of telephone booths, where he met his FBI contact.

They had barely managed to exchange more than a few words when the two men from the Dodge appeared.

Taking advantage of the moment, one of the men unleathered a suppressed automatic pistol and emptied the 13-round magazine into Chavez and his contact man. He turned and walked calmly out of the bus station, followed by his comrade. They returned to the Dodge and drove away without being challenged.

Because of repeated vandalism to the telephones, the phone company, in cooperation with the bus-station management, had installed two well-concealed video cameras. The cameras were on day and night, scanning the alcove and making permanent video recordings of everything that occurred there.

The cameras recorded Chavez meeting his contact, and their cold-blooded murders. The recordings were checked by the local police as soon as the bodies had been discovered. By midmorning of the following day, a copy of the tape reached the desk of Hal Brognola. With it was a handwritten note from the one man who could always be relied on to make the big Fed sit up and take notice.

When this man sent a note asking for his presence at a meet, Brognola knew that big trouble was brewing.

# CHAPTER ONE

*War Room, Stony Man Farm*

The War Room buzzed with conversation. The Stony Man combat teams sat around the large conference table, exchanging information and catching up with recent events. Also present was Barbara Price, Stony Man's mission controller. A couple of seats away, Jack Grimaldi, the Farm's resident pilot, sat in deep conversation with Carmen Delahunt, the red-haired member of Aaron "the Bear" Kurtzman's cybernetics team. Ex-FBI, Delahunt possessed a quick, decisive brain and the ability to act coolly under stress. Kurtzman himself was pushing his wheelchair across the floor in the direction of the steaming pot of coffee that had been set up on a small table against one wall. He reached the table just ahead of T. J. Hawkins, Phoenix Force's most recent recruit. The youngest of the Phoenix warriors, "Hawk" was already proving himself to be an asset. His combat experience in the Rangers and Delta Force was a welcomed addition to a team that could boast of an impressive array of experience. British-born McCarter with his SAS training, which had a fearsome reputation. Then Calvin James and his SEALs background, as well as training as hospital corpsman, had been a long-time valuable asset, as was Canadian-born Manning and his GSG-Nine antiterrorist activities.

The elevator door slid open to admit Hal Brognola and Yakov Katzenelenbogen. The Israeli, formerly the leader of Phoenix Force, had retired from active duty to take up a position as Brognola's tactical adviser. The long years he had spent under combat conditions, having to make split-second decisions, committing his men to life-or-death situations, had made him the ideal candidate for such a position in the Stony Man command structure.

Crossing the War Room with a stack of files in hand, Brognola took his place at the table. Dropping the mass of files on the table in front of him, the big Fed glanced around. The only face missing from the assembly was Mack Bolan's. There was a good reason for that. The Executioner already had his part of the upcoming mission under way.

"Okay, people, let's get to it," Brognola said, nodding toward Kurtzman.

Swinging his chair around, Kurtzman aimed a remote-control unit at the wall behind Brognola. A panel slid back, exposing a bank of TV monitors. Fingering the keypad, Kurtzman activated the video displays.

"All yours," he announced.

The closest screen to Brognola's position showed a silent, black-and-white image. From the camera angle it was obvious that the tape was a replay from a security setup. It showed a square area with a half-dozen pay phones fixed to one wall. The area was deserted at the commencement of the tape, then a man walked into the picture, and stood at the far end of the area, obviously waiting for someone.

"This has been edited," Brognola said as the picture jumped.

A second man walked into view, holding a carryall in his left hand. He went up to the waiting man and took his hand. They exchanged a few words, then turned to go. At that moment two other men stepped into view. One pulled a suppressed auto-pistol from under his jacket and emptied the entire magazine into the first pair. The moment their bodies hit the floor, the assassin turned away from them, pushing the pistol into the hand of his companion. This one concealed the weapon under his coat before he followed the killer. They started to walk out of the picture, and as they turned, looking in the direction of the security camera, the picture froze.

"That happened the day before yesterday," Brognola explained. "The hit man and his partner weren't aware of the security camera. It had been installed only a few days earlier, due to constant vandalism to the pay phones."

"It didn't help those poor guys much," Price commented. She had seen the tape earlier, but the second time around the cold-blooded murders still had the power to shock.

"The first man in the picture was Alan Moreland. He was FBI, the section chief for the guy who came to meet him. He was Paul Chavez, also FBI. He'd just stepped off a plane from Puerto Rico, where he'd been working undercover for the last seven months. Apparently he phoned Moreland as soon as his flight touched down, asking for a face-to-face. He wouldn't say what it was about, just that it was urgent. Moreland drove out to meet him at the arranged spot, but it appears the location wasn't as secure as they imagined."

"We got a tag on the hit team?" asked Carl "Ironman" Lyons, the Able Team leader.

"Yeah." Brognola nodded at Kurtzman, and the image on-screen changed to a close-up of the killer and partner.

"The backup man is Jose Cammera," Kurtzman explained. "Cuban exile. He's been in the U.S.A. for almost three years. As far as we know, he's never been in trouble with the law. Runs a car-body shop in Little Havana, Miami. The local cops are certain he's in the stolen-car business. He's also suspected of being involved in dealing in illegal weapons, but they've never been able to pin anything on him."

"I'd say he's stepped in it this time," Katz observed.

Kurtzman indicated the second man. "Our shooter is Raul Fuentes. Cuban national. Also G-2, Cuban secret police. But that wasn't his name when he took the same flight from Puerto Rico as Chavez. He booked the flight as Michael Vasquez, U.S. citizen, with an address in Miami. We have to assume he was picked up at the airport and given the gun by Cammera."

The face staring out across the War Room showed a man in his early forties. Fuentes was hard-looking, with eyes that seemed to burn with menace even in a frozen image.

David McCarter, the Phoenix Force leader, leaned forward, studying the face on the screen. "I suppose the logical question is, what's the tie between Fuentes and an undercover FBI agent working Puerto Rico?"

"Chavez had been playing it solo," Carmen Delahunt said, "getting himself accepted as a member of the Puerto Rico Independent Separatist Movement—PRISM—a radical group of dissenters on the island. The leader is a man called Jesus Salazar. These guys are hard-liners, extremists, and have been causing trouble for some time now. They're anti-U.S. in a big way. Again, though the local cops and the FBI have their suspicions, nothing has come up concrete on these people. I've got a file here that gives details on the group.''

"Going back to David's question," Brognola interjected, "I'd like to know myself how the Cuban secret police manages to tie in with a group like PRISM.''

"It could be that Cuba's interested in their politics," Katz suggested. "Let's face it, Hal, Castro has always disliked U.S. influence in Puerto Rico. He feels the island should be free from American domination and the taint of the big buck. That's no secret. Maybe he's funding the movement. It wouldn't be the first time he's tried something along those lines. The way things are going for him at home, Castro needs something to focus Cuba's attention away from domestic problems.''

Brognola chewed over the suggestion, finally shaking his head. "My feeling is there's something more to it. We've been getting reports of something in the wind from our source in Cuba. General unrest among the anti-Castro movements. Nothing solid. More like gut feelings. It could tie in to this Puerto Rico incident.''

"We'll keep digging," Kurtzman said. "It's early days yet.''

"Early days have a habit of overtaking you," Brognola replied. "I want round-the-clock input on this. The President hinted at the same when we talked, and he gave me the word. So give it your best shot and then some."

There was a hesitant silence before Katz spoke. "You holding something back, Hal?"

"More gut feelings."

"And what is it telling you?"

"That we could have something bad brewing in the Caribbean."

From where he sat across the War Room table, Katz could see the expression in Brognola's eyes. The Israeli, still adjusting to his new position within the Stony Man setup, hadn't lost the intuition that had stood him in good stead during his hectic years commanding Phoenix Force. Katz had always been a good judge of mood, and right now Hal Brognola was worried.

"Tell me about it, Hal," Katz said quietly. "What is it that you already know that's bothering you?"

Brognola pulled a cigar from his shirt pocket. He stripped off the wrapper and tucked the unlit cigar between his teeth. He glanced around the table, aware that every pair of eyes in the War Room was on him.

"When I talked with the President, he made it clear he wanted Stony Man on this and no one else. A few weeks ago Chavez submitted information that something was brewing on Puerto Rico that could have direct implications for the U.S. He'd picked up rumblings within PRISM—anticipation, he called it—as if something were coming up. He reported he was going to try to get a line on what it was all about. He was still trying to find out who was backing PRISM. They've come up too fast. Almost out of nowhere. The organization has money, contacts and equipment. Chavez got that much through. But he couldn't be specific because he hadn't worked his way into the group far enough to be trusted with too much detail. He had to move slowly.''

"Any indication where the backing is coming from?'' asked Calvin James, the black Phoenix Force commando.

"The fact that the Cubans are in the frame is new to everyone,'' Brognola said. "We knew nothing about them until Chavez got taken out by Fuentes. It puts a new slant on the whole thing. Because if the Cubans are involved, they could be in bed with people from the U.S.''

"Did I miss something?'' Katz asked.

"The twister,'' Brognola said. "Chavez's earlier reports, as vague as they were, pointed the finger at the possibility of unidentified Americans involved with PRISM.''

"Unidentified?''

Brognola smiled. "Is this what I'm going to get now you're home based? Questions every time I make a statement?''

Katz smiled. "I can't assess the situation without all the information. If that means digging, then I'll dig."

"Why do you think he upset me all the bloody time?" McCarter said in his typically blunt manner. "That bloke caused me more stress than all the terrorists we ever faced. Why do you think I used to smoke so much?"

"You still do, David," Katz said with genuine warmth.

"Yes, but now I do it for fun," McCarter replied.

He nodded to Brognola. "Don't let him give you a hard time."

"I think I can handle him."

"Rather you than me. To tell the truth, life's a lot less stressful now we've dumped him."

Katz's laugh rang out across the table. A stranger would have thought the pair was at loggerheads. In truth, the bantering that existed between the two had been created out of the fires of combat.

"Okay, okay," Brognola said, smiling briefly, "let's get back to it. The President has handed this over to us. Because of the implications concerning possible U.S. involvement, he thinks that an independent agency should handle it. And that means Stony Man. The FBI wasn't happy about losing the assignment, but the Bureau's been compromised with the deaths of Chavez and Moreland."

Brognola tapped the thick files in front of him. "This is everything the Bureau had put together, and it's all we have to go on. But remember this. Chavez was a good agent. His strong point was that he was no scaremonger. His reporting of any given situation was analytical, factual, nonspeculative. The guy knew his job and played it straight every time."

"Any hint as to what Chavez was doing back on the mainland?" Lyons asked.

Brognola shook his head. "Feedback from the FBI didn't add much. Moreland got a call from Chavez asking for a meet. Straight and simple. No indication what it was about. Everyone figures Chavez must have come up with something hot. Aaron did some checking through the news agencies and picked up on a dead man found by a cleaner in an apartment in San Juan the day Chavez flew out. He did some further digging and came up with San Juan PD files on the incident."

Kurtzman detailed what he had learned.

"The dead man was Luis Montejo, a Puerto Rican national with attachments to PRISM, it turns out. Montejo was listed as being a borderline criminal, always on the edge of slipping over into full-time lawbreaking, and had a reputation as a wheeler-dealer. The connection is that the apartment was the one Chavez had been renting. Could be PRISM got suspicious of the man and sent

Montejo to deal with him. Only it looks like Chavez turned the tables. The attempt on his life must have been why he wanted out of Puerto Rico. It appears he'd booked his ticket the day before. Maybe he'd found something hot or figured he'd been tagged. If his cover had been blown, there was nowhere else for him to go. Chavez must have decided the only safe way to get his information to the Bureau was personally. He made his try but got intercepted before he could make his report."

Brognola pushed the stack of files toward Barbara Price. She took them and began to separate them into the order she needed, then stood and worked her way around the conference table, dropping folders in front of each team member.

"I've included everything relevant to the operation," she explained. "If you need anything else, just ask."

"Our orders are to look into this and find out just what's going on," Brognola said, then hesitated. "The mission brief is clear and simple. If the need arises when you assess the threat, you take out whoever is behind it. If our feelings are correct on this, the potential could be grim for the U.S. So don't take prisoners. Use whatever means you can to stop the opposition."

"Phoenix Force will take the Puerto Rican end," Price said. "See if you can pick up on what Chavez had unearthed. You'll have to work from whatever you can get out of the files, because we don't have anything else to give you. There are a couple of tentative leads Chavez detailed, but take it easy. The way this has gone, we don't know who works for whom."

"I wish we had more for you," Brognola said by way of apology. "This has come at us fast, and the general feeling is something could be scheduled to happen soon. So I can't give you more detail at the moment. If someone is prepared to gun down a couple of FBI agents in broad daylight, following on an earlier attempt on the life of one of them, then there has to be something heavy in the wind. We're going to throw everything we have into getting you more information. Until then, we go with what we have. Our main lead in Luis Montejo."

"This is the kind of mission I like," McCarter said. "Clear and concise, with nothing left to chance. You make things too easy for us, Hal."

Lyons dropped his file on the table. "I suppose our piece of the action is Fuentes and his pickup man, with a trip down to Miami thrown in as a bonus?"

Brognola nodded. "The security-tape information has been kept out of the news. The FBI jumped on that the minute they heard what had happened to their people. They didn't want Fuentes or Cammera dropping out of sight. As far as they know, the killing hasn't been linked to anyone at the moment. Just a simple murder story on TV. They won't be aware they've been IDed."

"One of the company planes will fly you down to Florida," Price stated. "Covers are being drawn up for you all. That includes Phoenix Force."

"Your paperwork will be ready for you when you leave," Brognola said.

"What about weapons?" Hawkins asked. "We aren't going to be able to walk into Puerto Rico carrying."

"That's been fixed," Price assured him. "When you arrive, there'll be a one-off meeting with an FBI agent in San Juan. He knows nothing about Chavez or his operation. That's how close the Bureau was playing it. He's under instructions to provide you with whatever you need, then forget he ever met you. It took personal intervention from the President to sanction this. The Feds weren't too happy, but they admit they can't establish another agent undercover in the short term. They've been told a special unit is going in. No need for them to know any more."

"I would have preferred to keep this all in the family," Brognola said. "We just don't have the time to do it any other way. So stay on your toes, all of you. We want you back under your own steam"

He leaned back in his seat, taking a final look around the table. "So, any questions?"

"Is Striker in on this?" Gary Manning asked.

Brognola glanced up, nodding in the Canadian's direction.

"He's already involved."

"Cuba?"

"Yeah. Cuba."

# CHAPTER TWO

*Earlier at Stony Man Farm, Virginia*

"Right now we don't know who might be involved," Brognola had explained, "so we have to be suspicious of everyone. This is going to be strictly Stony Man all the way, Striker. The only contact you'll have in Cuba is one of our deep-cover agents, a Cuban named Ricardo Contreras, and the possible assistance of an anti-Castro group Contreras has connections to."

Bolan's response was a simple, short nod. He had no need to question Brognola's decision. The big Fed accepted the limitations of his choices, sifted through the options and came up with the most workable. Whatever the Justice man suggested would be the most acceptable way of getting Bolan into Cuba.

"Jack will get you onto Cuban soil with a high-tech helicopter. Night insertion."

"I'll gear up," Bolan said. He rose and made his way to the door, pausing to look back over his shoulder. "Take a breather, Hal. You look like hell."

Brognola gave a hard laugh. "You know something, Striker, I feel like hell. But our games don't have time-out because the umpire needs a break. Thanks for the thought."

Bolan closed the door behind him, heading for his quarters, his mind already forging ahead. He was formulating his plans for when he touched down on Cuban soil. He would be going in without sanction, with no official seal of approval, because that was the only way this mission could proceed. His piece of the action could involve bracing a foreign government's secret police on the one side and a strictly unlawful group of dissidents on the other. The fact that the anti-Castro groups opposed the government didn't automatically make them allies of the United States. They might easily be against Bolan's presence as much as G-2. The big American would have to rely on whatever Contreras had to offer. He accepted the problem as he always did, aware that he was unable to alter the status quo. All he could do was go in and create his own path to walk, between the two sides.

In his quarters he stripped off and had a long, hot shower. Then he dressed in blacksuit and combat boots. This was going to be a strictly operational mission, since, there was no time for establishing civilian credentials. His Cuban visit wouldn't even be graced by the cover of someone on vacation or business. He was gearing up for war, and he equipped himself for the eventuality.

Bolan strapped on the shoulder rig that held the Beretta 93-R, clipped the belt in place for his Desert Eagle .44 Magnum and the sheathed, razor-sharp Ka-bar fighting knife. He checked his handguns and made sure both held full clips. Extras went into the pouches of the combat harness. A small backpack held other required items. His final weapon was a 9 mm Uzi subgun. Bolan stripped the weapon, checked it and reassembled it. He snapped in a 32-round magazine that had a second one taped to it for quick reloading. A spare twin magazine went into the backpack. He placed the readied gear on the bed.

The only other things he needed were details of his contact, meeting place and a roll of dollar bills. Hard cash could often buy a way out of tricky situations when words and promises failed. The human need for money often overrode the most honorable intentions as far as loyalty and honor were concerned.

*Cuba*

MACK BOLAN FOLLOWED Ricardo Contreras for almost an hour from the meeting point. The lean, dark Cuban, who had been working undercover for the United States for the past five years, had little to say on the journey. The bulk of his conversation had been during the initial meeting, when he and Bolan had exchanged passwords. Finally satisfied as to the Executioner's credentials, Contreras had raised a hand, beckoning him to follow. After that, silence reigned supreme.

As he followed the Cuban, the big American was able to study his surroundings, noting that the dark, deserted streets held the same air of bleak despair that was found in any big city's run-down areas. Few lights showed from dark windows. Many of the buildings were derelict, the doors open to the night air. These were the parts of the city the tourists never saw.

Within the next few minutes, Bolan noticed their surroundings changing as they moved deeper into the outskirts of Havana. The streets became cleaner, though still narrow and poorly lit. The houses looked better maintained, and lights threw pools of illumination to the ground. Music drifted across the night air.

Bolan's guide came to a stop, beckoning the tall American to his side and pointing to a house on the far side of a small square. Pink-tinged walls fronted the house, with greenery spilling over the top.

Moving quickly, Contreras led Bolan across the square and in through a narrow wrought-iron gate, which he closed and bolted behind him. He led the way across the flagged courtyard filled with lush plants and up a short flight of worn stone steps. Pushing open a door, the Cuban ushered Bolan inside, closing and locking the door.

"Sit down, Mike," Contreras said. Bolan had chosen to use his Mike Belasko alias for this mission.

The Executioner sank into a worn but comfortable armchair, unzipped his jacket and dropped the backpack he was carrying on the floor beside him. He glanced around the cluttered room. Shelves held rows of books and magazines, and more were stacked on the floor beside a large wooden desk that held a typewriter. Contreras used his talents as a writer of Cuban history as his cover. It enabled him a reasonable amount of freedom to move about the country, investigating things other than Cuba's past.

"Coffee?" Contreras asked.

Bolan nodded.

Turning toward the small kitchen adjoining the main room, the Cuban filled the battered metal percolator with water and spooned rich coffee grounds into the filter dish. He replaced the top and plugged the lead into the socket. He set out a pair of mugs in readiness. Glancing over his shoulder, he looked at the American, who seemed every inch a warrior. It had little to do with the black clothing under the blue windbreaker or the weapons he wore along with the combat harness. This Mike Belasko would have been just as menacing in a tuxedo. The man appeared to be relaxing, but Contreras could see the alert look in his eyes. They were never still, roving back and forth across the room, picking up every detail. If Contreras had been an enemy of this man, he would have been frightened.

"It'll take a few minutes," he said. "Talk to me."

Bolan leaned forward, holding Contreras's gaze. "What can you tell me about Raul Fuentes, his connection with Puerto Rico and a Cuban named Jose Cammera?"

"Hell, you don't waste time," Contreras said, grinning. He dropped into a seat across from Bolan. "Raul Fuentes is a lowlife. He heads a special detail in G-2. Most of their work is done in the shadows, and Fuentes doesn't take prisoners. You understand what I'm saying?"

"I get the picture," Bolan said. "Fuentes made a trip to the mainland the day before yesterday. He'd followed an FBI undercover agent from Puerto Rico. As soon as the agent met his contact, Fuentes shot them both dead. Security cameras recorded the whole thing, which is why we were able to identify Fuentes. The man who picked up Fuentes at the airport was also picked up on the camera. He was Jose Cammera."

"Can I ask what your FBI man was working on in Puerto Rico?"

"Infiltration of a group known as PRISM, the Puerto Rican Independent Separatist Movement. Bottom line is they want the U.S. out of Puerto Rico and out of their business. Someone's funding them, and it could be coming from here."

"And your FBI man got too close?"

"It looks that way. Whatever he found died with him."

Contreras thought for a moment, his eyes on some distant object on the far side of the room.

"Maybe it has some connection with the rumblings I've been picking up from the streets about G-2 coming down hard on anyone mouthing off about the government. That isn't unusual in itself, but the feeling is the authorities have more-important matters on their minds and don't want to be bothered with pest control, as they call it."

"So they're pushing hard to close everybody down?"

Contreras nodded.

"How about you?"

"As far as I know, I'm not on their list. If they knew why I was in Cuba, I believe they would have visited me a long time ago."

Bolan's look told Contreras that didn't always ensure safety. The Cuban gave a half-embarrassed smile.

"That was a stupid thing to say," he admitted. "Maybe I've been in place too long. Makes you complacent. For all I know, they might have had me spotted a long time ago, and they're letting me run so I can identify my own contacts for them.''

''Has your Intel given you any reason to think something might be going down?'' Bolan asked.

The Cuban nodded. ''Little bits and pieces from different sources. But they tie together in a loose way. My feeling is there's a deal of some kind going down. Can't put a finger on it yet, but it has all the signs of being big. It could link up with your information.''

''I was told you had some contact with one of the anti-Castro groups,'' Bolan said.

''A very small group,'' Contreras replied, ''but it comes up with interesting information. It's headed by a brother and sister. They work in media and government departments, so they have their ears to fairly reliable sources.''

Contreras pushed to his feet, heading back to the kitchen. ''Let me know what I can do for you. If you need pointing in any direction, I'll do what I can.''

He had barely reached the kitchen when there was a rapid tapping on the outer door.

Contreras turned, his face creased with concern.

Bolan slipped the Beretta from its holster.

The urgent knock sounded again.

''Do you often get visitors this late?'' Bolan asked.

"No!"

Bolan picked up his backpack and retreated to the far side of the room, out of range of the door.

"I'll cover you," he said.

Contreras approached the door.

From outside, a woman's voice reached them, speaking in Spanish.

"Linda Ramos," Contreras said over his shoulder. "She belongs to the anti-Castro group I just mentioned. She's a friend and can be trusted."

Contreras unfastened the door and pulled it open.

The young woman who rushed inside, turning immediately to Contreras as he secured the door, was of medium height, and even from the fragmented view Bolan received, he realized she was beautiful. Thick black hair brushed her slim shoulders. She wore a white shirt, open at the neck, and dark pants. Her large dark eyes were bright with fear as she clutched at Contreras's sleeve.

"They are looking for Manuel," she said, words tumbling over one another in her haste. "Ricardo, they will kill him if they find him!"

Contreras caught her arms, holding her still.

"Explain," he said in English.

She stared at him in puzzlement, then, sensing she and Contreras weren't alone, she turned her head and searched the room.

She saw the tall, black-clad figure on the far side of the room, a pistol in his hand.

"Who is he?" she demanded in clear English. "What have you done, Ricardo?"

"Calm down," Contreras said. "This man is on our side. Come to help."

Linda Ramos stared at Bolan.

"To help? Who has he come to help, Ricardo?"

"Your brother perhaps," Bolan said, stepping into the light. He lowered the Beretta, removing its threatening presence. "Could be he's running from the people I'm looking for."

Ramos gazed into his clear, unflinching eyes and was calmed by the expression she saw. The doubt flickering away at the back of her mind was soothed, not only by Bolan's look but also by his presence. Though she couldn't have explained it in so many words, there was something about this American that told her she could trust him.

"Then please help him," she begged. Her words began to falter, weariness edging her tone now.

"When did all this start?" Contreras asked gently.

"This morning. Manuel came to the apartment. He looked terrible, as if he had not slept for days. He was bruised about the face. His clothes dirty. And he had a gun!"

"Go on," Bolan encouraged.

"He told me that he and others in the group had found the information they had been looking for, information that would expose Castro and make the people realize what he was doing to our country. But he had been found out, and now the secret police were looking for him. He said they were also looking for the others in his group."

Contreras glanced across at Bolan.

"Did Manuel tell you what he had found out?" Bolan asked.

"Enough to make me realize everything he has been working for has been worth all the sacrifices. And that the government is about to embark on a foolish expedition that could destroy Cuba, an alliance with Puerto Rican rebels who want to stage a coup that would topple the Puerto Rican government and end American influence in the country. He was about to tell me more when someone tried to break in. They were shouting for Manuel to give himself up, to surrender. We got out of the apartment with moments to spare. All we could do was to run. Somehow we became separated. I wandered around all day, trying to think how I could help Manuel. When it became dark, I went back to the apartment. I didn't know what else to do. The telephone rang twice. I answered the second time because I thought it might be Manuel. It was."

"And?"

"He told me to come to you, Ricardo. He said you would help."

"Of course I will help."

"Did your brother tell you where he was?" Bolan asked.

"Yes." Ramos frowned. "But then there were strange sounds on the line, and Manuel was cut off."

"Someone had a tap on your line," Bolan said. "We'll have to move fast. If Manuel told you where he was, he also told the people looking for him."

"Linda, did you come in your car?"

"Yes, I parked at the rear of the building."

"Then you must take us to where Manuel is hiding. Now."

The crash of boots on the outside steps told them their time had run out. Voices yelled harsh commands.

Contreras stared at Bolan, his eyes asking the question.

Bolan didn't waste time on explanations. He snatched up his backpack and turned, signaling Contreras and Ramos with the Beretta.

"The back door!" Contreras said, pointing.

Ramos ran ahead, pushing through a beaded curtain.

Bolan, hard on her heels, heard wood splinter as the bolted door behind them was struck by something hard. A second crash, and the door sprang open. The room echoed with the harsh yelling of the invading force.

The savage chatter of multiple autoweapons drowned any other sound. A hail of slugs hammered the walls and furniture, filling the air with splinters of wood and plaster.

As he moved away from the intruders, Contreras was stitched from shoulder to hip by the blast. His bullet-riddled body fell awkwardly, bouncing off the edge of a table before he crashed to the floor, blood bursting from the numerous holes in his body. Someone fired a second burst into the back of his skull, blowing it open and destroying what was left of his life in a moment of white-hot pain.

Bolan saw the man's cruel demise out the corner of one eye as he moved in behind Ramos, shielding her with his own body.

The woman snatched at the latch of the rear door, freed it and pulled it open.

Bolan reached her and grabbed her shoulder, pulling her away from the opening just as a slug tore a large chunk of wood from the frame.

Ramos gave a startled cry and stumbled to her knees.

Bolan stepped beside her, the Beretta searching the way ahead. He dropped to a crouch, glancing down the steep flight of stone steps that led to the narrow alley backing the rear of the building. A shadowy figure sprang for the steps. The Executioner tracked in and loosed a triburst, catching the man in the chest. He fell back with a shocked grunt.

"Move!" Bolan snapped.

Ramos ran down the steps, the soldier close behind. She reached the bottom moments before he did, feeling his bulk brush her aside. He peered along the alley and saw another dark outline as the first man's partner moved in to back him.

Bolan didn't waste time. He raised the 93-R and triggered a burst. The backup man spun along the wall, his dying cry lost in the crash as he collided with an overfilled trash can, taking it down with him.

"My car is this way," Ramos gasped.

Bolan followed her, conscious of the close pursuit coming up behind.

She reached the parked car, a sixties Oldsmobile, and yanked open the driver's door. As she tumbled inside, Bolan turned to fire a volley at the first armed figures who reached the bottom of the steps. His second burst dropped one man, pushing the others back under cover, their bravado deserting them for a moment. In those few precious seconds, Bolan piled into the car on the passenger side as the engine roared into life.

"Where is Ricardo?" she asked, eyes wide with alarm.

"He didn't make it," Bolan told her. "Now get us out of here. Fast!"

Ramos jammed her foot on the gas pedal, sending the big car lurching forward. At the far end of the alley, she swung the wheel, taking the car onto the street in a cloud of burning rubber. The soft springs on the vehicle threatened to take it out of control, but the woman demonstrated her skill by keeping it on track. She swept around another corner and took them along the semideserted street at ever-increasing speed.

"Is he dead?" Ramos asked.

"Yeah," Bolan said without looking up as he reloaded the Beretta. "There's nothing we could have done for him."

"He would be alive if I had not come. But I had to. Manuel is my brother."

"Is that supposed to make me feel better?" Bolan asked.

He caught the flash of defiance in the young woman's dark eyes. She faced him squarely, refusing to back away from his hard stare.

"Watch the road," he said.

She glared out the windshield, driving hard but not forgetting what she wanted to say. "Do you believe I am leading you into a trap?"

"It's happened before. A pretty girl, a sad story. Men have died for less."

"You do not know about my brother?"

"No."

"Then you will not know about our family, how they died because of their opposition to the regime. Hunted by the agents of the secret service until they were dead. It was only through the dedication of people who knew my parents that Manuel and I survived. We were only children then, barely able to understand. But we learned as we grew up. We took new names and rebuilt our lives, determined to fight against the people who rule our country."

"How does that make a difference here and now?"

"Only to show that we are both against the regime. It can only make a difference if Manuel stays alive to tell his story, to show to the people that this adventure will only bring more suffering to Cuba. If Cuban forces invade Puerto Rico, we all know what America will do. First Puerto Rico, then Cuba. America will devour us all."

"Don't make the States the bad guy in this," Bolan said. "The only reason we'd get involved would be if someone did make a move against Puerto Rico. We couldn't ignore that."

"I understand. So it is important that you reach Manuel and bring him to safety. Somewhere he can tell his story. But it will not be easy. The man who is leading the hunt for Manuel, Colonel Lopez, has his people everywhere. He is known to be generous to anyone who gives him information. His spies will be scouring the streets looking for Manuel and the rest of our group—and you, if they learn of your presence.''

Bolan knew she was right. The man known as Colonel Lopez would do his best to locate and capture an American loose on the streets of Havana. Capturing an American agent would be a big coup for him. The political propaganda would be a bonus.

The thought only reinforced Bolan's resolve not to allow that to happen. His priority was to complete his mission and get out of Cuba without being captured or allowing the United States to be compromised. He didn't fool himself into believing it would be easy. Bucking the odds always became a game of push and shove. Too far either way, and the numbers would fall with such rapidity that situations got out of control.

''How quickly can you get me to him?'' he asked.

''He is hiding out in an abandoned apartment building on the other side of the city. It will take about an hour to reach it. We will have to go by the back streets.''

''Take me as near as is safe for you, then go. Get far away and leave me to deal with whatever I find.''

''You will bring Manuel out safely?''

"I'll do my best. That's all I can promise."

She considered his reply for a moment, then nodded. "On one condition. I will not leave you. If you bring Manual out, you will need transport. I know the city. How to get through and how to travel outside it. Do not expect me to stand by and allow you to risk your life and not help. I will not. I do not fool myself. We are in a war here in Cuba. Being a woman does not excuse me from that war."

Bolan couldn't argue that point. She was right. It was a war, and it was hers. And so was the country.

"You have yourself a deal, Linda Ramos."

"And what do I call you?"

"Mike Belasko."

She concentrated on driving for a while, guiding the car along near-empty streets with the expertise of someone who knew the city well.

The night cloaked their movements. In the near distance the lights of the city proper threw a soft haze into the sky. The streets that they traveled now were dark for the most part. There was little in the way of public lighting, and only scattered light showed from the buildings they passed. The sidewalks were thinly populated. Here and there they passed groups of young men huddled together. The occasional dog ran out to challenge the passing car, then slunk back into the gloom.

Slums were the same wherever you went, Bolan thought. Poverty and deprivation had the same look the world over. The hungry and the desperate were a global fraternity.

A number of times Ramos pulled the Olds to the side of the street, turning into dark alleys, waiting until a prowling car or military jeep passed by. She seemed to have an awareness of their presence. Bolan began to have a growing respect for the woman's skills. She certainly had courage, though she concealed it beneath a calm exterior.

"How do you see Cuba's future?" Bolan asked to break the silence.

"If we go on as we are, the future will not be very good for us. It is time for a change. A new administration. The revolution had its chance. The Communist way has not brought Cuba a brave new society. Only hardship and a wasted generation. In a few years we will be into a new century. If Cuba stays as she is, we will be left behind. The changes Castro is making are too few too late. They are superficial. We must have someone stronger in charge. The old ways must be swept aside and quickly. This foolishness being planned is a desperate measure by a dying administration, a final act of defiance by a crippled ideology."

She stopped speaking suddenly, as if embarrassed by her strong words. She didn't have to worry. Bolan picked up the pride and the hope in her voice, the cry from the heart from a people who had endured the drab, repressive regime for so long. Their fate had been decided for them by a government now long past its credibility threshold, and these vibrant people wanted a chance to have a say in the way their country was to go.

Her answer echoed views he had heard before, coming from a people frustrated by the specter of communism that was dead but refused to lie down. The established hierarchy, entrenched and still holding on to the reins of power, aware of its fading style of government, wouldn't relinquish its grip on the country. Rather than back away and admit defeat, it clung with dwindling tenacity to a regime long past its prime.

Perhaps Cuba's future did depend on some change. But not the kind envisaged by the possible alignment with Puerto Rico, or the consequences of that alliance.

## CHAPTER THREE

Linda Ramos parked against the wall of an empty apartment building across the street from the building where her brother was hiding. With the engine switched off, she and Bolan sat in the darkness.

"If I run into trouble," Bolan stated, "I'll do my best to get Manuel out. If things go bad and I don't make it, get yourself out of here, Linda. No point in all of us going down."

She faced him, her eyes bright with the fear she felt inside. She leaned across and kissed him on the cheek. "Be careful, Mike Belasko."

She watched him remove the Uzi from his backpack, checking it as easily as another man might check his wallet. Satisfied, Bolan slipped from the car. Within seconds his dark figure had vanished from the woman's sight. She huddled down in the seat, silently mouthing a prayer. It was something she hadn't done for a long time.

She hoped it would help.

HUGGING THE SHADOWS, Bolan made the far side of the street without challenge. He took time to study the layout of the apartment building. Most of the floors were in darkness. Windows were broken or boarded up. Mounds of scattered trash littered the ground at the base of the building, and a burned-out automobile shell rested near the edge of the sidewalk.

Bolan held the Uzi at chest height, close to his body, and flicked the selector switch to single shot. He had a limited supply of ammunition, so he would need to make sure every shot counted if he was forced to use the weapon.

Turning to look back the way he'd come, the big American saw only a deserted street. Nothing moved. No sound disturbed the desolate silence. He remained where he was, checking and rechecking. It didn't pay to take anything for granted in his situation. One mistake was all it took, and once you were dead, you stayed dead.

Finally satisfied, Bolan crossed the sidewalk and reached the gutted wreck of the abandoned car. Then he was hugging the wall of the apartment building, sliding to a crouch, merging his black-clad form with the deeper shadows at ground level.

Ramos had told him that her brother was on the sixth floor, apartment number 622. If he was still there and Bolan managed to locate him, there was no guarantee that Ramos would cooperate. He was a hunted man, his anti-Castro activities exposed, and was probably branded as a traitor by the government he opposed. Even so, he might be unwilling to tell Bolan what he needed to know.

The soldier still had to try. Information was the lifeblood that nourished his mission. Without it, the mission would be scuttled. His presence in Cuba was totally without sanction. He was completely alone: no support, no backup. He knew that a situation had developed that had to be dealt with. Whatever obstacles stood before him would have to be overcome.

Easing his way along the base of the wall, Bolan reached the entrance. The door stood ajar, empty gaps showing where glass had once been installed. The wood was scarred and covered in graffiti. Stepping inside, he worked his way through the trash covering the floor. He mounted the shadowed stairs, the Beretta tracking ahead of him. He searched the stairs above him, ears tuned for any sound other than the faint noise he made.

He passed apartments where music sounded behind closed, barred doors. Despite the fact that the building was supposedly abandoned, there were those who were willing to risk everything for somewhere to live.

When he reached the sixth floor, he was greeted by silence. He traversed the stale-smelling hallway that was lined with apartment doors, counting off the numbers he could see. Then a distant sound reached him. Bolan froze, concentrating, and knew instantly what he was hearing.

Footsteps were coming up the stairs at the far end of the hallway, the matching stairwell that allowed access from the opposite end of the building. There was more than one pair, and Bolan heard the brittle rattle of bolts being snapped back on automatic weapons.

The opposition had located Ramos, as well, which meant any time Bolan might have had was dramatically reduced.

The numbers were falling with increasing acceleration.

Bolan moved on. By his reckoning, he was no more than a couple of doors away from the apartment. He checked off the numbers as he passed: 619, 620.

There was a gap before the next numbered door, and he paused outside 622.

There was no time for the niceties of life. Bolan hit the door with his full weight, smashing it open. He went in fast, breaking to the left, eyes scanning the poorly lit, near-empty apartment.

The dark-haired man scrambling to his feet, eyes wide with shock, had to be Manuel Ramos. The likeness to his sister was surprising.

"Quick choice, Ramos," Bolan said. "Come with me and I'll try to keep you alive. Or stay and die. Your other visitors want you dead!"

Ramos hesitated for a few seconds, still not comprehending what Bolan meant, until an armed figure lunged through the open doorway, swinging an autoweapon in his direction.

Bolan fired first, placing the 9 mm tumbler between the gunner's eyes, the coring slug skewering through his brain and blowing open a large exit hole. The gunner flopped back against the door frame, his expression showing total surprise.

The soldier hurried over to him and scooped up the Uzi the guy had dropped. He saw that it had 32-round clip in place, with a second taped to it. He took the clip and tucked it behind his belt.

"Now do you understand?" Bolan asked.

Autofire split the night apart. Slugs hammered the door frame and chewed holes in the cheap plaster. The salvo was covering fire for the gunners who pounded along the hallway, converging on the open door to Ramos's apartment.

Bolan had moved the moment the gunfire sounded. He grabbed Ramos by his shirt and propelled the man across the room and through the door that led into the single bedroom. The Executioner knew he was backing himself into a corner, but at the moment he had little choice. There was no knowing how many hostiles were crowding the hallway. He needed to shorten the odds before he and Ramos made their break.

"See if you can find us a way out," Bolan snapped, then turned back to face the shadowy figures crowding the apartment door, flicking the Uzi's selector to full-auto.

As the first pair shoved into the apartment, Bolan triggered the Uzi, laying down a savage blast that eliminated the two gunners. They were caught in a sizzling blast of fire, bodies shredded by the powerful hail of slugs. Blood sprayed across the walls as the gunners stumbled and fell, squirming in agony.

Without taking his eyes off the now-empty doorway, Bolan called over his shoulder. "Ramos? Anything?"

"Nothing. There are no other exits. Windows open on the outside wall. There is no way down."

"Can you handle that gun you've got?"

"A little."

"Well, you'd better improve if you want to stay alive."

"How did you know?"

"Linda."

"She's here?"

"Waiting downstairs with a car."

"They will kill us," Ramos said, reluctantly taking out the autopistol tucked in his waistband.

"If you feel that way, maybe you'd better just walk out and surrender."

Before Ramos could reply, there was a noisy scuffle beyond the open apartment door. Moments later something was tossed into the room. It thudded to the carpet and rolled across the floor.

"Grenade!" Bolan yelled, and shoved Ramos away from the open bedroom door. Turning his own body from the opening, the Executioner heard the blast of the detonating grenade. The room shook, and a cloud of dust rolled into the bedroom, followed by a shower of debris.

Even as the noise of the explosion filled the apartment, Bolan heard the oncoming gunners. They were using the grenade blast to cover them as they made an attempt to breach the apartment. Bolan swung away from the wall, dropping to one knee in the bedroom door and watching dark figures racing into the dusty apartment, skidding over the loose debris covering the floor.

He tracked the nearest and blew him off his feet with a short burst to the chest. The guy twisted in an awkward roll, landing facedown on the floor. Tracking onto another target, Bolan caught a second gunner in a blistering figure eight. The man went down screaming, the shrill sounds unnerving his two companions. They hesitated, realizing they might be the next victims.

The soldier obliged them. He emptied the magazine, the Uzi snapping empty even as the lacerated figures, spilling blood, crashed to the floor.

Bolan quickly ejected the magazine, reversing it to snap in the second. He cocked the weapon, covering the door, his eyes scanning the section of hall he could see. Nothing moved. He waited for a long minute before he moved, turning back to seek out Ramos.

He was slumped against the wall, his pistol hanging loosely from one hand. His shoulders were shaking, and when he raised his head sweat glistened on his skin. His eyes told it all. The man was too scared to even defend himself.

"Let's move, Ramos," he snapped.

When the man remained where he was, Bolan grabbed his shirt and hauled him from the room, leaving Ramos by the inner wall while he checked the hall. It was, as he'd thought, deserted. If there were more hardmen lying in wait, they were staying well out of sight.

One of the downed gunners groaned. Bolan crouched beside him, moving the man's Uzi out of reach first, then rolling the man's head so he could see his face. Blood streamed from the guy's mouth and nose.

"You understand me?" Bolan asked.

The man nodded.

"Why are you people doing this?"

The gunner tried to point a finger at Ramos. The effort left him gasping.

"That one is a traitor.... So are his friends. They have to die."

Ramos reacted to the accusation, pushing away from the wall, his face dark with anger. "It is you who are the traitors," he yelled. "You would take us into a war we could not win. A war that would gain us nothing except our own defeat."

"That I would expect from a coward."

"No," Ramos said. "A free man who makes his own decisions. Not a fool who listens to the ramblings of a leader ready to destroy the country to bolster his failing regime."

The wounded man didn't reply this time. When Bolan glanced down, he saw that he had quietly died. Picking up the Uzi, Bolan pushed to his feet. He took the weapon's magazine to add to his supply.

"It is not true," Ramos said, clutching Bolan's arm. "I might not have the courage to kill, but I am not a coward. At least I faced these people with words not guns. I denounced what they were planning. I ran only when I realized they were ready to kill me where I stood. I could do nothing more once I was dead."

Bolan couldn't argue that point.

"Let's get out of here. We can discuss the finer points when you're on safe ground."

"It will not be easy," Ramos said. "The city will be saturated with Colonel Lopez's men. He will do everything he can to silence me. The more I talk, the more people I will be able to convince that this is foolishness. If you stay close to me, you will be in danger yourself."

"Then we'd better stay out of the light," Bolan said.

"Tell me why you are doing this Why does an American risk his life coming to this city?"

"Because there's more to this than even you know, Ramos. Right now I don't have time to explain. The only thing we need to worry about is getting you out of here in one piece. You're needed alive to tell your story where it can do the most good."

Manuel Ramos studied Bolan for a long moment. He seemed to satisfy himself about the American's sincerity, nodding at the Executioner.

"Let's get out of here," Bolan said. "Take your car and get out of Havana."

"Linda will have to come with us now. I have somewhere we must go. There are people you need to meet who will tell you the same things I have found."

*Headquarters, G-2, Secret Police*

"LOPEZ, HAVE YOU FOUND Ramos yet?"

Colonel Oswaldo Lopez, of the Cuban secret police, listened to the speaker on the other end of the telephone and cringed inwardly. He kept his fear to himself, not allowing it to show on his face. Though he despised himself for his feelings, he *was* frightened of Salvano Cruz.

There was something about the man that planted fear in those around him. It wasn't a tangible thing. It was invisible, ethereal. But it was strong enough to warn people that Cruz was a dangerous man. To his enemies, he radiated terror. To those who worked for him, he generated fear and loathing.

Right now Lopez was on the receiving end of Cruz's anger.

"We are in close pursuit," Lopez said.

"You mean he's escaped from your men again." The slight rise in the tone of his voice indicated that Cruz was becoming very angry. "Colonel Lopez. Oswaldo, my friend, do not make excuses. Whatever the reason, at least do me the courtesy of admitting that you have failed to apprehend your quarry. I do not want to hear lies."

"Yes, he has got away. However, it appears he has an accomplice. I have been receiving reports that when my men raided the home of Ricardo Contreras, who was sheltering Linda Ramos, there was someone there. He killed a number of our people. It seems he also appeared at the apartment building where Ramos was hiding, just ahead of our people. There was more gunfire, and this man killed more of our people and got away with Ramos."

"Who is this man?" Cruz demanded. "I must know, Colonel."

"We will find out."

"When you do, tell me immediately so that I can hire him and ask if he has any friends, I need someone like that on my side."

The irony in Cruz's words took a few seconds to sink in. When they did, Lopez went cold. He understood the thinly veiled threat in Cruz's sarcasm.

"We will find Ramos and this assassin he has with him."

"Make certain you do. We do not have the time to waste on this foolishness. Time is the one thing we are running out of."

# CHAPTER FOUR

*San Juan, Puerto Rico*

Phoenix Force arrived in Puerto Rico on an early flight. Stony Man had booked them in as individuals, traveling under assumed names. The team had also been booked into a hotel with separate rooms. It was a preliminary security maneuver. Once the Commando team got together on Puerto Rican soil, they would act collectively as they always did. Arriving as individuals might fool anyone watching at the airport and allow Phoenix Force the time they needed to set themselves up for the main thrust of their mission on the island. It wasn't a foolproof tactic, but not one of the Phoenix Force commandos ever imagined it offered them total anonymity.

Once they were in the hotel and had taken time to establish themselves, David McCarter phoned the number he'd been given by Stony Man and had a short, precise conversation with their FBI link. A meet was arranged, to be attended by McCarter and Rafael Encizo. The compact, muscular Cuban's expertise would be especially useful on this mission, considering that this wasn't the first time he'd battled agents of the oppressive Castro regime.

While McCarter and Encizo were away, the rest of the team gathered in Gary Manning's room for final discussion over the way they were going to conduct their investigation.

"This Montejo character didn't have any kind of regular work," James said, "so it isn't going to be easy getting information out of his pals."

"The kind of people he ran with aren't the kind to take being questioned very gracefully," Manning agreed.

T. J. Hawkins leaned over to pick up one of the information sheets Barbara Price had supplied. He read through it again, making sure of his facts before he spoke.

"How about this guy Fernandez," he suggested. "According to preliminary information Chavez submitted, Montejo and Fernandez were buddies. Drank together. Played around with the ladies some. Like they were partners."

Manning nodded. "You could have something there, T.J."

"We'd need to walk light around this Fernandez. Chavez figured he was into PRISM pretty heavy going by what he put in his report. We go at him too strong, and he's liable to spook like a steer in a thunderstorm."

James reached across and took the sheet from Hawkins. He ran his eye over the data. "Says here that Fernandez has some kind of freight business outside San Juan. Runs a few trucks hauling goods. Could be he also does a little moonlighting for PRISM. What do you guys think?"

"It's worth a look," Manning agreed. "We'll put it to David when he gets back."

McCARTER AND ENCIZO returned to the hotel carrying a couple of lightweight cases that contained Beretta 92-F autopistols, complete with shoulder rigs, and 9 mm mini-Uzis. In addition, they'd brought an ample supple of ammunition clips. McCarter handed them out.

"If we need anything else, we're going to have to appropriate it ourselves," he said.

"So what's new?" James said.

"T.J. came up with a suggestion as to where we might start checking," Manning said.

"I see," McCarter replied. "Turn my back and he's after my bloody job. Have to watch this Yankee upstart."

"Do I get a raise in salary along with the job?" Hawkins asked, just as deadpan. "I'm not goin' to do it for peanuts."

McCarter grinned as he sat down and lit a cigarette. "All right, chum, what's this bright idea?"

Hawkins repeated his suggestion, pointing out the information in the data sheet.

"Sounds good to me," McCarter said. He leaned back, considering other options. "Right now we're on the thin edge where time's concerned. I'd like to go at this from a couple of angles. I'll take T.J. with me, and we'll go check out the place where Montejo was living. The rest of you go and track down this Fernandez bloke and see what you can come up with. We'll make the hotel the rendezvous point later today."

"Okay," James said.

"You set, T.J.?" McCarter asked.

Hawkins nodded. "Sure."

"I want you with me so I can pick up some ideas from you, hotshot," McCarter said dryly.

The sarcasm wasn't wasted. Hawkins picked up his mini-Uzi and snapped in a clip. "Well, they do say you're never too old to learn, boss. Maybe we'll find out if it's true."

McCarter picked up the phone and tossed it at the younger man. "Book us a rental car. My fingers are too frail to punch the buttons."

EASING THE CAR to a stop, McCarter cut the engine. He peered across the busy street at the shabby building. Beside him, Hawkins checked the sheet of paper in his hand.

"That's the one," he said eagerly, reaching for the door handle.

"Hold on. Let's not go jumping in too fast."

The younger man slumped back in his seat.

"Check the setup first," the Briton said. "If Montejo was in with PRISM, there might be some of his chums staking out the place. But they won't be holding up placards saying who they are."

Hawkins scanned the street. This was a neighborhood where Phoenix Force would be the ones who stood out. The parked car was one of many lining the street. More traffic weaved past street vendors hawking food and drink. In addition to being a busy area, the place was noisy, too. Music rolled out from open windows, competing with the traffic noise.

The avenue McCarter was parked on lay off the Calle Fortaleza, toward the cheaper end of town, where the hotels and souvenir shops catered to a less discerning class of customer. The building where Luis Montejo had rented a couple of rooms stood between a fast-food restaurant and a store that was crammed with electrical goods.

"I don't see anyone paying too much attention to the place," Hawkins said after taking a careful look around.

"And I don't see anything that makes me feel all that secure, either," McCarter grumbled. "Okay, we'll take a look. Listen. Take it easy. We don't want to start any fireworks if we can help it. On the other hand, I don't fancy my last resting place to be on Puerto Rico. If the temperature does get hot, we do our best to get out with the same number of arms and legs as we went in with."

"Trust me, David, I've done this kind of thing before," Hawkins said lightly.

"Recalling those instances is what's troubling me."

The Phoenix Force pair was armed with their holstered Beretta 92-F pistols. The mini-Uzis were locked in the trunk of the car.

They crossed the street with all the caution of men negotiating a mine field. The local drivers didn't seem to have been shown any other control than the gas pedal. Horns blared and tires screeched as the vehicles swept by the two men.

"Now I know why the chicken never got to the other side of the road," Hawkins observed. "He lived in San Juan."

Leading the way, McCarter entered the lobby of the building. The interior was no less shabby than the outside. Nothing seemed to have been disturbed for years, and that included the dust on all the flat surfaces. The air was stale and warm. A bank of mailboxes was secured to the wall just inside. Cards were stuck into frames, with room numbers and names written in shaky block letters. Some had the names scrubbed out and fresh ones written over them. The one for Luis Montejo was untouched, but the mail flap was open. McCarter peered inside. The box was empty, except for a lone cockroach that was scuttling around the small space with manic speed.

"Doesn't look like anyone has taken the room yet," McCarter said. He checked the number again, then pointed along the dim hallway. "Down this way."

With Hawkins close behind, McCarter walked along the corridor, counting off the doors. Montejo's was the last one.

"Go and check if there's a back way out," the Briton suggested, reaching under his leather jacket to ease the Beretta autopistol from its shoulder rig.

Hawkins had vanished from sight around the corner. He returned seconds later.

"A door opens on a parking area and an alley. If we turn left and follow the alley, it should take us back to the street."

McCarter paused at the door to Montejo's room. He took a pair of thin leather gloves from his pocket and pulled them on. Hawkins did the same. The Briton tried the handle. The door was locked. He put his shoulder to the panel and felt it give. Pressing his hip to the door just above the handle, and holding the handle to prevent the door from swinging inward, McCarter eased back then gave a sharp push. The door sprung off the catch with a soft crack. He eased the door open, fisting the Beretta, and peered inside. The dingy room was empty and in shadow. Someone had closed the shades.

Inside, with Hawkins beside him, McCarter closed the door. The Briton slipped the catch of the security chain into the slide. Holstering their weapons, the Phoenix Force commandos began to search the room.

Montejo's apartment, if it could be classed as such, consisted of a large room that comprised a living-and-sleeping area. There was a bathroom at one end, containing a shower unit and toilet. Montejo hadn't been one to gather very much in the way of belongings. There was no television, only a cheap plastic-cased radio. A plywood wardrobe held a selection of clothing consisting mainly of jeans and sweatshirts. Most of the clothes needed a good wash. Two pairs of shoes lay on the floor of the wardrobe.

"This guy knew how to live high," Hawkins muttered as he went through the pockets of the jeans.

McCarter was checking out the chest of drawers on the far side of the bed. Clothing again. A top drawer had been left partway open. The Briton saw that it was empty. Perhaps it had contained Montejo's personal belongings. If so, it looked as if someone had already been in the room to take the articles away.

He turned to the bed and tipped the mattress to the floor to see if anything had been hidden under it or in it. Nothing.

They spent fruitless minutes going through the room and came up empty-handed.

McCarter paced the room. He dragged back the thin carpet that lay at the foot of the bed, then tossed it down again. He hooked a foot under the base of a worn armchair and pulled it to him. Turning, he dropped into the chair, leaning his head back as he made another careful scan of the room.

"No bloody help at all, Luis Montejo, my son," he said softly. "No bloody help at all."

He fished his packet of Player's cigarettes from a pocket and lit one, staring around the room as if he were trying to will something to show itself.

"No cops," Hawkins said. "That's what's missing."

McCarter glanced at him through a wreath of cigarette smoke.

"It's been bothering me," Hawkins went on. "Montejo is dead. It should be down as an unlawful killing as far as the cops are concerned, because they don't know Chavez's background. But they do know that Chavez vanished after the killing."

"So what is the point?" McCarter asked.

"This place has been gone over. We know that. Anything that might have pointed a finger at Montejo is probably gone. But there isn't any sign that the police have been here. Why?"

McCarter shrugged. "I can't answer that." He felt he should have had an answer, because Hawkins had made a valid observation. There should have been evidence of some police presence.

"This is weird," Hawkins said.

"Maybe the local cops aren't as fussy on procedure as they are on the mainland," McCarter observed.

"Or maybe someone who wears a badge is in with PRISM, someone with clout enough to keep the cops away from here in case they figured something out."

"It wouldn't be the first time," McCarter agreed. "We'll probably never know the truth. If someone high up in the police department is covering PRISM's tracks, he'll most likely be out of our reach."

Hawkins didn't say anything. He knew that McCarter was probably very close to the truth.

The Briton suddenly sat upright. He dropped his cigarette and ground it under his heel. "And maybe we've been allowed to walk in here so someone could get a look at us."

He pushed to his feet. As he did, something white and crumpled slipped from where it had been wedged down the side of the chair's cushion and dropped to the floor. McCarter picked it up, turning it in his fingers as he began to smooth it out.

Hawkins turned at a sound outside the door. He raised his left hand and clicked his fingers. McCarter glanced at him, alerted by the warning. He slipped the object he'd picked up into a pocket, reaching for his holstered Beretta. He flicked off the safety as he eased the handgun from under his jacket.

Hawkins, his own weapon drawn, positioned himself to the right of the door, while McCarter moved farther to the left, so they had the door covered from both angles.

The sound outside was repeated, and the door shook as someone pressed against it. The low murmur of voices reached the ears of the men inside.

On an impulse McCarter turned to check out the window. He saw a shadow move in the alley outside. Someone was getting into position.

There was a moment's silence out in the corridor, then a brief exchange before the door was forcibly struck, sending it flying open to crash against the inner wall.

An armed group, wearing ski masks and toting sawed-off shotguns, burst into the room, fanning out as they stepped across the threshold.

As the intruders lunged forward, stepping away from the door, McCarter flattened against the wall, putting himself behind the armed men. Hawkins, on the opposite side of the door, did the same. The three-man team was confronted with an apparently empty room—until McCarter made his presence known. He stepped up behind the last man in and jammed the muzzle of his autopistol into the back of the guy's neck, twisting the barrel a fraction to let the man feel the cold steel.

"Your choice, friend," McCarter said in rapid Spanish. "Throw away the gun, or I'll put you down for good!"

The man, for whatever reason, hesitated for a fraction too long. McCarter didn't. He whacked the guy across the back of the skull with the Beretta, dropping him to his knees. Shaking his head, the shotgunner tried to push upright, turning to face his attacker, so McCarter kneed him in the face. Blood soaked the ski mask as the guy toppled sideways, moaning. The Briton scooped the shotgun from his limp fingers.

As he straightened, twisting at the waist, McCarter swung the shotgun in a sharp arc and cracked it against the skull of the second intruder as the guy lunged at him. The man fell against the wall, eyes already glazing over. The Phoenix Force leader reversed the shotgun and rammed the barrel into his adversary's throat. He gave a rasping gurgle, desperately trying to suck air into his lungs. He dropped his shotgun and clutched at his throat, out of the action.

As McCarter took out the first intruder, Hawkins moved in on the guy he'd marked. This one, tall and heavily built, recovered quickly. He spun and met Hawkins head-on, driving the butt of the shotgun at the Phoenix Force commando's face. Hawkins pulled to the side, feeling the stock brush his cheek. He let the guy step in closer, then slapped the barrel of his Beretta against the side of his enemy's face. The hard rap connected with the guy's cheekbone, and he grunted with pain. Spinning on his heel, Hawkins slammed his hip against the man's body, curling his left arm over the guy's head, snapping it down against his shoulder. With a quick pull, the man was flipped over his hip and slammed to the floor. The guy landed hard, breath gusting from his mouth. Hawkins followed through, his foot slamming down across his adversary's throat, making the man writhe in agony.

"Time to leave," McCarter said, leading the way out of the room with Hawkins close on his heels. The hallway was deserted. The Briton kept his pistol flat against his thigh as he reached the door, scanning the street. There didn't appear to be any panic on the street. McCarter put his gun away, waiting for his partner to follow suit, and then stepped onto the sidewalk.

Crossing the street, the two men headed for their parked car. Hawkins touched McCarter's shoulder.

"There's a spotter over by that red pickup truck."

McCarter nodded. "I see him. There he goes. Off to see where his pals are."

The spotter edged along the sidewalk and slipped inside the rooming house.

"Let's go," McCarter said, breaking into a trot.

Reaching the car, he slipped behind the wheel and jammed the key into the ignition. As Hawkins dropped into the passenger seat, McCarter hit the gas pedal and took the car away from the curb with a sharp squeal of rubber. Weaving his way through the traffic, he made a sudden turn, taking the car down a side street, then cut back onto the main road. He drove steadily, aware that they might have a tail. It was difficult to tell on a busy city street, so McCarter decided to make a detour, out of the city.

Gradually the traffic thinned. The buildings became sparser. They were passing through an industrial area, with car-repair businesses and scrap yards. The road itself had turned from asphalt to a dusty, rutted strip.

"Red Ford," Hawkins said. "He's been with us all the way, and is starting to close up now."

McCarter grunted. "We're on his turf. He probably feels safe out here."

Hawkins eased his Beretta out of its holster. "He could find out he's badly mistaken."

"Are you showing signs of hostility?" McCarter asked.

Hawkins grinned. "Having shotguns waved at me tends to bring out my worst side."

"Bloody glad to hear it. I was starting to think I'd have to deal with this all by myself."

McCarter swung the car around the end of a sagging chain-link fence, flooring the pedal, and aimed for a cluster of deserted industrial buildings. Weeds and dust hugged the edges of the foundations. Doors sagged open, and windows, long devoid of glass, stared out at the world like sightless eyes.

Guiding the car around the side of one building, McCarter swung it under a loading dock, braking quickly. He cut the engine and shoved open his door, pulling his Beretta and checking the area in a sweeping glance.

"How are we going to play this?" Hawkins asked.

"There's only one way to play," McCarter said. "These blokes want us dead. I want to stay alive. Just keep that in mind, and you'll know which way to play it."

The approaching roar of an engine heralded the imminent arrival of the tail car. McCarter spotted the vehicle as it swept over the crest of a low hump, then vanished behind a building. There was no time left to go for the Uzis locked in the truck of the rental car.

"You take that side," McCarter said, indicating the far end of the loading dock. "I'll cover this end."

Hawkins nodded, turning immediately and breaking into a trot as he made his way to the position.

Moments later the tail car rounded the end of a building and barreled in their direction. The vehicle slid to a dusty halt as the driver hit the brakes, doors flying open before it had stopped completely. Men tumbled out, their autoweapons up and firing as they spotted the Phoenix Force commandos. Bullets clanged against steelwork, flying off in all directions. Glass shattered as shots struck the rental car.

McCarter was first to return fire, the 92-F held two-handed, punching out 9 mm slugs with unerring accuracy. His initial burst of three shots took out the gunner on the far side of the car. The triburst caught him chest high, the rounds coring into him in a tight pattern. The gunner tumbled backward, his heart blown apart by the shots.

His initial shots fired, McCarter changed position, ducking and weaving as he moved through the spiderweb of steel girders that supported the loading dock. The gunners were forced to bring the fight to the Briton, which was what he wanted. He allowed them to break away from the car, forcing them to move into open space, albeit for only a few seconds, but it was enough.

He stopped running, swept the Beretta in a short arc, triggered once, then again, each time altering target acquisition. His first target went down with a bullet in his skull, the entry point just above his left eye.

Close by, a second gunner felt something slam his chest. Moments later he was gasping for breath as the slug burned through a lung, erupting into a livid spot of pain deep inside his body. He tried to continue, but the sudden tang of blood in his throat took him out of the fight. He stumbled to his knees, not caring about the conflict anymore, his mind and body closing down.

Hawkins's run ended as he reached the farthest point of the loading dock. He could hear the rattle of shots, felt the impact as slugs slammed against the metalwork all around him. He ducked, scanning the area, and saw two of the gunners converging on his position.

On his knees, with a heavy steel beam shielding his midsection, Hawkins leaned out a fraction as he picked up the soft crunch of gravel underfoot. He spotted the creeping gunner a full two seconds before the guy realized he was being observed. His lack of concentration proved to be his downfall.

Hawkins stroked the Beretta's trigger twice, sending 9 mm slugs into the startled gunner's chest. The man went down hard, letting out a short, scared yell before he lay still.

The downed man's partner quickly grasped what had happened and realized he wasn't dealing with an amateur. By the time the thought took shape in his mind, the gunner was already dying, a pair of 9 mm slugs in his heart.

Checking out McCarter's position, Hawkins saw that the Briton had already dealt with his adversaries.

"Let's go," McCarter called, and set off at a run. Following his partner, Hawkins wondered what the man intended. He became aware moments later when the rising crescendo of a car engine filled the air. It was the tail vehicle. One man had remained inside, keeping the engine ticking over. Now, seeing his buddies taken out, he had decided to quit the scene.

Hawkins broke clear of the steelwork, digging in his heels as he made a hard run to catch up with McCarter. He came alongside the Briton as the tail car, reversing wildly away from them, came to a rocking stop, the front end slithering in a broad skid as the driver hauled the wheel around. The man threw a startled look in the direction of McCarter and Hawkins, then worked the gearshift as he attempted to move forward. The car lurched, stalled, and the engine died. Both McCarter and Hawkins heard the man's angry curse. He fiddled with the controls, got the engine running again, then, for no other reason than panic, produced a stubby subgun and opened fire over the edge of the door.

McCarter shoved Hawkins to one side, then dropped to the ground himself. Bullets chewed at the ground, filling the air with dust and gravel.

Hawkins rolled, coming up on his elbows, the 92-F locking on the tail car as its rear wheels spun, raising a huge billow of dust. He settled on the driver's door, triggering the Beretta until the slide locked back on empty.

The stream of 9 mm slugs punched through the door and blew out the trim panel. A hail of those slugs ripped into the driver's side, opening a number of ragged wounds. The injured man began to scream, his rising wail of pain matching the scream of the engine. The car burst into motion, turning in a wide circle before slamming into a wide, solid steel girder.

The impact threw the driver against the windshield. He recoiled, rolling out of the door, still clutching the subgun. Bloody and incensed with rage, he staggered to his feet, yelling at McCarter and Hawkins as he hauled the weapon into target acquisition.

McCarter, a look of resignation on his face, raised his Beretta and put two shots into the driver's skull. The impact tossed the man over on his back, where he lay kicking at the dusty ground.

On his feet, Hawkins ejected the empty magazine and snapped in a fresh one. With the Beretta cocked and ready, he prowled the area, checking the downed gunners one by one.

McCarter looked inside the tail car, but it contained nothing of interest. It was an old vehicle, its upholstery worn and cracked, the floor littered with the usual debris that cars collected.

"Not a thing," Hawkins announced as he rejoined McCarter. "No wallets or ID. The only things in their pockets were ammo clips and cash."

"Bunch of the local PRISM street troops," the Briton stated. "If the rest of them are like these, I don't give much for their chances in a real head-to-head."

"They'll save the best for the real work," Hawkins said.

They returned to the rental car. Hawkins took the wheel and drove them back to the main highway. He kept an eye open for further interference, but nothing showed.

Once they were on a clear road, McCarter reached into his pocket and pulled out the crumpled paper he'd found in Montejo's room. Smoothing it across his knee, he studied it for a while, translating the Spanish.

"What is it?" Hawkins asked.

McCarter tapped the paper. "Could be our first solid lead," he said.

"Well, are you going to give me a clue?"

"Patience, my boy."

The Briton held up the piece of paper. "One receipt for the rental of a storage facility in downtown San Juan."

"Taken out by Montejo?" Hawkins asked.

McCarter nodded. "From what we know of him, Luis Montejo was no businessman. What would he be wanting with a warehouse?"

"More likely he rented it on behalf of PRISM," Hawkins said. "What do you think?"

"It's worth looking into, old son."

"How old is that receipt?"

McCarter checked the date again. "Near enough three weeks," he said, nodding at the implication of Hawkins's question. "You thinking we might be too late?"

Hawkins shrugged. "All depends on the timing of whatever is planned to go down. If PRISM needed to store something for an upcoming deal, the stuff could still be there. Or it might have been moved on. Either way, we won't know if we don't check it out."

"Get us back to the hotel. Time we found out what the others have been up to."

"Let's hope they had a quieter day than we did," Hawkins said.

McCarter didn't say anything, but he knew from past experience that quiet days and Phoenix Force seldom went together.

# CHAPTER FIVE

*Little Havana, Miami, Florida*

"Looks like a chop shop to me," Rosario "the Politician" Blancanales said, studying the front of the building through the rain-streaked windshield of Able Team's panel truck.

"Whatever the place is used for, they're not doing much business," Carl Lyons observed. He glanced at his watch. "Nearly two hours now, and no one has been in or out."

"Can't blame them," Blancanales said. "We come all the way to Florida and walk into a rerun of the great flood."

"It'll blow itself out," Hermann "Gadgets" Schwarz said.

"Listening to you two is like bugging a sunshine home for the elderly," Ironman complained.

"Maybe it's time we did a little recon," Blancanales suggested. "Sometimes a little shove is all it takes," he added, with a faint smile on his serious face. A powerfully built man, he had Special Forces training behind him, but could be very diplomatic when the situation called for it.

Lyons sat upright. "Pol's right. This isn't a damn stakeout."

He unzipped his leather jacket and pulled out his .357 Magnum Colt Python, checking the loads. He placed the big handgun on the seat beside him and started the engine. Easing the panel truck out of the alley where they had been parked, Lyons cruised across the rain-swept street and rolled to a stop in front of the body shop. He shifted into neutral, leaving the engine running.

"Two inside. One in here ready to roll and provide backup in case we get unexpected visitors," Lyons said.

"You guys go ahead. I'll mind the store," Blancanales volunteered. "And keep your eyes open. If Fuentes is in there, go easy. Don't forget Chavez and his partner."

Lyons tucked his gun away and opened the door. He stepped out onto the sidewalk, Schwarz close behind him. They crossed to the door set in the wall beside the main shutter doors of the shop. Lyons pressed the handle, and the door swung inward.

Shadows seemed to hang from every wall. Vehicles littered the floor of the cavernous shop, all in various stages of repair. Tools and equipment were strewed around the floor. Despite the setup, an air of desolation hung over the place. The only sound came from the rain pounding on the roof above their heads.

Lyons glanced at Schwarz. "They don't exactly look as if they're rushed," he said.

Schwarz stroked a finger across the roof of a parked car, tracing a line in the dust that lay on the vehicle. "Needs a wax job," he remarked.

They threaded their way across the shop, heading toward what appeared to be an office.

They were halfway across when a man appeared in one of the doorways. Despite the gloom, both Lyons and Schwarz recognized him as Jose Cammera, the man who had driven for Fuentes.

Cammera had a can of something in his left hand. He peered across the shop at the Able Team warriors.

"Who the hell are you?"

"You the owner?" Lyons asked. "I need some work done on my truck. It's outside."

"We're closed for business. Now haul your asses out of here."

"Door wasn't locked," Gadgets said conversationally. "Your sign doesn't say Closed."

Cammera stared hard at Schwarz. "You always so fuckin' loose mouthed?"

Lyons watched the man's eyes, sensing the agitation behind the words. Cammera was on edge about something. He was a rocket just waiting to have his fuse lit. The Able Team leader had been an L.A. street cop, and he still retained the ability to read a man's face. He didn't like what he was seeing in Cammera's.

"Hey, don't worry about it," Lyons soothed. "We'll find another place."

Cammera swiveled his eyes, studying Lyons. He seemed to register the blond man's no-nonsense attitude.

"Who told you about this place?" Cammera asked.

"Some guy in a bar," Ironman replied, knowing straight off how lame it sounded.

"You're lying!" Cammera tossed his canned drink into the shadows. "I never seen you mothers around the district. You know what? Something got a bad smell, like a cop!"

Cammera began to turn, as if he were going back through the door. But his right hand signaled his intention, slipping under the flap of his open coat, fingers grasping the butt of a handgun tucked in his pants.

Lyons eased to the left, reaching for his own weapon.

Moving in the same moment, Schwarz pulled out his Beretta 92-F. He turned sideways, presenting a slimmer target to his adversary as the Cuban swung the muzzle of his autoloader in his direction.

The interior of the shop echoed with the blast from Cammera's gun. The big slug punched a hole in the side of a dusty Corvette.

Schwarz felt the wind of the round as it passed him. He returned fire automatically, triggering the 92-F with a smooth pull. The 9 mm slug caught Cammera in the upper chest, slamming him into the edge of the door frame. He spun, collapsing to the floor with an odd sigh. He screwed up in a tight ball, his arms pulled under his body, his legs kicking against the base of the wall with jerky movements. There was a big, bloody hole between his shoulders where the slug had torn its way out.

"Check him out," Lyons snapped as he ran for the door, stepping over the dying man and sweeping the corridor with the muzzle of his Python.

Above the drum of the rain on the roof, Lyons heard the scrape of a foot against concrete. He flattened against the wall, watching the slightly open door of an office just yards ahead of him. Leaning forward, Lyons peered in through the opening and caught a quick glimpse of a shadow pulling back from the threshold.

He swore under his breath. One thing he had never gotten used to was flushing someone from a room. The guy on the interior had all the advantages. Someone entering had only one area to move in. The person inside the room could be anywhere: on the far side, or in the farthest corner to the side of the door. He—or they—could cover the door easily. All he had to do was wait.

Schwarz appeared at Lyons's side. "Cammera is out of it," he said softly.

"We've got someone in there."

"Fuentes?"

Lyons shrugged.

"How do we handle it?" Schwarz asked.

Lyons was about to reply when the sound of breaking glass reached his ears.

"See if you can find a rear exit," Lyons said, turning for the door that was ajar.

As Schwarz pounded along the corridor, the Able Team leader raised his foot and kicked the door, slamming it back against the inner wall.

From inside the room, he heard a frantic scrambling sound.

Taking a deep breath, the big ex-cop ducked low and went in through the open door. He stayed in a crouch, almost on his knees, moving quickly to the right of the door as he went through.

On the far side of the cluttered room, a lean, light-haired man was climbing through a window He was halfway through, his upper body twisted so he could look back over his shoulder. A large autopistol was clutched in his left hand. When he saw Lyons enter the room, he angled the pistol's muzzle and triggered a wild shot that chewed plaster from the wall well away from the intended target.

Lyons hit the floor. The guy might have been firing wild, but ricochets were still a danger. Lyons crawled across the floor, coming to rest against the side of a filing cabinet. He pulled his legs under cover an instant before the gun fired a second time. The slug clanged off the cabinet.

He pushed the Colt Python around the edge of the cabinet, tracking in on the window. He was rewarded by the sight of the shooter vanishing over the windowsill.

"Damn!"

He pushed to his feet, crossing the room to the window, searching the grimy alley beyond. Rain sluiced down between the buildings, misting the narrow lane. Lyons missed the guy first time around, then picked him out of the gloom. The shooter was already well along the alley, heading for the street.

He might have made it if Blancanales, alerted by the shots, hadn't boosted the panel truck into the mouth of the alley. As the vehicle burst into view, the shooter raised his weapon and fired. The slug struck the windshield, scoring the glass as it angled off. Blancanales hit the gas pedal, and the truck swept deeper into the alley. The front of the vehicle struck the shooter head-on, slapping him to the ground like a bug. The man crashed to the concrete, rolling before he came to a crumpled stop against the base of one wall.

Blancanales cut the engine and climbed out of the truck. He walked to where the shooter lay and bent over the motionless, bloody form. When he looked up, his expression told Lyons all he needed to know.

A door burst open down the alley and Schwarz ran onto the scene. He lowered his gun and joined Blancanales. Spotting something on the ground beside the corpse, Schwarz bent and picked it up.

"Bring him inside," Lyons called.

He took a long look around the room, wondering just what was in the place to cause such a reaction from the two men.

A computer sat on a desk across the room. Lyons glanced at the filing cabinet he'd used as cover, then walked over and pulled the drawers. They were empty except for scraps of faded invoices that were dated a couple of years back. Pushing the drawers shut, Lyons went over to the computer.

"That went all to hell in a hurry," Blancanales observed as he and Schwarz entered the room.

Schwarz pushed his pistol into its holster. "One thing doesn't change," he said.

"What?" Blancanales asked.

"Your driving," Schwarz said dryly.

"All right," Lyons said tautly, "cut the comedy. Let's check out this place and move before any of Cammera's buddies turn up."

Schwarz, who carried the nickname "Gadgets" because of his skill with electronics, was also trained in counter intelligence, which frequently came in handy. He pulled a chair to the desk and studied the computer.

"Nothing very fancy about this," he announced. "Standard industry model."

He turned on the computer and waited as the monitor lit up, then filled with text. Keying in a number of commands, he brought up menus, checking them quickly while his fingers rifled through the disks strewed across the desktop. He inserted a couple into the twin drives and accessed them, reading off the file lists that appeared on-screen.

"Anything useful?" Lyons asked.

"Hard to tell," Schwarz said. He accessed one file. "Looks like a simple text list. Trouble is it's in code. Have to break it before we can find out what it means."

"We don't have time for that," Lyons said. "Just take all the disks. We'll contact Stony Man. Get them to pick up the stuff and hand it to Kurtzman. Let him work it out."

"You got it," Schwarz said.

Blancanales had been checking the telephones. One had an answering machine, and the flap of the recorder was open.

"Tape's missing," he said.

"Try this." Schwarz handed Blancanales a small cassette tape. "Picked it up in the alley next to the shooter. He must have grabbed it out of the machine before he took off through the window.''

Blancanales slipped the tape in, rewound it and tapped the play button. There was only one message on the tape. It was short and to the point, the speech clipped and precise.

''Velasquez, we may have a problem. One of the team has gone AWOL. Son of a bitch jumped the base and vanished. Name to listen out for is Leopold Meecher. We have people looking for him, and it could be he might still be around Benedict. We'll try and contain the problem here. It sounds like he may have got religion and decided he didn't want to handle the action. He might decide to talk. Be ready to ship out if the shit hits the fan and they come looking down your end.''

After they had listened to it, Blancanales ran the tape again. ''Any thoughts?'' he asked.

''He talks like he's in the service, or used to be,'' Schwarz said.

Lyons looked at him. ''Military you mean?''

''Yeah.''

Blancanales found a thick manila envelope and dropped the disks into it.

''Put that tape in with the disks,'' Lyons said.

He picked up a phone and punched in the number that would connect him with Stony Man.

''We need some fast assist,'' he said when he got through to Barbara Price. ''A cleanup at the body shop. We also need a courier to pick up some material for Aaron at the hotel. Thirty minutes will be fine. By the time we get there I'll also need the location for a place called Benedict and a rundown on a guy named Leopold Meecher. Find out if there's any kind of tie in between Benedict and Meecher. I don't care how thin."

Lyons signed off and hung up.

"Let's get the hell out of here before the local cops turn up and ask questions."

ABLE TEAM'S DEPARTURE from the body shop was observed by the driver of a dark limousine parked in an alley across the other side of the street.

Reversing out of sight, the driver sat and watched the building. He was able to pick up the sound of shooting from where he sat. He resisted the desire to drive away. Instead, he kept the body shop under observation and was rewarded by the sight of three men leaving the building. They all climbed into the panel truck and left the scene.

The watching driver started his car and tailed the panel truck across town to a hotel. The men went inside and stayed there for just under twenty minutes. When they came out, they were carrying luggage, which they placed inside their vehicle before moving off again. Allowing traffic to distance him from the panel truck, the driver tailed the vehicle again. He realized its destination well before it pulled into one of the parking lots at Miami International Airport.

The three men from the panel truck made their way inside the terminal building. The man left his car and followed the trio inside. They went directly to the counter of an airline and picked up tickets that had obviously been booked for them. Forty minutes later they joined the other passengers boarding a domestic flight, and the moment he saw the displayed flight information the man knew where they were going: El Paso, west Texas.

And from there, they would move on to a town called Benedict.

Locating a pay phone, he made a call, advising his contact to expect visitors. He described the three men and also gave their estimated time of arrival at El Paso airport. From there, they would most probably charter a flight to their final destination, and he suggested they could be spotted when they showed up in Benedict.

After completing his call, he left the terminal building and returned to his car. He sat behind the wheel, considering his next move. There was no chance of returning to the body shop. He was convinced that Jose Cammera was dead. And so, too, most likely, would be Pringle, the man they had hired to oversee the shop. By now it would be swarming with police and federal authorities. It was time he moved on, back to Cuba.

His cover in America was no longer valid. The sooner he discarded it, the better. Jose Cammera, his contact and driver for the hit on Chavez, had been identified, which was why the three men had visited the shop. It was also possible that he had also been identified. And it seemed that they had gained some information on Benedict. Now they were following up on that information. If things were handled correctly, they wouldn't get very far once they reached Texas.

He started the car and left the parking lot, heading back toward the city. If the authorities had information linking him with the Chavez killing, he would have to be careful. Getting out of the United States was easy. He had money and contacts. He could leave by the end of the day and be back in Cuba tomorrow.

He decided that was what he would do.

When he did leave, Michael Vasquez would vanish for good. That was the name he went under in America.

Back home in Cuba, he could resume his real identity.

That of Raul Fuentes.

# CHAPTER SIX

*On the outskirts of San Juan, Puerto Rico*

From information provided by the Stony Man file, Phoenix Force found out that Abel Fernandez spent much of his time at a local gas station that had a small restaurant attached. They drove out to the place, parking across the dusty street, and took some time to check it out.

"Hey, isn't that Fernandez's truck?" James asked, indicating a run-down, canvas-backed Dodge.

The others followed his gaze. Parked on the edge of the gas-station lot was a dirty truck, with the name of Abel Fernandez painted on the door. A large Puerto Rican was bending over the hood, busy with the engine.

"Going on the description, that's our man," Manning said.

"So," James asked, "what do we do?"

"How about asking him straight about Montejo?" Encizo suggested.

"Say what?" James asked.

"We need some kind of catalyst, something to push these PRISM guys into making a move," the Cuban explained. "It's the only way we're going to start making headway. Agreed?"

"I see what you're getting at," Manning said. "So how are you going to do it?"

"Why don't I go over and do some talking to Fernandez? Tell him I've been looking for Montejo. I just arrived in town and want to join up with PRISM. I can get away with pretending to be Puerto Rican. Been away in New York for a few months. Now I'm back, and I want to do some business. I can say I got a load of contraband weapons to sell."

James looked skeptical. "You don't believe he's going to fall for that, do you?"

"Doesn't matter. He might call someone and have them come after us. On the other hand, maybe he'll try and take me on himself. I doubt it. But the way things are, PRISM is on edge. Because it looks like something is going down soon."

"I agree it'll probably get a reaction," Manning said. "I doubt it'll be pleasant."

"Sometimes you have to shake the pot and see if it rattles," Encizo said.

"I can't think of anything better at the moment," Manning said.

"Okay, so let's do it," Encizo replied.

Without waiting for further discussion, the Cuban opened the door and climbed out of the car. He tucked the mini-Uzi under his jacket as he strolled across the road and traversed the dusty lot to where Fernandez was working on his truck.

"This could be the start of something big," James muttered.

He checked his Beretta and placed his own mini-Uzi across his lap, finger resting on the trigger guard.

Encizo stood by the truck, talking animatedly with Fernandez. The Puerto Rican showed little interest at first, almost becoming belligerent as he tried to ignore Encizo's relentless banter. But eventually he seemed to change his mind. It probably had something to do with the weapon Encizo showed him. The two men went into a huddle at the rear of the truck, still talking. Almost ten minutes later Encizo parted company with the Puerto Rican and walked back to the parked car.

In the meantime Fernandez had climbed into the cab of his truck. He picked up the handset of a mobile telephone and began to talk into it, waving his free hand about to emphasize his words.

Encizo climbed back inside the car. "Let's go," he said, jerking his thumb. "That way."

"Wait a min—" James began to protest.

Encizo cut him off. "Just drive."

The black Phoenix Force commando started the rental car and swung back onto the road. As they pulled away from the gas station, Manning glanced around. Fernandez had left the cab of his truck and was standing, hands on hips, watching the car as it sped away.

"Well?" the burly Canadian asked.

"I wasn't sure how it was going until I showed him the Uzi," Encizo said. "Then he did start to show interest. I overdid the selling. Pushed a little hard, like I was real anxious to make an impression. Fernandez isn't exactly what I'd call bright. I could tell he wasn't sure how to take me. In the end he said I'd have to talk to some of his people. He gave me an address and said to go straight there. His people would be waiting."

"I'm sure that part's true," James said.

"He went straight to the phone as soon as you left him," Manning added.

"Wants to give his buddies plenty of time to load up," James observed dryly.

AS BAD DAYS WENT, this one had the makings of an epic.

That was the way Calvin James felt about it, and he didn't give a damn who knew it.

The growing suspicions the Phoenix Force warriors had about Abel Fernandez and his arranged meeting were compounded the moment they reached the warehouse address.

It was isolated, on an empty stretch of road that ran alongside what had once been a small airstrip. Old vehicles and abandoned hangars stood exposed to the elements. Grass grew thickly everywhere, even sprouting up through cracks in the concrete runway. Nothing moved.

"High noon all over," James muttered. "Any minute now, Gary Cooper will show up."

"If he does, you can take him on first," Manning said.

"That's where we're supposed to meet Fernandez's associates," Encizo stated, indicating the large freight warehouse.

"Well, we don't want to keep them waiting. Do we?" James said.

He drove the car to the front of the building.

With their mini-Uzis under their jackets, the Phoenix Force commandos assembled by the door.

"You want to go first?" James asked.

Encizo grinned. "Real old lady you're becoming," he said.

"Yeah? Providing I do live to reach old age, being an old lady wouldn't be so damn bad."

The Cuban eased open the side door and checked the interior. At first the lead appeared to be a dud. Or so the team realized as they breached the warehouse and found the place apparently empty.

Then someone opened up with a light machine gun, spraying the place with bullets. The firing had been badly judged. Whoever was operating the weapon hadn't allowed James, Encizo and Manning to get far enough into the light before touching the trigger. So instead of three dead men, all he achieved was to create a great deal of dust and concrete flakes.

The gunner was being cursed by his two companions, still arcing the LMG back and forth, and it took vital seconds before he realized that the intended targets had vanished.

Phoenix Force hadn't quit the place. They had simply gone to ground, drawing their own weapons and spacing themselves out prior to a response.

James, with Manning, crouched behind a stack of empty wooden crates. On the far side of the area, Encizo, his Uzi held ready, scanned the raised section on top of which the gunner and his partners were waiting.

Yards from where the Cuban crouched, a flight of metal stairs led up to the raised section.

Catching the eye of his partners, Encizo indicated the stairs. Manning nodded, turning to say something to James, who nodded in turn. He drew back a few steps, lifting his Uzi, and began to fire into the raised section, his bullets tracking along the length of the platform.

The moment James opened fire, Gary Manning, crouching, scooted across to where Encizo waited.

"You or me?" the Cuban, pointing at the stairs.

"Just make sure you cover me," the Canadian said.

Manning hit the stairs, his powerful legs driving him upward.

From his position Encizo laid down a second volley of covering fire, his bullets chewing at the railing that circled the section. The trio of gunners was driven back by the cross fire, giving Manning the edge he needed.

The moment he reached the top of the stairs, Manning executed a low dive across the floor, rolling away from the opening. He caught a blurred glimpse of the three men, one cradling the LMG in his arms, the others carrying standard 9 mm Uzi subguns.

One caught sight of Manning's rolling figure and yelled a warning to his buddies, snapping his Uzi into target acquisition. He fumbled with the trigger, his finger missing the metal first time. He didn't get a second chance.

Manning's Uzi tracked onto his lean torso. The Canadian stroked the trigger, feeling the weapon kick back against his palm as it fired, sending a stream of 9 mm slugs into the gunner's chest. The man twisted around, shock registering on his face as the bullets did their work, and then he fell, clutching his body and screaming in pure fear.

At floor level Calvin James had pulled back from his firing position, his own Uzi trained on the area above him.

Manning's opening shots caused the other men to step back, attempting to bring their weapons into play.

From below, James saw one man's head and shoulders loom into sight. The Phoenix Force warrior didn't wait. He lined up the Uzi and triggered a short burst. The 9 mm manglers hammered into the back of the shooter's skull, impacting and coring deep into his brain. The stricken man sank to his knees, blood starting to trickle down his face.

The lone survivor, struggling to heft the LMG, saw the second of his buddies go down. With a wild yell he triggered the weapon, sending a stream of bullets into the floor, dragging the muzzle around to where Manning was pushing up off the floor.

The big Canadian swung the Uzi's muzzle to target the machine gunner.

Just then, Encizo appeared at the top of the stairs.

Both Phoenix Force warriors fired at the same moment, their combined firepower driving the machine gunner back across the floor. He slammed against the railing, lost his balance and toppled backward with a brief scream. His bullet-riddled body crashed to the concrete floor of the warehouse. The now-silent LMG spilled from his fingers and clattered to one side.

James crossed to where the corpse lay, hauling the LMG well clear of the guy's hands, even though he was certain he was dead. There was no profit in being careless. Too many men had died from assuming an enemy was out of action. The man also had an Uzi slung around his neck from a nylon strap, and James removed this, as well.

Crouching by the body, the black Phoenix Force warrior searched the pockets. There was some loose change, but nothing of value to Phoenix Force. As he started to stand, he noticed something on the man's left arm, midway between wrist and elbow: a tattoo that spelled PRISM.

James stared at the word, which identified the man with the organization. The way in which it had been worn suggested that it was there to be seen in defiance of the legally elected government, a way of saying that PRISM refused to stay out of the spotlight.

"Hey, guys," James called, "you find anything unusual on those two up there?"

Manning appeared at the railing. "Like tattoo marks that spell a certain word we've come to love and admire?"

"Yeah."

"Both these guys have them," Manning said.

"That's what I figured you'd say," James replied. "You find anything useful on them?"

The big Canadian shook his head. "These boys travel light."

"Damn," James muttered. "We needed more than a tattoo."

"At least we've confirmed our friend Fernandez is up to his neck in PRISM business," Encizo said. "I say we go back and make him see we're slightly pissed off."

"I guess by now he'll be thinking how smart he's been," Manning commented.

"Okay," James agreed. "Let's go and have a talk with Mr. Fernandez. Show him he isn't as clever as he believes."

Before they left the warehouse, the Phoenix Force warriors collected the Uzi SMGs from the dead PRISM rebels, plus extra magazines.

It took them just over forty-five minutes to retrace their steps to the gas station. The truck Fernandez had been working on was gone.

"Let me go and talk to the girl inside," Encizo said, indicating the young Puerto Rican waitress watching them through the window. "Maybe she can help."

Manning smiled. "Help you with what?"

"Eat your heart out," the Cuban said. "Watch and learn."

He sauntered across to the wooden building that served as the gas station's restaurant. The door swung shut behind him as he vanished inside.

"The charm will be oozing all over the damn floor by the time he's done," Manning commented.

"Personal sacrifice for the mission," James said. "Wonderful to see."

"Depends how far he has to go."

Encizo was outside again within five minutes. He made his way back to his waiting partners, turning to wave over his shoulder before he reached the car.

"Just what did you promise her?" James asked as Encizo slid onto the rear seat.

The Cuban closed the door. "You don't expect me to give away such intimacies, do you?" he said smugly.

"Did you find out anything?"

"Fernandez's truck business is about eight miles south along this road. The girl doesn't like the man. It seems he's tried to come on to her a few times, and she told him where to get off."

"That it?"

"The girl is called—" Encizo began, but Manning interrupted him by starting the car and swinging it back onto the road in a cloud of dust.

THEY DROVE by the trucking yard, Manning slowing the vehicle so they were able to check out the untidy area. It was ringed by a sagging chain-link fence. There was a ramshackle workshop at one side, surrounded by piles of scrap and empty crates. The single truck parked in the yard was the same one the men of Phoenix Force had seen outside the gas station.

Manning slowed a few hundred yards farther along, then swung the car around, facing back the way they had come. He stopped and cut the engine.

"How do we work this?" Manning asked.

"Check the place out on the quiet," James replied. "If we find anything interesting, we follow it up."

With their strategy decided, the Phoenix Force trio moved out. Manning eased the car off the road and parked in the shadow of an abandoned trailer. The rusting hulk allowed them to watch the yard without being seen.

They were about to separate when a dusty, dark-painted panel truck slowed and made the turn into the yard. It rolled up alongside the parked truck. Two men got out and met Fernandez as he exited the workshop. The three men had an agitated conversation, Fernandez finally giving in and walking to the rear of his truck. He raised the canvas sheet at the rear, dropped the tailgate and hauled his bulk onto it. The panel truck was backed up to the tailgate and the doors opened. The two men hauled a number of long packing cases from the panel truck and hoisted them onto the tailgate, from where Fernandez slid them inside the truck. There were at least eight of the boxes. The only clear thing the Phoenix Force warriors could make out was the color of the boxes—olive drab.

"Military equipment boxes," James declared.

"Doesn't actually indict him," Encizo argued.

"How about this," Manning said. "The guy from the panel truck, closest to us, with the mustache."

"I see him," Encizo said.

"The last time I saw that face was when we were looking at files we brought from Stony Man."

"You sure?" James asked.

"I'm sure. That guy was in a photograph alongside Montejo."

With the loading complete, the two men returned to the panel truck and drove off. Fernandez fastened the truck's tailgate and secured the canvas drop sheet, then went back inside his workshop. He didn't come out again for more than an hour. When he did, he climbed into the truck, swung it around and drove out of the yard.

"Let's go," James said.

Manning started the car. He pulled back on the road, well behind the truck, and tailed it.

The truck coasted along at a steady forty miles per hour. Whatever else he was doing, Fernandez had no intention of being stopped for speeding.

An hour later they were still trailing the lumbering truck.

"This road is taking us to nowhere," Encizo said, glancing up from the map he was studying. "There aren't any towns up ahead. Just countryside."

"Maybe he's going to meet someone," James suggested, "to pass on whatever he's carrying."

"He's turning off the road," Manning said.

Up ahead the truck made a left onto a single-track trail that led deep into the forested area that bounded the road. Manning followed, still keeping at a distance from the truck. He eased off the gas pedal, allowing the car to slow to a crawl. The trail was rutted, and dust still hung in the air from the passing of Fernandez's truck.

Manning checked his rearview mirror. "We're generating too much damn dust," he said. "If there are any lookouts, they'll spot it."

"Pull over," James said. "We'll go in on foot. Fernandez isn't driving all that fast."

Manning steered into a deep clump of trees and hid the car from sight.

"Let's go, guys," James said.

The Phoenix Force trio set off at a steady trot. The trail wound in and out of the trees, following the contours of the land. They tailed the truck for almost half an hour, and the light was starting to fail when the vehicle rolled to a squeaking halt by a derelict building. It looked as if it might have been a farm storage shed at some time in the past. Now it was deserted, and the forest had started to reclaim it.

Fernandez climbed from the truck and made his way to the building. He produced a key and released a padlock on a door, vanishing inside.

"This gets better all the time," Manning said.

The Phoenix Force warriors eased their way down to the building. While Manning and Encizo took one side of the structure, James made for the truck.

He had a clear view of the vehicle and was about to go for it when the door in the building opened and Fernandez stepped outside. He went directly to the truck and dropped the tailgate.

By the time James reached the rear of the truck, Fernandez had the canvas sheet raised. He was sliding the first of the packing cases to the tailgate prior to unloading. The Puerto Rican was so engrossed in his task that he failed to notice James's presence. His first indication that he wasn't alone came when James caught hold of his ankles and yanked him backward.

Fernandez hit the edge of the tailgate with his chest, gasping, and bounced off, dropping to the ground. He was winded but far from out of the fight. Even as James bent over him, reaching for the gun that Fernandez carried in his belt, the Puerto Rican lashed out with his left foot, catching the Phoenix Force warrior hard across the side of the head.

James fell to his knees, shaking his head to clear the aftereffects of the kick. He felt disoriented for a few seconds, which was all the time Fernandez needed to follow up. He rolled to his feet, curling his right arm around James's neck and squeezing hard.

The air was cut off from the black man's lungs, and he resisted the urge to panic. He knew he still had time to react before the lack of oxygen began to weaken him. He was aware of Fernandez's left hand groping for the holstered autopistol. James reached up and grabbed the man's wrist, twisting sharply.

Fernandez let out a startled cry as one of the bones snapped. His fingers splayed out in response to the sharp, biting pain, and the arm around James's neck slackened a little.

Seizing the moment, the Phoenix Force warrior threw both arms up and back, his fingers closing over his adversary's head. He pulled down, leaning forward, and dragged the man over his shoulder. The Puerto Rican landed on his back, thudding against the hard ground. Before he could roll to his feet, James grabbed one of his flailing arms, wedged a foot against the side of his neck and stamped down hard.

Bone crunched and Fernandez's head lolled at an odd angle. His body shuddered violently, then became still.

James slumped against the side of the truck, dragging air into his lungs. His head pulsed dully from the kick he had received.

"Maybe Katz had the right idea," he said to himself. "The Farm's a damn sight more peaceful than being out here."

He pushed upright and moved to the tailgate. He released the catches on the packing case and raised the lid. Inside, nestling in foam recesses, were four LAW rockets. Judging by the depth of the case, there could easily be another layer beneath. Eight to a box. James pulled himself onto the tailgate and went into the truck. The interior was stacked with six more identical cases, plus a number of other boxes. James made a thorough check and found M-16s, grenades and ammunition.

Encizo and Manning appeared. They cast critical eyes over the contents of the truck.

"Looks interesting," Manning observed. "Fernandez didn't cart these all the way out here for fun. I wonder who he was going to meet."

"If we hang around long enough, we'll probably find out," Encizo said. He glanced at James. "You did okay."

"Glad you guys were able to enjoy the show," James replied.

"You were handling things okay," Manning countered. "We didn't want to cramp your style."

"Yeah? I'll do the same for you guys some day."

Manning climbed onto the truck and checked over the load. "At least we got what we came for."

"Not yet," Encizo said. "It's going to be interesting to see who comes to collect this stuff."

"It looked like Fernandez was starting to unload. Maybe we should do that," James suggested. "Put everything inside the building and hide the truck."

"Why hide it?" Manning asked.

"If Fernandez was simply going to hand the weapons over, why bother to unload everything? He could have left it inside the truck and just transferred it when his people turned up."

"Good point," Manning agreed. "Okay, let's do it."

It took them twenty minutes to move the cargo from the truck to the inside of the building. There were some folded canvas sheets in the truck, which they used to cover the stacked boxes. While James kept watch, Manning closed the doors of the building, snapping the heavy padlock back in place.

Encizo climbed into the truck, drove it a few hundred yards back down the track and concealed it within the deep foliage. When he returned, the others noticed a pleased expression in his eyes.

"What?" James asked.

"Remember that our friend Fernandez had a mobile phone fitted in his cab? I called the hotel and caught David. Told him what had happened and where we were. He and T.J. are on their way to join us."

"Best news I've heard all day," Manning said.

They settled down to wait.

IT WAS just about eight o'clock when McCarter and Hawkins arrived. Encizo's directions had been precise enough to bring them directly to where the others were waiting.

"Anything happened?" McCarter asked.

"Nothing," Manning said "We don't know when the stuff is being picked up."

"Maybe it isn't being picked up," Hawkins volunteered. "Maybe this is just a stash. Weapons to fall back on if somebody needs them."

James groaned. "Why is this guy so smart?"

"It's a privilege of youth," Hawkins said, grinning.

"They also say the smart die young," Manning said.

"I thought that was 'the good die young,'" Hawkins argued.

Before anyone could add to the exchange, Encizo raised a warning hand. "Quiet, children," he said. "And learn from an old man. I hear a chopper coming."

They fell silent, ears straining.

"Coming in from the north," Hawkins said.

"Right," Encizo agreed. "And what is it?"

Hawkins concentrated. "Sounds like a Huey."

McCarter, who knew his aircraft, nodded. "All right," he said. "Fun time is over. Here we go. Let's spread. Watch and listen. Wait for my signal. When you hear it, go in fast. I want some prisoners. We need information on these PRISM cowboys, and dead men won't help us."

Phoenix Force moved out from their vantage point, forming a half circle around the building where the weapons were stored.

Above them the night sky, lit by a pale moon, pulsed to the approaching noise of the incoming chopper. The aircraft zoomed into view, hovering over the building. A searchlight fitted beneath the helicopter's fuselage swept back and forth, the keen finger of light probing the shadows.

James watched the shaft moving toward him. He shrank deeper into the thick foliage, pulling in his legs a split second before the light reached his position. It remained stationary for long seconds, then moved on. He immediately changed position, taking himself closer to the storage building, eyes searching in case men were already on the ground.

The rest of Phoenix Force did the same, having to hug the earth as the beam of light swept the area. Only after a thorough crisscrossing of the landing spot did the Huey start to drop.

The moment it touched down, the side door slid open and a group of armed men, clad in camouflage fatigues, exited. They spread out to cover the area and protect the chopper.

Last to emerge was a stocky, hard-faced man carrying an autopistol. His uniform bore no insignia of rank, but it was obvious he was the man in charge. His crisp commands were obeyed instantly.

Three of the armed men moved to the building, one of whom produced a key and freed the padlock. The doors were pulled wide, and the men vanished inside. Moments later one emerged to give the thumbs-up sign.

Curt orders from the commander of the group sent two more of the men scurrying inside. The transfer of weapons from building to chopper took place with little waste of time.

DAVID MCCARTER HAD watched the loading of the weapons with mounting frustration. Phoenix Force wasn't as well equipped as he would have liked to take on the new arrivals. They hadn't been able to outfit themselves with all the gear they usually carried with them. They had weapons, but not the backup, such as a walkie-talkie, so he could talk to his men.

Glancing back and forth, the Briton pinpointed his concealed men. He was unable to actually see them, but he knew where they had concealed themselves. He had told them to wait for his signal before moving in. It was up to him to give the order that would send them into action—and possible danger.

This was the part McCarter liked least of all. He would do it because as commander of Phoenix Force, it was his decision to commit the team.

But as luck would have it, the decision was taken out of McCarter's hands. The action that followed forced his hand and plunged Phoenix Force into the thick of a firefight.

James, still not fully secure in his position and aware that he was close enough to be spotted, decided to draw back. Once he made that decision, there was no point debating it. He made his move—and was spotted by one of the men from the chopper.

The guy jabbed a finger in his direction. The commander of the group yelled to another of his men, who plucked a flare gun from his belt and triggered it.

The flare lit up the area, throwing everything into stark relief.

James was caught in the open, on the move but exposed to enemy guns.

There was no opportunity to stall what was about to happen.

McCarter didn't wait. He pulled the mini-Uzi to his shoulder, aimed and fired in a single fluid movement. The weapon crackled briefly, sending its deadly message across empty space. The Briton's short, controlled burst took out the target closest to James a fraction of a second before he triggered his own weapon.

The 9 mm slugs tore into chest and throat, turning the would-be assassin into a staggering, bleeding hulk. He toppled forward, crashing facedown on the ground, his membership to PRISM canceled in a burst of agony.

The moment McCarter opened fire, the other members of Phoenix Force broke cover and bore down on the other rebels.

With the sound of McCarter's volley ringing in his ears, James took a headlong dive, landing on his left shoulder and rolling in a controlled motion that brought him to rest in a prone position, his own weapon cradled to his shoulder, ready to take on any of the rebels he found in his sights.

The first target the black Phoenix Force pro saw was one of the PRISM hardmen advancing from the front of the building, weapon up and firing. The Phoenix Force commando touched the trigger of his Uzi, sending a hot burst at his target, his slugs hitting the man a fraction ahead of those from Encizo's weapon.

Caught from two directions, the rebel spun, his body exploding in a burst of misty red fragments of chewed cloth and flesh. He fell hard and stayed down.

McCarter, weaving in and out of blocks of shadow and light, advanced on the helicopter, firing on the run. He saw Manning angling toward his position, taking out one rebel without breaking stride.

"I don't want that chopper to get off the ground!" McCarter yelled above the crackle of gunfire.

Almost on cue the Huey's rotors began to turn, cutting the air as they built up speed.

The Briton sensed a blur of movement to his left, twisted and saw a rebel lunging at him, wielding a machete. The wide blade slashed across and down, aimed at McCarter's neck. The Phoenix Force commando ducked. He heard the weapon swish overhead and rammed his left shoulder into his attacker's lower body, feeling ribs crack. The man screamed in pain. McCarter raised a foot and drove the toe of his boot into the guy's testicles. The blow was delivered with every ounce of strength the

Briton could muster. It landed with terrible force, lifting the hardman inches off the ground. He collapsed in agony, both hands clawing at his injured flesh.

By this time McCarter had moved on, his headlong flight bringing him closer to the chopper. The rotors were starting to drag up dust and leaves, filling the air with flying debris.

He slammed up against the fuselage, hunching his shoulders as he heard an autopistol fire close by. The shot had come from the rebel commander. The man had scrambled for safety inside the chopper and was firing from the open hatch, clinging to a cargo strap as he leaned out. He was concentrating on McCarter and failed to see the onrushing figure of Gary Manning.

The burly Canadian closed in fast, took a flying leap and went in through the open hatch. He slammed bodily into the rebel commander, his shoulder tackle driving the man across the cargo area and into the stacked boxes of weapons. The pair crashed to the deck in a fighting tangle.

McCarter took the opportunity to haul himself up into the chopper. He pushed past Manning and the rebel and moved quickly to the flight deck, where he rammed the muzzle of the Uzi into the pilot's neck.

"If you want to try flying this with a hole in your head, just ignore me," McCarter barked. "If you don't cut the bloody power right now, you'll be able to try it!''

The pilot shut off the power and raised his hands. He was dedicated to his cause, but he had never seen any sense in being a martyr.

The chopper sank back on its skids, the rotors already starting to slow as the powerful engine began to wind down.

Behind McCarter the flurry of activity ceased abruptly, following a heavy blow. Glancing over his shoulder, he saw Manning drag himself to his feet, flexing the fingers of his right hand. The knuckles were red and scraped.

"Hell of a jaw that guy's got," the Canadian muttered. He bent to scoop up his Uzi, then quickly searched the unconscious rebel, relieving him of a knife and a compact backup pistol.

Outside, the firing ceased just as swiftly as it had commenced.

Hawkins appeared in the hatch. "Clear," he said. "You guys okay?"

"Struggling through without your help," Manning replied.

James and Encizo joined Hawkins.

"Not such a quiet night after all," James observed.

McCarter brought the reluctant pilot into view. He pushed the man to the hatch. "He's clean. No hidden weapons."

Encizo stared at the man for a moment. "And he's Cuban, too," he said.

"You all look the same to me," McCarter observed dryly. He jumped down from the chopper, leaned against the fuselage and fished a battered packet of cigarettes from his pocket. After lighting up, he studied the Cuban pilot. "Still understand English?"

The man nodded.

"Understand this then, chum. You have two choices in front of you. Fly us to wherever you were taking this load of weapons and gamble on staying alive. Alternatively you can be a hero to the cause and die right here on Puerto Rican soil. Your choice. I'm giving you five minutes to decide."

The man eyed McCarter, his mind working busily as he tried to assess the threat. He had already seen the ruthless efficiency of these men. They had taken out his compatriots without pause or mercy, decimating them with clinical expertise.

"Believe what he says," Encizo said, addressing the man in his own language. "This one does not take prisoners. He has no wish to waste his time with you. At least if you cooperate, there might be a chance for you. A bullet in the head finishes it for you here and now. No chance for escape. No way back home."

McCarter, who understood some Spanish, caught the general drift of Encizo's speech. He held a smile back as he caught the gleam of anticipation in the pilot's eyes. During Encizo's conversation, McCarter added emphasis to the threat by pulling out his handgun, easing off the safety and edging to the side, so he was partly behind the pilot. The Briton's final move was to lock back the hammer of the 92-F, close enough to the pilot so that he couldn't fail to hear the metallic sound.

The pilot's intake of breath was part answer. He turned imperceptibly and caught McCarter's cold, hard stare. He raised a slightly shaking left hand.

"I will take you where you want to go," he said, having to swallow in order to wet his dry mouth.

McCarter kept the gun in plain sight. "Don't try anything stupid," he warned. "I'd soon as kill you later as now. Makes no bloody difference to me. I figure out you're taking us into a trap, chum, I'll spill your brains all over the canopy of this chopper and fly the damn thing myself."

He pushed the pilot toward the chopper's hatch, the muzzle of the Beretta wedged snugly against the man's spine.

## CHAPTER SEVEN

*Benedict, West Texas*

They flew in from El Paso in a twin-engined Beechcraft. The pilot was a lean, taciturn man with a face as eroded as the land and quiet eyes that didn't miss a single thing. He spoke only in answer to a direct question, giving away nothing but absorbing a great deal.

The land they flew over was wild and desolate, rocky escarpments and bone-dry semidesert, baking beneath a relentless, sun-scorched sky. Hazy, blue-tinged mountains thrust jagged peaks up out of the emptiness. Unending miles of distance gave the eyes no comfort. This was a place far removed from the overpopulated Eastern Seaboard or the frantic West Coast excesses of California.

Here the attitudes that prevailed were those of the early frontier. The inhabitants of the Trans Pecos region neither asked for nor welcomed interference. They lived their lives on their own terms.

These were the people who had wrestled a living from the land in the formative years, putting their mark on it. They'd fought for every inch, carved out empires and earned a place in the history books. Even though the generations came and went, the values remained, and so did the stubborn pride. It made the people what they were.

The only thing immovable was the land itself. It remained as it always had, implacable, indifferent to man and his ambitions. Man had his victories, his minor conquests, but in the end the land always won the final battle.

Benedict survived by providing for the surrounding cattle ranches and the independent oil companies that pulled black gold from the earth. There were also the sheepherders, who struggled to maintain their isolated outfits strung out across the craggy escarpments and skinny grass slopes.

The town was large enough to have its own radio and TV station, serving the outlying community. It was a working town, not given to frills, and the only people who visited were usually connected to the insular business ventures that concerned Benedict. Those who did come were observed, treated with civility and marked as outsiders from the moment they arrived.

Able Team picked up the vibes quickly. From the moment they stepped out of the cab that had brought them from the local airstrip and walked into the lobby of their hotel, they were aware of being scrutinized by everyone they saw.

Stepping up to the desk, Rosario Blancanales took in the decor with a slight smile on his face. "You see this place?" he asked in genuine wonder.

Carl Lyons, filling in the register, shook his head in sympathy.

"He believes everything he saw on 'Bonanza,'" Schwarz told the desk clerk. "Be real disappointed if he doesn't see Ben Cartwright."

The clerk smiled indulgently. He'd heard it all before from out-of-towners.

Picking up their bags, Able Team headed for the stairs. As soon as the men had settled in, they congregated in Lyons's room.

"Plan of action?" Blancanales asked, crossing to the window to peer down into the street.

"Contact Stony Man. See what Aaron has come up with," Lyons said. "Then we decide how to handle it this end."

He picked up the phone and punched in the number. With the receiver to his ear, Lyons listened to the soft pulsing and clicking that told him the call was being diverted and relayed to the Farm. When his call was answered, he asked to be put through to Brognola.

AARON KURTZMAN PICKED up the phone and acknowledged Hal Brognola.

"Okay, put him through," he told the big Fed.

Moments later Carl Lyons was on the other end. "You have any luck?" he asked the computer specialist.

"Luck doesn't have anything to do with it," Kurtzman advised gruffly.

He tapped a key on his board, and the information flashed up on his monitor.

"Since I talked to you back in Miami, I've been doing some hard digging. Then I'd only identified Benedict's location. Now I got more, and I figure this should tie in to the info you got from that telephone message. Carl, you owe me on this one. Back in 1978 there was an Army base out in the Badlands. About fifty miles out from the town, as close as I can put it. It was a low-profile base, used for special training, practical testing for weapons and covert operations. In 1982 it was closed down and forgotten about. It had something to do with shortage of funds. As far as the official word goes, Benedict Base is strictly nonoperational."

"Got it."

"Your AWOL guy, Leopold Meecher, is a communications technician who saw action in Grenada, Panama and the Gulf. He's thirty-four years old, unmarried, and pretty much a career soldier. His current rank is sergeant."

"Present whereabouts?"

"According to my information, he's on special assignment."

"Who with and where?" Lyons asked.

"Officially nothing listed. But you seemed to have answered that part yourself," Kurtzman said. "I haven't given up yet."

"It has to be the right guy," Lyons stated. "I don't believe in coincidence. Too much ties together. All we have to do is find him."

"Could be I can help there. I ran a deep profile on Meecher and came up with a name—Karen Ann Russell, age twenty-seven. She lives in Baltimore and is listed as Meecher's only contact. No relation, so I'm assuming she must be the girlfriend. It's an interesting item, so I did some snooping. Karen Ann Russell booked a flight from Baltimore to Dallas, then she bought a rail ticket to Benedict, Texas. And there's a room booked in the name of Russell at the Lone Star Hotel in Benedict."

"Sounds like she's going to join Meecher. Thanks, Aaron. We'll move on this. You have any luck with those disks?"

"Nothing yet, but I've got the team hard at work."

"Can you patch me through to the boss man?"

Brognola answered Kurtzman's ring.

"Any feedback from the other guys?" Lyons asked.

"Phoenix Force has been up against some hard resistance," the big Fed told him. "They've made some progress but not enough to make much sense at the moment.''

''Striker?''

''No word yet.''

''Talk to you later,'' Lyons said, then cut the connection.

LYONS RELAYED his conversation to Blancanales and Schwarz.

''Looks like Aaron's given us the edge,'' Schwarz commented.

''We *need* to get to Leopold Meecher,'' Lyons said. ''Right now he's our only lead to whatever's going on.''

Blancanales turned away from the window. ''Fine, but what's going on, guys? I mean, we're out chasing a bunch of shadows. Okay, we got one of the creeps who killed the FBI agents. But the other one is still roaming around. Now we're here in the back end of Texas on some wild-goose chase looking for a guy who might or might not be a deserter from the Army. What the hell has all this to do with a Puerto Rican activist group and a hint the Cubans might be involved?''

Schwarz glanced at him, then across at Lyons, who didn't appear to have a satisfactory answer.

Blancanales waited for a few moments, then nodded. ''Okay, fine, now that you've cleared that up for me, why don't we hit the streets and do something?''

He took out his Beretta 92-F and checked the action. Jamming it back into the shoulder holster, he headed for the door.

''I guess we'd better go with him,'' Schwarz said. ''He's in a weird mood.''

Down in the lobby Blancanales asked the desk clerk where they could rent a vehicle.

''What are you looking for?''

''Better be something in the four-by-four range,'' Blancanales said. ''We need to go off-road.''

The clerk smiled. ''Hell, once you get clear of town, most everything is off-road. No six-lane freeways around here.''

''Right,'' Blancanales said. ''Can you recommend a rental agency?''

''Sure. There's one a couple of blocks away. Make a left outside the hotel and keep on walking.''

The clerk produced a business card, which he passed over.

''Thanks for your help,'' Blancanales said. ''It's appreciated.''

Able Team left the hotel and followed the clerk's directions. It was hot, the air close and still because of the bulk of the buildings around them.

"If this was a TV movie, the clerk would be on the phone now, calling the bad guys and setting us up," Schwarz remarked.

"They already tagged us," Blancanales said. "But don't look around or you might scare them off."

"This another of your jokes?" Lyons asked.

"No. Remember I was looking out the window when you made your call to Stony Man?"

"Yeah. So?"

"I saw a car park across the street just after the cab dropped us off. I checked when I came into your room. It was still there."

"And?" Schwarz asked.

"It was waiting when we left the hotel. It's behind us now. Way back but following us."

"And you brought us out into the open?" Lyons asked.

"How else do we flush them out?"

"Not by setting us up as walking targets," Lyons said tightly.

"You carrying your gun?" Blancanales asked.

"You know I am."

"Forgotten how to shoot back?"

This time Lyons only mumbled something rude.

They reached the rental agency without incident. The lot held a collection a vehicles, a mix of regular cars, as well as off-roaders.

Blancanales went into the office and spoke to the clerk behind the counter. He presented her with the card the deskman had given to him. He also produced the credit card Stony Man had furnished the team with, and went through the process of filling out the required forms the woman gave him.

Half an hour later Able Team drove away from the agency in a two-month-old Jeep Cherokee.

"Pretty snazzy color," Blancanales commented.

"Sure," Lyons agreed. "Red. Anybody trailing us will see it a mile off."

"You mean like the car tailing us?"

"Yeah. Like the car tailing us."

Blancanales put his foot on the gas pedal and picked up speed, guiding the Cherokee through the traffic.

"Let's head out of town. We don't want to lead them straight to Meecher if they are who we think they are," Lyons said.

"Question," Schwarz said. "How did these guys know we were coming? Or do they tail every new face in town?"

"We missed Fuentes back in Miami," Blancanales said. "Maybe he didn't miss us."

"He figured the game was up? Watched us go to the airport and checked our flight?" Schwarz didn't sound convinced.

"Give me a better explanation, and I'll go for it," Blancanales said.

Schwarz slumped back in his seat. "I can't."

"The only contact we've had is Stony Man," Lyons reminded Schwarz.

"The cabdriver who brought us in from the airstrip. Don't forget him."

"He didn't have the opportunity," Blancanales countered. "That tail car was already on to us when we were dropped at the hotel."

Blancanales drove them out of Benedict and along the blacktop that cut south, through a landscape that became less populated by the mile. Soon they were coasting along a road that was bounded on both sides by empty, eroded terrain, ridged layers of broken earth and sun-bleached vegetation.

"I can see why the military would site a base out here," Lyons said. "This is like the backyard of the moon."

Blancanales took a sharp right, leaving the main highway behind and pushing the four-by along a narrow asphalt strip.

"Our boys are still following," Schwarz commented.

"I noticed," Lyons said. "It's time we reeled them in."

He checked the way ahead. About three hundred yards along the track was a sudden dip, then the trail curved around a crumbling outcropping of sandy stone. Lyons decided it was going to be the most advantageous spot for an ambush.

"Pol, slow down once you take that curve. I'm going to drop out. Once that tail car shows, you stop. I'll cover you guys from behind."

"How do we deal with these jokers?" Blancanales asked.

"We take it as it comes," Lyons said coolly, which apparently explained everything.

Blancanales watched the dip coming up. As the Cherokee rolled down the slope and he swung the wheel, Lyons opened the door, holding on to the handle. He waited until they cruised around the bend, then felt the four-by slow as Blancanales touched the brake.

Pushing open his door, Lyons jumped out, shoving the door shut behind him. His feet hit the ground, and he skidded on the loose shale for a moment before gaining his balance. Without a backward glance Lyons moved to the side of the track, pressing close in against the slope as the tail car swept around the bend in a cloud of dust that obscured his prone figure from the passengers. He already had the big Colt Python in his hand.

Yards ahead the four-by slowed and came to a stop.

Immediately the tail car's brake lights glowed red, and it slithered to a halt. The rear doors burst open, and armed figures tumbled out, two from the left side, one from the right. They toted stubby Ingram MAC-10 submachine guns, and the way the men carried the weapons told Lyons a great deal about them. These men weren't amateurs.

The moment the Jeep came to its abrupt stop, Blancanales and Schwarz piled out, autopistols at the ready. They hit the dirt in rolling dives, each man clearing the stalled vehicle and presenting separate targets for the gunners from the tail car.

Someone yelled an order.

The gunners moved forward, weapons angling toward the ground and the moving shapes of Blancanales and Schwarz.

The lead guy from the pair who had exited from the left of the tail car paused in midstride. He raised the Ingram and triggered a short burst that sent .45-caliber slugs after Blancanales's rolling form. They chewed at the ground, filling the air with dust and shreds of vegetation.

Lyons pushed himself away from the bank of earth, the Python clamped in both hands. He lined up on the eager gunner and planted a single .357 slug in the back of the guy's skull.

The impact tossed the man forward, arms flying wide, a dark whiplash of blood erupting from the wound. He dropped facedown on the ground, raising a cloud of dust that was his final act in the land of the living.

The shot from their rear alerted the other two gunners. They swung around, seeking the source of the shot. By this time Lyons had already moved, dropping to his knees and hauling himself up against the rear of the car.

Schwarz, pushing to his knees, heard the boom of Lyons's shot. He tracked in on the other two gunners as they twisted around, seeking the big ex-cop. Schwarz didn't wait a second longer. He swung up the barrel of his weapon and triggered a pair of 9 mm slugs into the body of the gunner on his side of the car. The man was spun by the impact, then smashed hard against the side of the car, his un-fired weapon springing from his hand as it slammed against the roof of the vehicle.

The third gunner, suddenly realizing he was on his own, triggered his weapon and swept the muzzle back and forth in a last-ditch attempt at correcting the reversal of the situation. He was caught in a return of fire from both Lyons and Blancanales, who had pushed upright, spitting dust. The salvo of bullets put the gunner down in a bloody moment of pain.

There were a few strained seconds of silence, then the engine of the tail car burst into life as the driver decided he didn't want to join his ex-partners. He slammed the gearshift into reverse and jammed his foot on the gas pedal.

Lyons stepped away from the car as it fishtailed in reverse, the rear sliding as the tires lost traction. The vehicle curved into the rocky bank, metal collapsing with a thump. Splintered stone showered over the trunk, and the car came to shuddering halt.

The Able Team leader moved around to the driver's door as it was kicked open from the inside. The wheelman lunged out of the vehicle, brandishing an automatic pistol, which he swung in Lyons's direction, his face twisting in anger. The autopistol barked, the slug winging by Lyons's head. Feeling the wind of its passing, the former LAPD detective reached out and grabbed the driver's collar, yanking the guy off-balance, the Python slamming across the driver's gun arm. The guy yelled in pain, the autopistol slipping from numb fingers. Lyons spun him and pushed him against the side of the car, ramming the Python's muzzle hard against the back of his neck.

"Stay here," he snapped, running his hands over the driver's body in a search for a backup weapon. He found a compact autopistol holstered against the guy's spine.

Blancanales, slapping dust from his clothing, glowered at the prisoner. "Let me finish him off," he muttered. "Look at the mess I'm in."

"Only after he's been helpful," Lyons said.

The driver glanced back and forth between the two men, unsure as to whether they were serious.

"He can't tell us anything," Schwarz said, coming up to the car. "Can you, hotshot?"

The driver licked his dry lips. He'd witnessed the efficiency of Able Team, the direct and uncompromising way they had dealt with his partners. He knew little about how the men operated. Along with the rest of his team, his orders had been to trail the three new arrivals and take them out at the first opportunity. It was what he was paid for. Right now money seemed the least of his worries. A big bank account was no good to a dead man.

"Opportunities to stay alive in situations like this aren't all that plentiful," Blancanales said. "I should burn you here and now."

He snapped up the Beretta's muzzle and aimed at the captive's head. Lyons let him alone for a moment, then reached up to push the muzzle away from the driver, who followed it with his wide-open eyes.

"He's got a point," Lyons said. "Leaving you alive isn't smart."

"What do you want from me?" the driver asked, sweat beading his face as he looked from one man to the next.

"Why were you tailing us? And why the hit?"

The driver stared at Lyons as if he'd just been asked to explain a black hole.

"I'll make it easier. Who hired you?"

"You might as well just shoot me. If I talk, I'm as good as dead."

"Either way, I wouldn't take out anything long-term," Schwarz advised.

"We know about Leopold Meecher," Lyons said, playing a blind card. "Maybe you should have completed your contract on him first. I guess you blew it."

"The other guys will shut him—"

The driver clamped his mouth shut, inwardly cursing himself for saying too much.

"Whoops!" Blancanales said softly.

Schwarz had moved to check out the tail car. It had out-of-state plates and a rental sticker. He opened the glove compartment and riffled through the contents. Nothing of value. On impulse he pulled down the sun visors. Taped to the back of the visor was a photograph. Schwarz pulled it free and walked over to Lyons, showing him the photograph.

It was an ID photograph of a man in Army fatigues, staring straight into camera. His face was lean, and his hair was cut in a close crop. On the pocket of his fatigue jacket was the name Meecher.

"Now, that's what I like," Lyons said. "Cooperation."

Schwarz searched the three dead gunners. They carried no identification. The only useful thing he found was a folded map in the pocket of one of the men. Schwarz opened it up and found it was a map of Benedict. A number of locations were ringed in pen.

"Let's go," Lyons said, prodding the gunner in the ribs.

The guy started to move forward, then he half turned, grabbing for the Python and forcing it away from him. At the same time he slammed his left knee into Lyons's side, knocking the Able Team commander to one side. As Lyons fell away from him, the man dropped, throwing himself toward the gun he'd been forced to abandon on the ground. His fingers closed over the butt, and he rolled over on his back, sweeping the gun up, finger already on the trigger.

Blancanales yelled a warning, dropping to a crouch, his Beretta tracking in as the guy on the ground fired his first shot. It passed between Lyons's side and arm, then impacted against the inside of the car windshield, showering glass across the hood. A moment later Blancanales fired, three close shots that slammed into the guy's skull and hammered him to the ground.

"Son of a bitch," Blancanales muttered. "Did he really think he could take us all out?"

"I guess he must have," Lyons said. "He came damn close to making it with me."

"See Texas and die," Schwarz stated as they trooped back to the Cherokee.

"It's 'See Naples and die,'" Blancanales corrected him.

"They haven't told Texas that," Schwarz replied.

"Let's go and find Leopold Meecher before these morons shoot up the whole damn state," Lyons suggested.

# CHAPTER EIGHT

*Benedict, West Texas*

The hotel where Karen Ann Russell had booked a room was on the south side of town, close to the Mexican quarter and the railroad stockyards. It was the kind of neighborhood where taking a late-evening stroll was inadvisable.

Lyons eased the Cherokee across the street and slowed as he neared the building. On the day it had been built, the Lone Star Hotel had probably gleamed like a silver dollar. Now it was bleached out and decidedly run-down.

Blancanales leaned forward, eyes picking out a figure just ahead of them on the sidewalk. He took a longer look to convince himself that he wasn't mistaken, then quickly realized he wasn't. He was looking at Leopold Meecher. The man was carrying a brown paper bag bearing the logo of a local burger takeout.

"That's him," he said, pointing out the crop-haired man in faded jeans, "Leopold Meecher."

"He looks to be in a hurry, too," Schwarz observed.

"Could be he has reason," Blancanales said. "Like he wants to stay alive."

Instead of entering the hotel by the front entrance, Meecher turned into the alley along the side of the building. Lyons gunned the engine and rolled up to the alley. It was too narrow for the vehicle to enter.

"Damn!" Lyons banged his fist on the steering wheel. "Get after him," he said as Blancanales slipped out of the vehicle.

As Blancanales headed along the alley, Lyons moved the Cherokee to the curb as soon as he saw an empty space. He was out of the driver's seat and following on Schwarz's heels the moment he had locked the vehicle.

Entering the alley behind his comrade, Lyons caught up with him. Ahead of them Blancanales had vanished from sight. The alley, littered with trash, dim where the high buildings obstructed the sunlight, echoed to the sound of their footsteps. Reaching the midpoint, Lyons put out a hand to stop Schwarz, then pulled open his jacket and drew the Colt Python. Beside him Schwarz did the same with his 92-F.

"Where the hell did Pol and Meecher go?" Lyons asked.

Ahead of them a shadow moved, followed by a figure wielding a stubby autoweapon.

"Tell me later," Schwarz said, and rammed his shoulder against Lyons, knocking him to the far side of the alley.

The autoweapon opened up with a harsh rattle, sending a burst of slugs down the alley. The stream struck the ground between the Able Team warriors, chipping concrete that flew in all directions.

Schwarz, hugging the grubby wall on his side of the alley, cupped the Beretta in both hands and fired a snap-shot that laid a 9 mm slug inches from the gunner's feet. The guy stepped back, surprised by the swift return fire. He hesitated, trying to decide which of the two targets to go for, and allowed Lyons that scant extra moment to aim.

The slug from the big ex-cop's Colt took a chunk of flesh and muscle from the gunner's left shoulder. He spun halfway around, a stream of blood erupting from the gory wound as he stumbled and went down on one knee.

"Go!" Schwarz yelled. "I'll cover you."

The Able Team leader didn't hesitate. He took off in the direction of the wounded gunner, his feet pounding the concrete.

Schwarz, scanning the alley, saw a second gunner appear. The guy stepped out from an alcove, tracking the muzzle of his autoweapon in on Lyons's racing figure. Schwarz didn't waste time warning his teammate. He simply turned the Beretta on the new gunner and triggered two shots that hit the guy in the chest and slammed him to the ground.

Lyons reached the gunner he'd hit in the shoulder. The dazed man, in pain and shock from the powerful slug, was on both knees now, head down. Lyons kicked the autoweapon away from him, bent to frisk the guy and removed a handgun from a shoulder holster.

Schwarz walked past his team leader and checked out the man he'd put down. He was dead. Both slugs had drilled into his heart.

"Pol?" Lyons asked.

"Over here," Schwarz said.

Lyons turned to see Gadgets approaching a door that was recessed in the wall. Blancanales was on the floor just inside the open door, propped against the wall, rubbing at a sore spot on the back of his skull. Farther inside lay Meecher. He had also taken a hit on the back of the head. The difference was that Meecher's injury had been caused by a bullet, which had blown open the back of his skull, depositing a bloody mess on the floor beside him.

"On your feet," Lyons said, prodding his captive with the toe of his shoe.

The wounded gunner pushed groggily to his feet, and Lyons shoved him over to where Schwarz was helping Blancanales to stand.

"I'll check back there," Schwarz said, and headed along the passage, deeper into the hotel.

"You okay?" Lyons asked.

"Give me a minute and I will be," Pol replied.

"They waiting for him?" Lyons asked.

Blancanales nodded. "He spotted me as he opened the door. Walked right into a waiting gun. He didn't stand a chance." Pol waved his hand at the wounded man Lyons was covering. "He put a slug in the back of Meecher's head. His buddy whacked me with his SMG. Next thing I heard was a heap of shooting."

"What about the woman?" Lyons asked. "Any sign?"

"She's along here," Schwarz called out.

"Go ahead," Blancanales said. "I can watch this creep."

Lyons followed the sound of Schwarz's voice. He had to push past a couple of gaping guests. The door to a room stood open, and Schwarz was on his knees beside the prone figure of a young woman. He saw long blond hair and a lot of blood.

"How is she?"

Schwarz shook his head. He had a towel pressed over the woman's body. When he lifted it, Lyons could see where someone had used a knife on her.

"Damn!"

He searched for a telephone and dialed the emergency number. As soon as the operator came on, Lyons asked for an ambulance. He gave the location and hung up.

The woman had opened her eyes. She stared around her. She was in pain and scared.

"Karen Ann Russell?" Lyons asked.

She continued staring at him. Without warning, she reached out to grip his hand in hers. "We didn't want to hurt anyone. All Leo wanted was to get away somewhere so he could think things out."

"Don't worry about it now," Lyons said. "We'll get you to hospital as soon as we can."

"Leo? Where's Leo?... Oh, no... He's dead, isn't he?"

Lyons nodded. "We didn't get here soon enough."

"Those bastards are to blame. He wouldn't have run away if they hadn't wanted him to..." She lapsed into silence, breathing hard.

"Just rest," Schwarz advised. The hand holding the towel over her wounds was glistening red with her blood. She was bleeding to death from internal wounds, and there wasn't a thing he could do to stop it.

"Listen," she said. Her voice was softer now, every word formed with difficulty. "Leo told me some of the names. He was scared he wasn't going to get out of Benedict, so he started to tell me things. Colonel Ray McClain, U.S. Army. Brannon... Arkadian. He's in the Air Force. And there was a Navy guy, Barret. Douglas, I think. Don't have rank. Leo was going to tell me more. Wanted me to write it all down. Then he decided we should eat because he figured we'd be at it a long time.''

''He went out to pick up food, and that was when those men showed up?'' Lyons asked.

Russell glanced at him. ''Yeah. Leo always had bad timing... but he was a nice... guy....''

Her voice trailed off. Lyons looked down and saw the light fade from her eyes. A thin trickle of blood seeped from a corner of her mouth.

''Guess what I can hear?'' Schwarz said.

They all heard it. The approaching wail of sirens.

''Cops,'' Schwarz stated.

''Great,'' Lyons said. ''That's all we need. The Texas Rangers.''

Lyons and Schwarz rejoined Blancanales, who was looking groggy. The hit on the head had taken more from him than anyone had realized.

The Able Team leader took a look outside. Cruisers from the Benedict Police Department had blocked off both ends of the alley, and armed officers converged on the scene.

The three men laid down their weapons and held their hands in plain sight as the police officers closed in. In Lyons's right hand was the leather wallet that held his badge and ID, cover supplied by Stony Man in the event of such an occurrence. It took a couple of minutes of fast talking before the police officers showed signs of easing the tension.

Even so, Able Team was taken into custody and driven at high speed to police headquarters. There, in the presence of a senior detective, Lyons made a call to Stony Man and Hal Brognola.

"No excuses," Lyons said, explaining the situation to the big Fed. "It just went hard on us. No warning. One minute we were close to grabbing Meecher, the next the whole thing blew up in our faces."

"How's Pol?"

"Nursing a headache and giving himself a hard time. He figures he should have stopped it. He's lucky he didn't stop a bullet the way Meecher did."

"Tell him to quit blaming himself," Brognola said. "And that's an order. So what's your next move?"

"Maybe the local cops can give us some kind of background information on this military base. And the guys we tangled with. I'll be liaising with Detective Craddock on that. He's a good lawman."

"I asked if he'd give you his cooperation. He seemed obliging enough."

"I'll get back to you when we have anything useful to report."

"Okay. If Bear comes up with anything on those names, I'll get it to you."

Lyons replaced the receiver. He picked up the mug of coffee that had been brought to him earlier. It was still hot. He was certain it had gotten stronger, too.

Detective Tom Craddock entered the room. He was a tall, lean man with a face that reminded Lyons of a young John Wayne.

"Anything?"

Craddock perched on the edge of the desk. His face was creased by an expression of confusion and a little irritation. "All we can get on those boys you tangled with is the normal stuff—ID and some background. I tried the military angle like you suggested, but I can't get a damn thing on them. We've tried all our data bases, but all we get are lock-outs, restricted information. Damn it, Travis, I don't like being told I can't get information on a suspect. Who the hell are these guys?"

Lyons took the sheet Craddock handed him. He scanned the data. The information, apart from name, birthplace and a little background, did nothing to advise Lyons who the men were working for and why they had killed Leopold Meecher.

"It's like a big chunk of their lives has been wiped out," Craddock said. "Big zero. I don't buy it. Those guys have been doing something. I want to know what."

"That makes two of us," Lyons said.

"Maybe your partners are having better luck with Lester," Craddock said. "You want to take a look?"

Chuck Lester was the survivor of the alley encounter, and up to now his name was all they had been able to get out of him.

Lyons, going under the cover name of Jim Travis, followed Craddock out of the office and down to the basement, where the cells were located. There were a number of interview rooms, with adjoining offices fitted with one-way glass. The room Lyons entered was dimly lit. He could see into the next room through the panel set in the wall.

Lester, his arm and shoulder heavily bandaged, sat in a chair, facing Lyons's direction across a table. The top of the table was littered with plastic coffee cups and an ashtray. On the near side of the table, their backs to Lyons, sat Blancanales and Schwarz, calling themselves respectively Royce and Danson for the mission. A small speaker set in a corner of the room relayed to Lyons and Craddock what was being said on the other side of the mirror.

"—going down for a good while," Blancanales was saying.

"More than a good while," Schwartz added. "I'd say life."

Lester didn't appear happy at the prospect, but the fact hadn't helped to loosen his tongue. He slumped back in his seat, occasionally reaching up with his good hand to rub his bandaged shoulder.

"You believe what you like about us," Blancanales said, "but you know you're in deep. You murdered a man today. No question. The police have the murder weapon, and your prints are on it. No way you're going to wriggle out of that. Plus you're involved in the murder of Karen Ann Russell."

"So you got me," Lester said "What else do you want?"

"How about the people who hired you?"

"Who said anyone hired me? I had a beef with the guy, so I whacked him. End of story."

"The hell it is," Schwarz snapped. "What do you figure, we just fell out of the tree? That was no grudge shooting. Not with the hardware you guys were packing."

"So figure it out yourself, hotshot," Lester replied. "I don't have to say a fuckin' thing."

Lyons turned to leave the observation room, then glanced at Craddock.

"I'd like to try something," he said.

"Be my guest."

Lester's head snapped around as Lyons entered the interview room.

"Now we got all the three stooges together," he said.

"You're a funny guy, Lester," Lyons said. "Try this for a laugh. Seeing as how you have important friends who can remove all your records from the files, officially you don't exist. Makes things easy all around. The local cops don't want to know. It's going to save them a pile of paperwork when we take you off their hands. When you vanish, nobody is going to miss you."

Lester's smirk vanished. "What the hell do you mean? What do you mean vanish?"

"Disappear. You're a disposable item, Lester. And we can pretty well do what we want with you." Lyons nodded at Blancanales and Schwarz. "Get him ready to be moved. We can deal with him and be out of here before sunset."

Lyons turned to go. As he reached the door, he heard the clatter of a chair being pushed back.

"You can't do this! No fuckin' way you can do this...."

"You want to give me odds on that, Lester?" Lyons asked.

The man's face had paled. His mind worked furiously as he debated his options. In the end personal survival won over loyalty.

"If I cooperate?"

"If you cooperate, Lester, maybe we let you stay alive. It depends on the quality of the information you give us," Blancanales said.

"You guys are bastards," Lester muttered, slumping against the wall.

Lyons glanced at the mirror, and he sensed that Craddock would be grinning all over his face.

"First thing you've got right today, Lester," he said under his breath.

"DID HE GIVE YOU much?" Craddock asked.

He had taken Able Team to a local diner and, as they sat over their meal, the Texan cop gently tried to pry some information out of the closemouthed trio.

"Wasn't that much to tell," Lyons told him. "According to Lester, he and his partners were hired to take out Meecher because he was ready to spill information on some low-profile military operation. Meecher was AWOL. He'd ducked out when he found out what the operation was about and didn't like it."

"Whoa," Craddock interrupted. "What the hell are we talking here, boys? Military operation? Around Benedict? And since when did going AWOL merit getting shot?"

"Something's going on at some base out in the desert," Lyons explained. "Lester clammed up after that. He either doesn't know what's going on, or he's really scared of whoever is running the show."

"I never heard of any military base around here," Craddock said. "You sure he said Benedict?"

Lyons nodded. "Like I told you when we first met. We came here because of information we received. We were told Benedict and we were given the name Meecher. We found both. Too late for Meecher, but the way Lester told us it looks like we're on the right track.''

Craddock leaned back, toying with his coffee mug. ''This is way over my head,'' he admitted. ''Way I see it, the thing to do is step back and let you fellers get on with it.''

''Anybody in your department who might be able to give us some information on this base?'' Schwarz asked. ''Maybe someone who's been around awhile?''

Craddock shook his head. ''No one currently in the department,'' he said. ''But there's a guy named Cappy Dwyer. Used to be on the force. Retired a year and a half ago. Born and raised in the county. Knows it better than anyone.''

''Will he help?'' Lyons asked.

''One way to find out,'' Craddock said. ''We go and ask him.''

Schwarz suddenly leaned forward, his hands catching hold of Blancanales as he slumped over the table.

''Hey, the food isn't that bad,'' Schwarz said.

They sat Blancanales upright. His face was pale, damp with sweat, his eyes out of focus. He reached up to touch the back of his skull where he'd been hit.

"Said you should have had that checked," Schwarz told him.

"He will now," Lyons said. "Let's go."

THIS IS A WASTE of time," Blancanales grumbled from the hospital bed. "I can't stay here."

Lyons shook his head. "No choice," he said. "Doc's orders. And mine. You stay for forty-eight hours and leave when he gives you the all-clear."

"A damn headache."

"Concussion," Ironman corrected. "Now shut up moaning and make the most of it."

"See it as R&R," Schwarz suggested.

"Sure," Blancanales said. "How are you guys going to manage without me to back you up?"

Schwarz shrugged. "Be hard, but we'll just have to try."

"Take it easy, Pol," Lyons said. "Craddock will keep in touch. Let you know what we're doing."

He and Schwarz turned to leave.

"Hey!" Blancanales called, and as they turned, he added, "Take care. Okay?"

Lyons raised a hand. "Don't we always?"

IN THE HOSPITAL parking lot, Craddock was just getting out of his car. He had a tall, lean man with him. Tanned, with faded blue eyes, the newcomer eyed Lyons and Schwarz with exacting scrutiny.

"Look like city boys to me, Tom," he drawled.

"Don't let that fool you, Cappy," Craddock said. "They know where it comes from."

"We'll see."

"This is Cappy Dwyer," Craddock said by way of introduction.

"Tom figures I might be able to help you boys," Dwyer offered. He pulled off the long-peaked baseball cap, running his fingers through his thick dark hair.

"He explain what we're looking for?" Lyons asked.

"Yeah. I maybe recall that place. Been some time since I was out that way."

"Think you can find it again?"

Dwyer smiled. "We'll give her a damn good try."

"Keep an eye on the patient?" Lyons asked Craddock.

The cop nodded. "I'll see he behaves."

*Badlands, South of Benedict*

"SHE'S OVER THAT WAY," Dwyer said. "I'd say about ten to fifteen miles. You'd never tell from ground level until you hit the wall. They built the place close to the surface."

"Underground?" Schwarz asked.

"Yeah, like they didn't want anyone to know it was there." He grinned sheepishly at his last remark. "Stupid thing to say. Course they didn't want anyone finding it. That's why it was damn secret."

Lyons glanced across at the ex-cop. "You certain we're in the right direction? Easy enough to get lost out here."

"Hell, boy, I was raised in this country. Jesus, don't go believing all that crap they feed you about the desert changing its shape and all, so no one can find a spot they visited the week before. Only time I was away was when I was in the service. Now, I might not be able to pick up a particular grain of sand, but I sure as hell can find a particular spot."

"I hope so," Schwarz muttered.

They traveled for another half hour, following the directions Dwyer gave them from time to time. The man seemed to have an instinctive knowledge of the terrain. There was nothing indecisive about his guidance. His instructions were sharp and precise.

Lyons turned his attention from the Texas landscape and sank back in the seat of the four-by, feeling the chill from the air conditioner wash over him.

"If I'd been in charge at the Alamo, I would have let Santa Anna keep Texas."

"Don't let any of the locals hear you say that," Dwyer said. "Likely to string you up."

"Figure they're tough, do they?"

"Texas isn't a place," Schwarz said. "I heard someone describe it as a state of mind."

"That's pretty deep," Dwyer observed.

"Too deep for me," Lyons grumbled. "How we doing, Cappy?"

"We should be getting close."

"Hold it," Lyons said, touching the brake and bringing the truck to a stop. He opened his door and climbed out. The move from air-conditioned comfort to the furnace blast of the open desert hit him like a fist in the face. He took a moment to adjust to the unrelenting heat.

Schwarz joined him moments later. "You see something?"

"Off to the east. Flash of something."

"Somebody watching us maybe?"

"Could be," Lyons said.

Then they heard the sound of helicopter rotors slicing through the air. As they all turned, a dark blot in the shimmering sky began to take shape. Within minutes it grew into the outline of a Bell UH-1 Huey. The bulky outline of the chopper, painted in drab olive and bearing Army ID, swept down on Able Team's location, dropping lower. Rotor wash sucked dust into the air, throwing it about in stinging clouds. The moment it touched ground, armed figures in combat uniforms dropped from the open hatch and formed a cordon around Able Team. They all carried M-16s.

A tall, lean figure with the rank of lieutenant stepped to the front. He scanned the three men and their parked vehicle.

"We've been expecting you," he said. "Pretty good timing, Dwyer."

The older man shrugged. "Don't I always deliver?"

Lyons turned slightly, just enough so he could get a look at Dwyer's face.

"You got something to say?" Dwyer seemed to be enjoying himself.

"To you?" Lyons asked. "Not a thing."

Dwyer's confident smirk was his undoing. No one was prepared for Lyons's sudden move. He barely seemed to put any effort into the back-fist that impacted with his victim's face. Blood gushed from his crushed nose, dripping onto Dwyer's shirt. He staggered back, bellowing like an injured bull, hands cupping his face.

The lieutenant, stiff with anger, snapped a curt order to the sergeant standing near Lyons. Without hesitation the man rammed the butt of his M-16 into the Able Team leader's side. The impact dropped Lyons to his knees.

"Try anything like that again, mister, and I'll forget we're supposed to take you in able to walk," the lieutenant said. He caught the eye of the sergeant. "Hiller, get this pair in the chopper and do it now."

"On your feet, asswipe," Hiller yelled.

Lyons, gripping his aching side, fell in alongside his silent partner, making a promise to himself that Sergeant Hiller was going to be taken care of when the opportunity presented itself.

The lieutenant stayed behind to talk to Dwyer.

"As soon as you get back to town, deal with the one in the hospital. There are too many loose ends starting to show. No delay. Take him out."

Turning away from Dwyer, the lieutenant made his way back to the waiting helicopter. Lyons and Schwarz were already inside. As soon as the lieutenant was on board, the aircraft rose from the ground in more swirling dust, then made a tight curve and sped through the air.

Lyons raised his head. Schwarz sat silently by, waiting to see what happened next.

Whatever else they had done by coming out here, they had located Benedict Base and its occupants. All they needed to know now was what was going on.

THE BASE WAS DIFFICULT to spot even from the air. The buildings had been camouflaged to blend in with the desolate surroundings, and they did so with great success. It was only as the Huey came in to hover over the landing site that Lyons, peering through the dust-streaked port, was able to spot the outline of structures. Very little was more than a few feet high. Even the air ducts, which brought out the used air and sucked in the fresh, had been fitted at a low level. The base had been constructed with concealment in mind. The dust, constantly moved around by the wind that was forever drifting across the open terrain, helped to conceal the raised outlines.

The Huey touched down, the pilot cutting the power immediately. As the rotors stopped turning, there was a sudden shift in the ground beneath the chopper. Lyons realized they were on an elevator platform. The Huey sank below ground level. Figures moved out of the shadows and manhandled the craft off the platform, which immediately began to rise again. The moment the platform had returned to its original position, lights came on around the Huey.

Lyons glanced across at Schwarz, who acknowledged him with a slight nod.

The Huey's hatch slid open, and the two men were hustled out of the chopper and across the underground hangar. They were marched along unadorned corridors until they reached a central square. A door swung open, and they were pushed into a room.

The desk was standard military issue, and behind it sat a hard-faced Army major, a predatory look in his eyes.

"You see a red nose on me? No? That's because I'm no fuckin' clown. So don't treat me like one. You two are here because you have been interfering in our operations. That means interfering with the United States Army, and I do believe that's an offense. That aside, I could have you shot right now, and nobody—I mean nobody—would ever find your bodies. So let's quit the playacting. You men are in deep shit."

His piece said, the major studied the two Able Team warriors and waited.

"We supposed to beg for mercy, or what?" Lyons asked.

Schwarz shook his head. "I think the major is waiting for us to tell him who we work for and what we've found out about his unauthorized operation."

"And who we've already told what we've found," Lyons added.

Boots scraped on the concrete floor, and behind Lyons the Able Team commander half turned. He caught a glimpse of Hiller stepping in close. Then pain engulfed Lyons's side as the sergeant hit him with the M-16 again. This time he used a lot more force, and Lyons went to his knees, teeth clamped together to keep from crying out. Hiller followed through, grabbing a handful of Lyons's hair and yanking his head back until he could stare into the big ex-cop's eyes.

"You're a breath away from being dead, boy, so go careful."

Hiller clubbed Lyons across the side of the face.

The major stood and walked around the desk. His hand was resting on the butt of the autopistol resting in the military high-ride holster on his right hip.

"I don't know who you are, son, or who you work for. But this time you're up against the U.S. Army. Not some bunch of back-street juveniles."

Hiller snapped out an order, and two of the armed soldiers stepped up to Lyons and hauled him to his feet.

"Think on it, son," the major advised. "You're in a lot of trouble. Now, I don't give a damn whether you stay alive at the end of this. But until then, I'd advise you to cooperate. Tell us what we need to know, and things could go easy on you. Stay hard, and I'll have you broken into little pieces.

"Hiller, place these men in the detention cells. Let them consider their options for a while."

As they reached the door, they heard the major's voice again.

"And don't worry about your buddy back in Benedict. Somebody will be calling on him during visiting hours."

Lyons, followed by Schwarz, was escorted out of the office. There was another trek along anonymous, drab corridors, followed by a descent to a lower section. Finally the two men were pushed into a bare, harshly lit room. The heavy steel door clanged shut, and they were left alone as the locks clicked into place.

They examined the room. Apart from an air duct set near the ceiling, the walls were smooth. The door fit snugly into the frame, leaving nothing to grab hold of. Schwarz stood beneath the light. It was a fluorescent twin-tube set behind toughened glass. He examined it carefully, shielding his eyes from the glare with one hand. Finally he stepped back, shaking his head.

"Well?" Lyons asked.

Schwarz crossed the room to sit down at the base of the wall, his arms resting across raised knees.

"No doubt about it," he said. "It's a light fitting."

For a couple of minutes Lyons stood in the center of the room, breathing slowly and deeply as he unwound. Then he, too, went to sit against the wall directly across from Schwarz.

"How's the side?" Schwarz asked.

"Sore."

"That Hiller is a mean son of a bitch," Schwarz commented.

"Only while he has an armed squad backing him."

"His type are easy meat on their own."

"His time's coming," Lyons replied.

"You figure this room is bugged?"

"Bound to be."

"So they're listening to everything we say?" Schwarz asked.

"Yeah."

After that, not another word was spoken.

*Nassau, the Bahamas*

WHEN MCCLAIN CAME OUT onto the veranda, his face betrayed his inner feelings.

"You look a little flustered, Ray," Lawrence Boyette said. "The weather getting to you?"

McClain dropped onto the padded chair, reaching for the tumbler of bourbon. "Reports are suggesting we have problems. I'm allowed to react to those."

"Yes. I've heard about the interference in Puerto Rico and Texas," Boyette said. He showed no outward signs of being disturbed.

"A little more than interference, I'd say. Men are dead. There has also been a loss of weapons. A possible compromising of security. And don't forget the Cuba upset. Everywhere I look, something is going wrong. We have two prisoners at Benedict Base. Until they're interrogated, we can't assess how much they know. Just what has to happen before *you* react?"

"I'm a businessman, Ray. I don't react. I absorb facts and make my decisions based on the information I receive."

"Goddamn, Lawrence, this is getting out of hand. All of a sudden we're knee-deep in dead bodies. What next?"

"Relax, Ray, we don't have to quit yet. Our people are on to it. We knew the risks when we went into this. Every war has its skirmishes."

"I don't need a lecture on the nature of warfare, Lawrence. What I do need is an assurance that we're not going to get blown out of the water on this."

"That's an odd expression coming from an Army man, Ray. Perhaps you really wanted to be in the Navy."

"Very droll. Leave the jokes to the comedians. Have your people come up with anything on this group who hit us?"

"A blank at the moment. They're professionals, no doubt about that, but as far as we can ascertain they don't belong to any of the recognized agencies."

"And you still expect me not to worry?"

"Oh, come now, Ray, we're too old to panic because of a few loose cannons."

"I worry when I don't know who set them loose. How do we figure they got on to us? What do they know about us?"

"All in good time, Ray. For the moment we carry on as we have been. Isn't much else we can do. Too much has been pushed into this operation for us to back out now. It'll all be happening soon, and when it does all these incidents will go away. Our people in Texas are already arranging to close down the opposition there. And I'm sure we can stabilize the Puerto Rican and Cuban situations. So don't worry. Everything is on schedule. There's no need to up and run. Have faith, Ray, and you'll be the man of the hour yet."

"Lawrence, there are times I suspect you're full of shit. Today is one of them."

"Coming from you, Ray, that is a rare and sincere compliment."

# CHAPTER NINE

*Southwest of Havana, Cuba*

Dawn thinned the blackness, pushing the night aside. The shadows fled like vampires seeking the sanctuary of darkness, away from the rising glow of the new sun.

Linda Ramos pushed the Oldsmobile up a rutted track that was overhung by lush fronds and thick foliage. The city lay far behind them now. The terrors of the night were like a bad memory—but like a disturbing dream, they skittered around the corners of the mind. She couldn't entirely erase the images of death, the crash of gunfire and the frantic escape from the hungry guns of Lopez's henchmen. The visions stayed with her. The sounds, distant and seemingly detached, still echoed in her consciousness. The coming warmth of the day failed to remove the chill that clung to her, and she shivered with the remembrance.

"Slow down," Manuel warned. "We're not on the highway now."

Her brother's voice snapped her back to reality. Linda glanced at him. He looked tired, his face unshaved, but his smile comforted her. As it always had in the past.

"Are you okay?" he asked.

She nodded, covering her bad feelings with a quick grin. "Just tired. I'm not usually out this late. My brother worries about me."

"Funny girl."

He reached out to touch her hand. "I was proud of you last night. The way you helped."

"What else could I do, Manuel? Those men were after me, too. I could have died the way Ricardo did. It was only because Mike was there that I got out alive."

Manuel Ramos glanced over into the back of the car, where the man they knew as Mike Belasko sat silently watching their surroundings. He hadn't spoken very much during the past few hours, allowing Manuel to guide his sister out of the city and into the countryside. He spent his time observing, silently mapping the way they had come, searching the darkness for any signs of pursuit. His hands were never empty of a weapon. His manner was that of a soldier permanently on duty, ready for combat at any given moment.

Manuel felt safe in the presence of the big American.

"Follow this trail. We will reach a narrow stream. Stop there," Manuel said.

"Where are we?" Linda asked. "Where are you taking us?"

"To meet his friends," Bolan said, leaning forward, "others who are concerned about what's happening to Cuba and are trying to change things."

Manuel stared at the American. "How do you know?"

Bolan smiled. "Trust me," he said lightly. "I've done this before."

Manuel Ramos gave a gentle laugh. "Of that, I have no doubt. Tell me something, Mike Belasko. Just who do you represent?"

"No one you have to be afraid of. I came to Cuba to meet Ricardo Contreras. He was going to give me information about people who are involved in some kind of conspiracy involving Puerto Rico and a group called PRISM."

"If you believe in fate, Mike, then we were destined to meet."

The car rolled on along the track. When the stream came into sight, Linda slowed, stopped and switched off the engine.

"We walk from here," Manuel said, opening his door and stepping out of the car.

Bolan pushed open the rear door. He climbed out of the car and stood by the open door, checking the area. It was quiet.

Too quiet.

"Stay here," he said.

Manuel turned to question the order and saw the Beretta appear in Bolan's hand.

"What is it?" he asked.

The Executioner simply raised a hand to silence him, gesturing for him to stay by the car. He moved to the driver's door and spoke to Linda. "Get the car turned around. Do it as quietly as possible and keep the engine running."

Linda looked up at him.

"Just do it," Bolan said quietly.

He signaled Manuel to his side. "What am I looking for?" Bolan asked him.

"Across the stream there is a slight rise. On the other side a deserted farm. Only a small house and outbuildings. I was to meet five men there. My friends, as you guessed."

Bolan nodded and moved to the side of the trail. He slipped into the undergrowth and began to work his way toward the stream. He crossed it yards up from the track, pushing through tangled foliage until he was able to look down on the overgrown area that surrounded the ramshackle building that had once been home to someone.

The bright morning light showed everything in stark relief—especially the three bodies on the ground in front of the house.

Bolan checked the area thoroughly.

Manuel had said five men.

He turned and returned to where he had left Manuel and Linda. Catching Manuel's eye, he beckoned the man to him.

The Cuban sensed something was wrong as he followed Bolan back to his vantage point.

"Are they there?" he asked.

"Only three of them," Bolan said over his shoulder.

Manuel moaned softly as he took in the scene. "How could this happen?"

Bolan didn't answer. He was scanning the surrounding area, picking up nothing that suggested anyone was waiting for them.

"We have to go to them," Manuel insisted. "They are my friends."

Covering the Cuban, Bolan followed him down. Manuel went to each man in turn, his distress growing when he found the first two were dead.

The Executioner could see the bloody bullet wounds in their bodies, the final kill shots through the heads. He also noticed the burn marks on arms and hands, and the raw bruising on their faces. Someone had made them suffer before killing them.

He heard Manuel gasp, turned to see him bending over the third figure and wiping at the blood covering the man's face.

"He is alive," Manuel said. "Diego is alive!"

Bolan knelt beside the battered figure. He had been shot a number of times in the body, and bore an ugly head wound. The man *was* still alive, but barely.

"Diego, it is Manuel. Can you understand me?"

Diego's eyes rolled in his head as he tried to focus. His mouth moved, silently at first, as he struggled to form words. When he did speak, slowly and in a halting whisper, Manuel had to bend close to his mouth to pick up the words. He spoke back to the man in Spanish, gently coaxing him until he had all the information he needed. When Manuel looked across at Bolan, his eyes were moist with tears.

"Diego and the others came here as we had arranged. We were going to make a decision how we would get out information out to the public. But one of our group had betrayed us. His name is Rico Jorges. As the others waited for my arrival, they were surrounded by a squad of Colonel Lopez's killers. Jorges said they had been watching us for days, just waiting for the right moment. They seemed to know I had important information.

"Jorges was angry because he did not know where I was. Diego and the others were tortured and beaten. But they did not know where I was. If Jorges had checked with those in the city, he would have found out I was being chased. But he just went ahead and had everyone shot. He himself went around and put the final bullet in each man's head.

He did not realize that Diego was still alive when he and his men left."

Bolan glanced at Diego, who had fallen silent. When the Executioner checked for a pulse, there was none.

"He kept himself alive long enough to name your traitor."

Manuel stood slowly, wiping Diego's blood across his shirtfront. "They were all good men," he said, failing to keep the emotion from his voice. "They loved their country but not what is being done to it. And now they had given their lives for it."

"It's always been that way, Manuel," Bolan said. "Good men seem to be the ones who have to die in order to keep the faith intact."

"There is one more thing," Manuel said. "I said there were five men. Antonio Batiste is not here. Diego told me that Lopez's men took him with them. He had information they needed to get out of him, so they are keeping him alive for now."

"Your group is getting smaller by the minute," Bolan said.

"Then get me somewhere where I can tell my story," Manuel stated. "Away from this place where I do not know who to trust anymore. But do it quickly, Mike, because I do not think we have very much time left. What is going to happen is set to take place within the next few days."

"Let's get out of here."

They crossed the weed-choked yard, retracing their steps. Bolan's mind was searching for a detail that hung tantalizingly close yet just out of his reach. There was something significant connected with what Manuel had just said about time being short.

As they neared the stream, a flicker of movement to Bolan's left caught his attention. He glanced that way and made out the crouched form of a man shielded by the thick undergrowth. The imagery was familiar. It was a kneeling man, an object raised to shoulder level.

The image moved, and sunlight winked briefly on the barrel of an autorifle.

Bolan reacted instantly. He threw his full weight against Manuel and slammed the Cuban to the ground. The big American hit the earth alongside the man as a weapon fired and the bullet gouged the earth inches beyond them.

Bolan tracked around and triggered a triburst in the direction of the sniper. His shots passed close. The guy jerked back in surprise, the top of his head rising inches above the foliage.

It was enough of a target. The Executioner held his position long enough to take solid aim and triggered a second burst. There was a flash of red among the greenery, and the sniper toppled backward, his head glistening and bloody.

"On your feet and head over there," Bolan snapped, pointing to where he had dropped the sniper.

They ran hard, feet pounding the ground, knowing that the sniper wouldn't have been alone.

An autoweapon thundered behind them. The earth erupted around their feet as 5.45 mm rounds snapped and chewed at the ground.

There was more gunfire off to the right, but they were moving targets, and those were the hardest to hit.

The sniper's cover loomed before them. Bolan slammed a hand between Manuel's shoulders and propelled him into the bush without ceremony. They crashed through, confronted by the dead sniper. The man's weapon lay on the ground beside him, an AK-74 with a 30-round magazine.

Bolan snatched it up, jamming the Beretta back into its holster. He saw that the dead man also had a 9 mm Uzi hanging by a strap from his shoulder. He took that weapon, too. The 30-round magazine had a second, reversed magazine fixed to it with black adhesive tape. He hung the Uzi around his neck.

"Cut toward the car," Bolan ordered. "We need it to get out of here. Let's hope they haven't hurt Linda."

Bolan talked as he moved, urging Manuel on.

Bullets snapped at the foliage, filling the air with shredded leaves and twigs. They made angry hissing sounds as they whipped through the undergrowth, some of them coming uncomfortably close to the two men.

It was as they pushed their way up the slope that the numbers fell into place. Bolan could have done without the solution to his query at that moment, but the answer reached him unbidden.

*Within the next few days!*

The date that was coming up fast was one Mack Bolan could never forget, him and millions of Americans all over the world.

The Fourth of July.

American Independence Day!

The date had to be significant within the framework of the conspiracy that seemed to be growing with every encounter Bolan faced.

If he was right—and the soldier was more certain with each passing moment—then the need to push forward became that much more important.

And right now the need was to extract himself and Linda and Manuel from the situation in which they found themselves.

He didn't waste time working out the odds or how difficult it might be breaking through the opposition. In a combat scenario, under pressure, the only way was forward, taking the fight to the enemy and using every moment to his advantage.

Bolan had been through so many firefights that he went into reaction mode automatically. His warrior persona took over and led him through the engagement.

The pursuers came through the tangled undergrowth with the stealth of rampaging elephants. The enemy was either clumsy or had a death wish that cloaked them in arrogance. They had to have believed they had Bolan on the run, scared and running in circles.

So let them think that, the soldier decided, and cut off to the side. Manuel Ramos ran on, unaware that Bolan had vanished from his rear.

Turning aside plunged the Executioner into denser foliage. The green fronds closed around him, hiding him from the trio of hard-eyed gunners that crashed into view, each man shouting to the others. They stayed together, making a neater target, losing any numerical advantage because they failed to fan out.

Bolan allowed them to walk past his hiding place, then stepped clear of the foliage. Bolan triggered the AK-74 and laid them low with a withering burst. The 5.45 mm hollowpoints, tumbling as they struck flesh, caused massive wounds. The three went down, bodies jerking.

Manuel Ramos had stopped, drawn by the gunfire. He stared at Bolan, almost transfixed, until the American's yell spurred him on again.

They reached the crest of the slope. Now Bolan moved ahead, cautioning Manuel to stay behind him. Peering through the undergrowth, the soldier was able to see the car.

It was where they had left it, but Linda wasn't alone. A single armed man stood near the rear of the car. He was alert, his attention heightened by the shooting.

Bolan eased the AK's selector switch to single shot. He shouldered the weapon and aimed, waiting until he had full target acquisition, then triggered the assault rifle. The heavy slam of the shot kicked the butt into his shoulder.

The lone guard was punched off his feet by the impact of the slug. It cored through his chest and into his heart, dropping him to the ground.

"Let's go," Bolan said.

Realizing that the assault rifle's magazine had to be nearly empty, Bolan tossed the weapon aside and unslung the Uzi.

He covered Manuel as they ran for the car.

Linda saw them coming and had the presence of mind to climb behind the wheel and turn on the engine. As Bolan and Manuel piled into the Oldsmobile, she put it into gear and floored the gas pedal. The heavy car lurched into motion, swaying as it rolled along the rutted track, kicking up dust.

"If Jorges has betrayed us," Manuel said, "I can understand how they traced Linda to Ricardo."

"Where do you think they took Batiste?" Bolan asked. "If he has vital information, we need him alive, too."

"I believe I know where they will have taken him. To the home of Salvano Cruz. He is the man behind this whole thing, the one who has persuaded Castro to embark on this foolish adventure. He is a dangerous and evil man."

"Then that's where we have to go."

"I can get you there," Manuel said, "but it would be suicide to go against Cruz. He is too well protected."

"Let me worry about that," Bolan replied. "First we need to get rid of this car. By now every cop and G-2 agent in Cuba will be on the lookout for it."

"That can be arranged," Manuel said.

"In the meantime you can tell me what it is that's got so many people wanting to kill you."

# CHAPTER TEN

*Cordillera Central Area, Puerto Rico*

They had been in the air for almost forty minutes. The night was still bright with moonlight, and it was easy to make out the heavily forested terrain below them. Ahead the peaks of a mountain range framed the horizon.

Hawkins was watching the pilot. Behind him, in the cargo area, the rest of Phoenix Force was gathered around a map James had found in the cockpit.

"From the heading I'd say we were on course for the Cordillera Central," McCarter said. He traced a line from where they had taken off to the spot on the map that indicated the mountainous, forested area that formed the island's central spine.

"It's the place I'd choose if I wanted to hide men and weapons," Encizo said. "Pretty isolated, but within striking distance of San Juan."

"We'll soon find out if we're right or wrong," McCarter stated, folding the map.

Gary Manning joined them. He had been opening one of the weapons crates and removing M-16 autorifles. The Canadian had checked the weapons over, then loaded each one with a 30-round magazine. He passed the weapons out to his partners, along with extra magazines.

"We don't know how many we're going up against," he explained. "Better we go in ready for the worst."

"Cheerful bugger," McCarter muttered as he made his way to the cockpit, where he took over from Hawkins.

As the Briton ran his eyes over the instrument panel, the pilot glanced around and saw him. His eyes revealed his nervous condition. He was genuinely upset in McCarter's presence.

Leaning forward, the Phoenix Force commander raised his arm and tapped the glass of his wristwatch.

"How long?"

The pilot thought for a moment. "Very soon," he answered.

"Make certain it is."

Shortly after that, the pilot began to alter course. He did it gradually, hoping that no one would notice the slight drift. But someone did.

David McCarter. He had been talking over his shoulder to Hawkins when he felt the slightest change in the pitch of the chopper's engine. It was a minimal sensation but enough to alert him. He remained calm, keeping the knowledge to himself, and carried on talking to Hawkins. But his eyes settled on the pilot, and he kept a careful watch.

If he hadn't been watching, he would have missed the moment when the pilot reached across and flicked a switch. There was no effect in the cockpit. The realization hit McCarter moments later. The pilot had activated some kind of emergency alert, which had most likely shown itself as a warning light on ground-based monitoring equipment.

McCarter strode forward and sprang at the pilot.

As the Briton neared him, the pilot jerked to one side, avoiding the blow McCarter aimed at him. He yanked at the controls, sending the chopper into a sudden spin and drop.

The sinking motion threw the Stony Man commandos off-balance, tossing them back and forth across the swaying cargo area.

McCarter, clinging to anything he could get his hands on, dragged himself toward the pilot. The Cuban bent forward, reaching for something at his feet, and came up with a stubby fire extinguisher. Without hesitation he hurled the object at McCarter, catching him full in the chest. The Briton stumbled, and his brief incapacity allowed the pilot the time to evacuate his seat and attack. The pair crashed to the deck, each struggling for supremacy.

Bracing himself against the side of the chopper, Hawkins edged his way along to where McCarter and the pilot lay struggling. He launched a hard kick that slammed into the pilot's ribs, rolling him off McCarter. Hawkins followed up, his right knee catching the pilot in the face as the guy scrambled off the deck. The pilot crashed back against the bulkhead, spitting blood from his mouth where his lips had been crushed against his teeth. He met Hawkins's attack full on, slamming a hard elbow into his adversary's stomach.

The younger man sucked in his breath, looped an arm around the pilot's neck and hauled him close. Hawkins increased the pressure, felt the pilot kick, his face darkening as he fought to break free. This time the Stony Man Warrior followed through, maintaining his grip on the Cuban until there was a sudden stiffening in the pilot's stance. Moments later he went limp. Hawkins let him drop to the deck as the sinking chopper swept in at tree level, catching the upper branches and almost overturning.

The spinning rotors sheared through foliage, then buckled and shattered. The helicopter dropped into the thick blanket formed by the treetops. Its forward motion carried for yards before gravity took over and it began to crash through the green canopy.

The men of Phoenix Force were thrown in every direction, all coordination lost as they tried to maintain control of their bodies. They clung to cargo straps and handles, anything that would hold them in one position, and succeeded to a degree.

The descent of the chopper was brought to a sudden, bone-jarring stop as it became wedged between the thick trunks of a pair of close-standing trees. The fuselage, already split and broken, creaked and groaned under its own weight, threatening to break free with each second that passed.

"Everybody okay?" McCarter asked.

The gloom within the chopper made it difficult for him to make out his partners.

He received the responses he wanted. No one was badly hurt. Other than scrapes and bruises, there were no major injuries.

Manning and James managed to open the cargo hatch. Peering out, they were relieved to see that the helicopter had come to rest no more than four feet from the forest bed.

"Our chum the pilot activated some kind of homing device just before everything went to hell," McCarter said. "That probably means we'll have his mates on our necks pretty soon. Best we can do is get off this crate and into the forest. Once we do that, it's up to us to hit these beggars where it hurts. Find their base and put it out of action."

Phoenix Force took its weapons and exited the downed helicopter. In addition to their rifles, they all took one of the LAW rockets from the consignment, except for McCarter, who took an extra one. Once on the ground he slung his M-16 over one shoulder and the Uzi over the other. He followed the rest of the team to a safe distance before turning to look back at the chopper.

Taking one of the LAWs, the Briton pulled the pins and extended the firing tube, activating and cocking the weapon. He laid the LAW across one shoulder, placing his eye to the sight, and fired. The rocket streaked from the tube and ripped through the downed helicopter's fuselage. The explosion that followed tore the chopper apart and destroyed its cargo. Multiple explosions blew a raging fireball into sky above the forest.

"That's one delivery PRISM won't be taking charge of," McCarter said. He tossed aside the used LAW tube. "Now let's get out of here."

*PRISM Rebel Base, Cordillera Central*

MAJOR ANGEL NUNEZ passed through the flap of the tent, ducking his head to avoid brushing against the sloping side, and made his way to the far end of the tent. A number of men clustered around a powerful Russian-made transmitter-receiver.

Nunez halted abruptly at the rear of the group, his impatience growing. He hadn't yet been noticed. After a few seconds his patience snapped.

"Well? Do we have anything further to report?"

One of the men straightened, turning with almost insolent slowness to confront the Cuban.

"We can't raise the helicopter. The radio must be switched off."

"Is the signal still coming through?" Nunez asked.

The PRISM rebel nodded. "It's closer now," he said. "Maybe two or three miles away."

"Form your search party," Nunez ordered. "Once we know where that helicopter is, we move out."

"What do you think has happened?"

Nunez shrugged. "Could be mechanical breakdown. On the other hand, we could have problems. Unexpected visitors."

The Puerto Rican's eyes gleamed with excitement. "Maybe we'll get to see some action."

Nunez didn't answer. The idiots would find out for themselves, he thought. When they got a bullet in the gut, the romance would soon go out of their rebellion.

He wished he didn't have to deal with these Puerto Rican rebels. They were an undisciplined rabble, with nothing going for them apart from their zeal. Nunez was under orders to see that they achieved their aims, which was akin to creating miracles. He was a professional soldier, and his instructions had come from the Cuban high command.

The long-term plan was that Nunez and his unit, comprising Cuban special forces, were to aid PRISM and oversee the successful coup. Once that had been achieved and PRISM was in control, Cuba would send in more troops to enforce the takeover and ultimately place Puerto Rico under her protection. Nunez, who had the confidence of a number of influential members of the government, and especially those involved in the organization of the proposed coup d'état, knew the whole thing could go disastrously wrong.

Cuba's involvement in the internal affairs of another country would be viewed with dismay by many. But there was a need for the regime to make some positive act, to show the world that Cuba was still a force to be reckoned with, not an impoverished island state slowly strangling itself by clinging to the redundant Marxist creed that had left it isolated. While the rest of the Caribbean islands had their feet planted firmly in the present, there were many who saw Cuba wallowing in the backwaters, struggling to maintain its own economy while holding on to the restrictive practices of communism.

Whether the truth lay somewhere between those two viewpoints, there was certainly a need for Cuba to establish itself as a country to be noticed.

So the Puerto uprising presented itself as one such opportunity. There had always been sympathy within Cuba to the Puerto Rican conditions, with its domination by America and the underlying desire of many native Puerto Ricans to free themselves so that they could regain the control of their island nation.

With the emergence of a charismatic, populist leader for the vociferous but impotent PRISM group, those observing Puerto Rico saw the possibility of an uprising on the horizon.

Jesus Salazar, the leader of the PRISM movement, was a handsome man in his early thirties. Salazar wanted his country back. For too long the island had been a pawn, used with casual disregard to the desires of its native population. The Spanish had dominated it, bringing their culture to the island, and due to Spain's continual wars with the other colonial nations, Puerto Rico had been invaded by the French, the Dutch and the British. Though these attacks finally fell by the wayside, the status quo remained until the Spanish-American War placed Puerto Rico in U.S. hands.

Salazar, always at the forefront of political agitation, had long harbored the desire for a free Puerto Rico. He had joined a number of separatist groups during his college years, but had abandoned them due to their lack of commitment. It was only in his late twenties that Salazar had, through a combination of luck and making the right contacts, been accepted into the more radical subculture of Puerto Rican resistance. Through his work as an independent journalist and writer, Salazar had been able to meet people who were to have a great influence on his life. His own ambition, fueled by his need to activate *real* resistance against American rule, brought support from a number of sources. Money began to flow his way. So did offers of material help from outside Puerto Rico. Salazar began to see that his resistance movement—PRISM—was fast becoming a reality.

He gathered people around him who were sympathizers and who also had special skills to bring to the group. With their help he evolved the intricate plan that was to come to fruition within the next few days. One of the greatest tributes to Salazar's dream came from the Cuban government. Assistance, in the form of a force of specialists, was offered by Fidel Castro himself.

Salazar was politically immature but had the potential to learn. He had little experience of actual insurgency. His combat skills were negligible, being little more than a couple of firebombings during his teenage years and a single incidence of weapons hijacking. In all that time Salazar had never once used a weapon in anger, though he felt he could if the need arose. His skills lay in organization and generating support. He also had the oratorical ability to get his message across. So the Cuban offer was accepted.

The specialists, led by Major Nunez, spent long weeks training PRISM members. They left nothing to chance. But despite the intense training, the rebels were still untried in combat. The back-street violence they indulged in, plus the car bombings and assassinations, did little to ready them for actual combat situations. When the actual coup took place, the bulk of the fighting would fall to Nunez and his men.

Over the past few days, however, even Nunez had been forced to admit that things were veering away from the prescribed plan of action.

An infiltrator had been discovered within PRISM. Although he had managed to flee the country, flying back to America, he had been assassinated by a Cuban operative. His discovery had, of course, worried all those involved in the PRISM operation. How far had the undercover man got? What information had he escaped with? His elimination had been swift, before he had been able to pass along any information to his American masters. But the possibility of the operation being compromised had to be faced.

Nunez had received instructions from Cuba to continue. Too many people were involved to back out now, and conditions were right. No overt moves against PRISM had been made, so it was possible to assume that the authorities had little to go on. The risks were as great to abort the operation as they were to continue.

Now, though, other incidents had occurred. It seemed there was some sort of strike team loose on the island. Already they had clashed with PRISM, and members of the resistance movement had died. The strangers moved around with confidence, resisting all attempts to stop them, and now it seemed likely that the strike team could be responsible for the crash of the helicopter bringing in the weapons PRISM had gathered for the upcoming assault on San Juan.

For Nunez the possibility of confrontation came as a relief. He was wearying of the time he had spent in the isolated forest camp, stuck in a kind of limbo with the PRISM revolutionaries. His own men had taught the Puerto Ricans everything they could. The honeymoon was over. It was time to move into the real world. Nunez welcomed that. His life had been spent in combat situations, and he craved the heat of battle once again.

If things went well, Cuba might once again take her place as a force to be reckoned with. It was something long overdue. Sitting in the shadow of

America didn't bode well for the island nation. Cuba's destiny surely had to be greater than being a second-rate, fading outpost of Marxism. There was only one way to make the world sit up and take notice. That was by doing something that couldn't be ignored, by lighting a flame that would burn to the other side of the globe.

And perhaps that flame would be ignited this very night, when Nunez and his force clashed with whoever was upsetting the operation that would wrench Puerto Rico away from the United States and set her free once again.

But only long enough for Cuba to step in and take full control.

## CHAPTER ELEVEN

*Benedict County Hospital*

Rosario Blancanales picked up the TV remote-control unit and pressed the Off button. The screen went blank, wiping away the frantic action of the cop show he'd only been half watching. The Able Team commando was feeling unsettled. Barely a day into his enforced rest, and he was fidgeting like a kid on his first date. Inactivity got to Blancanales quickly. He was a man who needed to be doing something. Sitting on his butt in a private room of a hospital was something he could barely endure.

Increasingly he was worrying about his partners. He hadn't been happy about Lyons and Schwarz going off on their own, but he hadn't been allowed to voice his opinion about it. The dizzy spell in the diner had left him without a valid argument, and at the time even he had agreed that he wouldn't have been much use to his buddies if he passed out in the middle of a firefight. So against his better judgment, Blancanales had allowed himself to be admitted to hospital, where an eager doctor had run tests and declared that a forty-eight-hour rest period was needed, with a review of his condition after.

Blancanales had given in. He said he would stay as long as he didn't have to remain in bed. The medic finally agreed, and Blancanales stayed fully dressed, relaxing in a comfortable chair in a quiet room.

Now, with nothing else to occupy his mind other than the bland, mind mush of television, Blancanales was starting to experience what it had to be like to be stir-crazy. His active imagination was working overtime, for no other reason than it needed to stay alert. He wondered what his partners were doing, where they were, what they had found out. He didn't even know whether they were still out in the desert or back in Benedict.

On reflection he decided they couldn't have returned. If they had, they would have contacted him by now. For all he knew, they hadn't found the isolated base. Could be they were still wandering around looking for it. Maybe Cappy Dwyer hadn't possessed total recall after all. Maybe the guy had been fooling, hoping to have a few dollars tossed his way for trying. Blancanales hopes that wasn't the case, because Carl Lyons didn't have much patience with people who tried to take him for a ride.

He glanced at his watch and saw that it was four forty-five. It was going to be a long night.

### *Headquarters, Benedict Police Department*

TOM CRADDOCK CLOSED the file and dropped it on his desk, where it was swallowed by the mass of paper covering its surface. He reached for the mug of coffee and had it partway to his lips when he realized it was stone-cold. Pushing to his feet, he made his way to the washroom, where he emptied his mug and rinsed it out. Back in the squad room he crossed to the percolator and refilled his mug. He took a long swallow as he returned to his office, slumping back in his seat.

"Landry," he called, "you got that stuff yet?"

"On my way."

Craddock looked up as he heard footsteps nearing his open door. Officer Kris Landry stepped inside, a thick file in her hand. She was a tall, young woman in her midtwenties. Black-haired and strikingly attractive, she looked better in her uniform than the rest of the department put together.

"You find anything interesting?" Craddock asked.

Landry shrugged. "Depends what you figure is interesting," she said. "Just what are we looking for?"

"If I knew, we wouldn't still be here," Craddock answered.

"This dinner you promised me better be worth all this extra work. Not one of your damned Mex chili burgers."

Craddock grinned. "No sweat. This time it'll be on a plate. I promise."

Landry dropped the file on the desk, frowning as she looked over the mass of paperwork. "Jesus, what a mess, Tom. You like this at home? No wonder your wife walked out on you."

"That was for a rodeo rider up north," Craddock replied.

Landry laughed as she went to get a cup of coffee. She returned and leaned her hip against the edge of Craddock's desk.

Watching her, Craddock sensed there was something on her mind.

"What?"

"Lester's details we got from central computer," Landry said. She pulled a folder from the pile and flipped it open. "Something I noticed on his service record. Probably just a coincidence. Here."

She pulled out a sheet and passed it to Craddock.

"What am I looking for?"

"Military service. Lester was in Vietnam from 1969 to 1972. He was in a special unit known as Team Casper, and they did deep-penetration operations."

"I got it," Craddock said, scanning the information. "Am I missing something?"

"Maybe you weren't around that day a couple of years back. The guys were talking about their service records, what they did, where they were." Landry smiled at the blank expression on Craddock's face. "Team Casper. Vietnam. I recall Cappy Dwyer saying he'd been in a Team Casper. He was there in 1971. I guess he must have known Lester. Some coincidence."

"TOO MUCH of a coincidence," Blancanales agreed as Tom Craddock relayed the information over the phone.

"Sit tight," Craddock said. "I'm on my way over to the hospital."

"You expecting trouble?" Blancanales asked, but he shouldn't have asked the question because his own mind was already working along the same lines. "Don't answer that."

Replacing the receiver, Blancanales spent at least thirty seconds considering his position before he picked up the phone again and punched in a number sequence.

"I need Kurtzman," he said.

The Bear came on moments later.

"I need information on a special squad in Vietnam, Team Casper, and a guy named Cappy Dwyer and another one called Chuck Lester. Run a check on them and see if you can locate others in the team. Maybe they're some of the guys we've tangled with since we arrived in Texas. Find out who was in command, and what he's up to now."

"You got a connection?" Kurtzman asked.

"Could be," Blancanales replied. "We just made Dwyer and Lester. I'm getting a bad feeling. Could be Ironman and Gadgets are in trouble."

"Anything else?"

"Benedict Base. I need a location, Aaron, and I need it fast. You got anything yet?"

"No. I've got the team working on it, but we're running into problems. Somebody is putting up blocks. I'd say they don't want anyone finding out exactly where the place is located."

"Find it, Aaron."

"Call me in a couple of hours. I just thought of something off-the-wall. But it might work."

"Okay."

Blancanales was sitting on the edge of the bed, the phone on his lap. Breaking the connection, he went to replace the receiver. His mind was busy analyzing the information he had received, and he missed the cradle, the phone slipping from his fingers, swinging from its cord.

"Damn!" Blancanales muttered, leaning forward to grab at the dangling phone.

His ears picked up the soft brush of cloth against cloth, and movement behind him. Someone was leaning across the bed.

Blancanales twisted, turning to face whoever was behind him, and caught a glimpse of a man in street clothes.

Hands reached out toward him, the toggles of a garrote held between closed fingers. The thin wire was already descending in a blur. Blancanales threw up his right arm, deflecting the wire from his head. The loop dropped over his arm, closing as his attacker pulled it tight.

Blancanales felt the cutting pain as the wire bit into his flesh. Blood spurted from around the loop as the attacker drew back, dragging his victim across the bed. Aware that if he resisted, the wire would slice through to the bone, Blancanales offered none. He rolled across the bed, teeth clenched tight against the pain in his arm. Reaching the edge, the Able Team commando appeared to be dropping to the floor. Instead, using his forward momentum, he swept his right leg around and slammed it deep into the groin of his attacker. The man grunted, doubling over, and Blancanales kicked out with his other foot, the heel smacking into the guy's face. Bone snapped, and blood gushed.

Feeling the wire garrote go slack, Blancanales lunged forward, his shoulder connecting with his attacker's chest. He pushed the man back across the room, shoving hard, keeping the momentum going. They collided with the medicine cart standing against the wall, scattering the contents across the floor. The cart rolled along the wall, with Blancanales's attacker bent across its top, arms flailing wildly as he tried to regain his balance.

The Able Team Warrior slammed a hard elbow into the guy's throat, then hooked an arm under his thighs, lifted and tipped him backward off the cart. The guy landed with a heavy thump, the back of his skull striking the floor with a solid thump. Shoving the cart aside, Blancanales bent over the prone figure, catching a handful of the guy's jacket and hauling him upright. The slack expression on his adversary's face and the loose way the guy's head fell forward told Blancanales the fight was over.

CRADDOCK HAD INSISTED they check the hospital. Something told him Cappy Dwyer was back from his desert trip. It was more instinct than anything, but Craddock had learned long ago to always play his hunches.

Landry was driving the big patrol cruiser. She handled the vehicle with ease, swinging off the street and along the approach. The parking lot was on their right, and Craddock scanned the parked cars.

"Anything?" Landry asked.

"Not yet," Craddock told her, then almost in the same breath he said, "Son of a bitch. He's over there."

Landry followed his gaze.

Cappy Dwyer was hunched behind the wheel of a parked Ford. Landry saw tendrils of smoke curling from the car's exhaust. Dwyer had the engine running.

"Kris, take the car around and block him off," Craddock said, pulling his handgun from its holster as he spoke. "Drop me here."

Landry touched the brake and allowed Craddock to step out of the cruiser.

As the police vehicle pulled away, Craddock moved between the rows of parked cars, his eyes fixed on Dwyer. He was still a couple of rows away when the man sat stiffly upright. His own gaze had settled on Craddock's approaching figure. Dwyer knocked the Ford into gear and floored the gas pedal. The vehicle lurched forward, tires screaming. The Ford spun, the rear fender clipping the side of a parked truck. Dwyer hauled the wheel around, clearing the end of the row, and gunned the vehicle toward the exit.

Craddock set off at a run. He was moving parallel to Dwyer, with a single row of vehicles between them. Dwyer's anxious face kept turning in his direction. The ex-cop didn't look scared, just angry.

"Give it up, Cappy!" Craddock yelled above the roar of the Ford's engine. He let Dwyer see the Beretta autopistol he was carrying.

Dwyer's response was to haul his own weapon into view. He laid it across the window frame of the door and triggered two quick shots at Craddock. A car window exploded to one side of the cop. He slackened his pace, falling a little behind Dwyer's car. He raised his Beretta, two-handed, and settled his aim on the Ford. The 9 mm slug blew a hole in the right rear tire of the speeding car. As the rim dropped to the pavement, showering sparks, Dwyer struggled to hold the vehicle on a straight course. It veered to one side, hitting the line of parked cars as it bounced along the row.

The cruiser swung into view at the end of the line, blocking the exit. Landry shoved open her door and raised the shotgun she had snatched from the rack. The muzzle of the pump-action weapon settled on the front of Dwyer's vehicle. Landry triggered a single round, the blast piercing the Ford's grille and puncturing the radiator. Steam spewed out in clouds.

Dwyer lost control of the Ford. It slewed to the left and plowed into the rear of a parked vehicle, coming to a shuddering stop.

Craddock raced between parked cars, coming up behind the Ford. He saw Dwyer kick open his door and scramble out. The former cop was still holding his autopistol.

"Lay it down, Cappy!" Craddock yelled. "Now!"

Dwyer turned to face him, his face twisted in defiance. "Go fuck yourself," he screamed, and pulled the pistol into target acquisition.

Craddock fired twice, the slugs catching Dwyer in the chest, spinning him off his feet. He slammed facedown on the pavement. Craddock ran over to the man and kicked the autopistol out of his reach. There was no need. The 9 mm slugs had drilled through Dwyer's chest and blown out between his shoulders. The pulped and bloody wounds were flecked with shredded lung tissue.

By the time Kris Landry joined Craddock, Cappy Dwyer was dead.

BLANCANALES WAS in a treatment room when Craddock found him. His arm had been cleaned up, and the wound was being stitched.

"You okay?" Craddock asked.

Blancanales nodded. "Better than my visitor."

"Sorry I couldn't get here sooner."

"I heard shooting."

"Dwyer was playing wheelman," Craddock said. "He figured he was a fast gun, as well."

"Somebody is getting touchy," Blancanales said. "Nervous enough to send out a hit man."

"Let's say you're right. What I want to know is, who? Somebody is pulling the strings. I'd like a name."

Wouldn't we all? Blancanales thought.

He also wanted to know where Lyons and Schwarz were.

*Stony Man Farm*

HUNTINGTON WETHERS tapped the final key, sat back and watched the information scroll down his monitor screen. His eyes ached, and his back was stiff from a long session hunched over his keyboard. The discomfort was going to be worth it, he decided, because he was beginning to make some kind of sense out of the jumble of information he had dredged up. Right now he was attempting to pull it into shape, something that could be understood without the need of a translator.

Sensing movement behind him, Wethers glanced around and saw Carmen Delahunt studying his screen.

"How's it going?" she asked.

"I'm getting there. The input from your FBI source helped," Wethers told her.

"Glad to be of service."

Wethers pushed his chair back and stood. He crossed the lab and poured himself a mug of coffee.

"Where's the boss man?" he asked, noticing that Kurtzman was missing.

"With Hal. Aaron has been working on something for Pol. He's still trying to locate Carl and Gadgets."

"Still on the missing list?"

Delahunt nodded. "Afraid so."

Turning back to his monitor, Wethers saw that the scrolling had stopped. He stood examining the data he had pared down to the bone. After a while he activated the printer, and it began to disgorge hard copy.

"Seems to be making sense now," he said. "Carmen, would you give Hal, Barb and Aaron a call? We need to talk."

Delahunt picked up a phone and contacted Brognola. The big Fed acknowledged her request. A few minutes later the three entered the lab.

Wethers turned to meet them, holding the printout in his hand.

Before anyone could utter a word, Akira Tokaido let out a whoop of triumph, spinning his chair away from his screen and jumping to his feet.

"Hey, I got something," he said triumphantly. "Transfer of funds from a London bank to a company in Puerto Rico. One of the names connected to the company is Jesus Salazar."

"Where did the money come from?" Kurtzman asked.

"That was the tricky bit," Tokaido said. "It's like unraveling spaghetti. The usual dummy corporations, dead ends, lock-outs. But I did pin it down. The original transfer came from a small company owned by Boyette Inc. The guy who runs the whole show is one Lawrence Boyette. It's a big corporation with fingers in a lot of pies, including armament. And Boyette's profile shows he was a colonel in the Air Force."

"Ties in with the information I've put together," Wethers said. "Boyette was a high-profile figure during the Cuban missile crisis. There was a lot of talk about him and some other high-rankers. Something about them wanting to push the button and nuke Cuba. Boyette was ready to take Castro down."

"That's right," Brognola said, crossing the room. "Boyette decided that talking to Castro and the Russians was a waste of time."

"According to my data," Wethers added, "Boyette had powerful friends in the military and the government. Still has, the way it reads. And they all lean toward the hawks rather than the doves."

"Boyette was always gung-ho and to-hell-with-the-consequences," Brognola said. He leaned against the edge of Tokaido's console, tugging his tie loose and unwrapping a fresh cigar. "At the time of the Cuban crisis, the rumor was that Boyette and his pals almost succeeded in launching U.S. missiles on Cuba. They managed to override control codes and tried to engage missile launch without presidential sanction. It got that close before they were forced to step back. If Boyette had made it, we might be living in a different kind of world today."

"Was that why Boyette resigned from the Air Force?" Wethers asked.

"The story goes that Boyette had one hell of a stand-up fight with the President. He felt the military had been made impotent by the administration. Decisions concerning military intervention had been taken out of their hands by the politicians. He felt he was unable to serve under such restraints, so he quit. He made it clear he still believed he had been right. Giving in to Cuba made America weak. It wasn't right to have a Communist dictatorship ninety miles off the American continent."

"That was when he took over the Boyette family business," Wethers said. "He plowed everything he had—time and money—into creating a financial empire worth billions. It controls electronics, chemicals, media and one hell of an armament division. He's still a hawk, though, and hasn't relented on his feelings about Castro. He funds Cuban-exile groups and anything that might hurt Cuba and Castro."

"So why would he fund PRISM?" Barbara Price asked. "Assuming that the money he's sent to Salazar *is* being used by the group, that tells us he's handing money to dissidents who want the U.S. out of Puerto Rico. Who is he getting at? America or Cuba?''

"How about one giving him the opportunity to go for the other?''

The question had come from Katz. No one had heard the Israeli enter the computer lab. He joined the group, aware that his cryptic words had set them thinking.

"Okay, Katz, we give in," Brognola said. "I know you're dying to give us the answer. So go ahead."

"I've been playing around with all we've got so far, moving the pieces and trying to come up with a sensible scenario. The one piece I couldn't get to fit was this suggestion there was American involvement. So I did some hypothesizing."

Katz turned to Price. "You asked who Boyette might be trying to get at by funding PRISM?"

Price nodded.

"Think about this," Katz said. "PRISM stages a coup d'état. Cuba offers help—weapons, special forces to back up their brothers in the struggle against a common enemy. We all know how Castro feels about American influence in Puerto Rico. And he's still smarting over the defeat his military got when the U.S. went into Grenada and kicked out his advisers. Castro would like nothing better than to see us out of Puerto Rico."

A thoughtful silence hung over the group as they debated Katz's proposal.

"Wait a minute," Delahunt said. "If Puerto Rican rebels try for a coup, we'll go in and stop it."

"Yes," Katz agreed.

"And Cuban intervention wouldn't be viewed very favorably."

Katz had a smile on his lips. He could see the Stony Man brains probing and pushing, picking up on the germ he'd planted.

"Go back to 1962," Katz suggested. "Use that as your basis."

"The missile crisis?" Wethers asked.

Katz nodded. "Fit that into the current situation. The common factor being Lawrence Boyette."

There was silence again until Brognola chomped down on his cigar with enough force to bite through it. "Dammit, Katz! That's a hell of a hypothetical conclusion."

"But it fits, doesn't it?"

Tokaido leaned forward, the beginning of a smile playing around his lips. "Boyette is still ticked off because Cuba backed down over the missiles. He missed his chance in 1962. All this time he's been figuring a way to make it happen, a reason for the U.S. to hit Cuba hard. A legitimate excuse."

"Like Cuba becoming involved in a rebel strike against the Puerto Rican government?" Wethers said in disbelief.

"Cuba backing PRISM is a strike against the U.S.," Katz advised.

"Sure," Wethers agreed, "but enough to go to war over?"

"More of a retaliatory attack that would cripple the Cuban military. Take out their airfields, defense systems. Hit power stations," Brognola said.

"Boyette hasn't got the capabilities to do that," Price argued. "He's a civilian."

"With connections that run very deep in the military setup," Katz said. "He has a lot of friends who agree with his views. Members of the military who don't like the Cuban situation and who would jump at the chance to give Castro a bloody nose."

"You realize we're talking conspiracy here?" Price said. "A deliberate plot to involve Cuba in an action that would leave her open to a military strike by the United States. It would have to involve high-ranking personnel from the military. I mean, aren't we actually talking treason?"

"Not quite, since they're not plotting to overthrow the government" Brognola said. "But it's a conspiracy, and unconstitutional. And the way I see it, it could eventually lead to treason."

"How do you get Cuba to agree to help PRISM?" Tokaido asked. "Taking this hypothesis further, first you have to get Cuba involved. Like 'Hey, Fidel, my man. We want you to invade Puerto Rico to give us an excuse to come over and blow you off the map.' "

"Good question," Brognola said, turning back to Katz.

The Israeli was ready for that. "We already know that there is some kind of military involvement from within the U.S. That's why Able Team is in Texas. We also have a Cuban down for the murder of two FBI agents, one of whom was investigating PRISM. Somewhere there's a connection that will lead us to the people directing all this. Striker's in Cuba now, looking into that side of the matter."

"It still doesn't tell us how Cuba got involved," Wethers argued.

"You haven't been analyzing the information coming in," Katz said. "Take time and check it out. Makes for interesting reading."

"Castro is at a low ebb," Brognola said. "His standing isn't all that good with the population. Nothing's really working for him. He needs the boost of a big victory. On the other side we have Cubans who want to topple him, enough to get into bed with American backers. They get their man and his people to work on Castro. And believe me, there are some clever ones around. They take Castro aside, show their concern, tell him the people need something to take their minds off day-to-day problems. They convince him it's time to stand up and be counted. All they want is Castro's say-so, and they can offer their advisers for PRISM's cause. Castro is promised a victory over the U.S., a time of pride for Cuba, a return to greatness."

"It sounds a little naive," Wethers said.

"Remember Germany before the Second World War," Katz said. "Who would have thought someone like Hitler could take a nation back into war fever after the 1914–1918 mess? But he did. And they believed him, believed that they could conquer the world."

"Castro could fall for it. The hard sell. Playing on his emotions, and we all know Castro is a patriot at heart. Politics apart, he loves Cuba. He'd like nothing better than a victory for her before he dies. He could allow himself to be persuaded, not knowing that his Cuban allies are setting him up.

"If the plot runs its course and the U.S. hits back at Cuba, Castro is going to go down like a lead balloon. He'd find himself alone. Nobody would stand behind him then. He'd be thrown to the wolves. And that would be the time for the guy who engineered it all to step in as Cuba's new leader."

Price stared at Katz. "Hypothetical, Katz? No way. I think you've just told us exactly what's happening."

"Let's work on that basis, people," Brognola said. "I want everything you can get on Boyette.

And work on the names we got from Able Team and the military personnel named by Karen Ann Russell. Go back and see if they link up to Boyette. I'm betting we find they're in this together. Check Boyette's movements. His known associates—whoever they are. Look into military deployment, anything that doesn't look right. Equipment and weapons movements that can't be accounted for. I don't give a damn how you do it or who you upset. If there are any problems, let me know."

"We have a connection between the hit men Able Team tangled with and one of the names Karen Russell gave them," Wethers said. He showed his printout to Brognola and Kurtzman. "The hit teams were current and former members of Team Casper. And Captain Ray McClain, U.S. Army, was the guy who formed the unit in Nam. He still has control over Team Casper, though according to official records it's on standby, not active service. Could be that Team Casper is using Benedict Base to operate out of."

"Maybe they're going to be used to go into Cuba as a covert force," Katz suggested. "They could fly in from the base."

"All done without presidential authority," Kurtzman said.

"How can they get away with this, Hal?" Price asked.

"Come on, Barb, you of all people should be able to understand the way the game is played. *Covert* is the magic word. Some of these groups are so deep they never see the sun. Political—military—they run their projects and hush-hush schemes with a free hand. They do so away from prying eyes, with layers of command to shunt questions aside, to delay and confuse."

"Put like that, it's scary," Price said. "So how do we fight them?"

"Like we always do," Kurtzman replied. "Down and dirty. No rules except we go out to win."

Price shook her head. "Land of the free," she said softly.

Kurtzman nodded. "That's right." He held out his mug. "And I don't pay a damn penny for my coffee! Now fill me up, would you, Barb, and let's hit these sneaky mothers where it hurts."

# CHAPTER TWELVE

*Cordillera Central Area, Puerto Rico*

The first shots in the exchange between Phoenix Force and the PRISM rebels came when a Puerto Rican decided that the moving shapes ahead of him were those of the opposition.

He was incorrect. The shapes he fired on were nothing more than tall fronds. The volley of autofire from the rebel's AK-74 tore the fronds to shreds.

There was no one to point out the rebel's error, because seconds after his initial fire, others in his group responded themselves, convinced they were under attack.

The previously silent forest exploded with the chatter of autofire and men calling out to one another.

Despite the commands coming from Major Nunez and the other Cuban advisers, the PRISM rebels kept up their fire.

By chance some of the gunfire came close to the advancing Stony Man warriors. They immediately went to ground, returning fire, and set in motion the subsequent exchange.

It wasn't an unusual commencement to a hostile action. Firefights were often set off by a nervous finger on a trigger. An overactive imagination and the automatic response of a single individual could plunge both parties into a confrontation neither side might have really wanted at that precise moment in time. Once the action had been initiated, there was no going back, no returning to the period of calm. It became a matter of survival, one side against the other, with every man determined that he wouldn't become one of the casualties.

David McCarter, a veteran of countless actions, closed his mind to the vicious hum of lethal slugs crisscrossing the air above his head. Flat on the forest floor, he issued his orders to the rest of the team, and knew they would face whatever lay before them with the professional calm and efficiency that had served them well over the years.

The Phoenix Force commandos chose their ground and selected targets, offering only token fire until they were able to pinpoint the opposition with certainty.

The first hit went to Rafael Encizo. The fiery Cuban had found himself a solid tree trunk behind which to make his stand. He studied the forest mass in front of him, biding his time, knowing that when someone made a move he would see it.

It took no more than thirty seconds before a dark figure detached itself from the surrounding gloom. Encizo made out the extended outline of the man's rifle as he advanced. Raising his M-16 and sighting, the Cuban expatriate triggered a short burst that was targeted on the man's chest. The rebel went down hard, kicking and screaming, his own weapon firing as his finger jerked back against the trigger.

A rapid exchange between a number of the rebels resulted in a soft crack overhead, and suddenly the area was bathed in brilliant light as a flare ignited. The illumination revealed a number of the PRISM rebels out in the open, caught without immediate cover.

Three PRISM rebels were cut down in the opening seconds. The suddenness of the attack and the terminal results created confusion among the PRISM rebels, few of whom had experienced hand-to-hand fighting. They were more used to inner-city terrorism, the four-against-one principle usually enacted in a back alley, or the indiscriminate bombing of someone in his car or house. This was different. A man had to depend on his own courage, his ability to face another on equal terms. When they saw their companions dropping, with blood spouting from ragged holes and inhuman sounds erupting from their throats, the PRISM hardmen realized just what they had let themselves in for.

FOR MAJOR NUNEZ, the firefight became an object lesson in combat survival. Within the first moments of the action, he realized that the Puerto Rican rebels were even less ready for action than he had first imagined. The training he and his men had drilled into the PRISM members seemed to fly out of the window with the sound of the first shot.

Immediately Nunez had ordered everyone to cover. His own men had done so, but the Puerto Ricans had hesitated, unable to make up their minds where to go. That in itself might not have been so bad, but then one of them had walked into the sights of the enemy and had been cut down. That error had been compounded by one of the PRISM rebels deciding they needed to *see* where they were. He had fired a flare, bathing the whole forest area in revealing light.

Chaos became the name of the game.

The rebels caught in the open were taken out in the opening seconds. The others, either through anger at the deaths of their comrades or because of total panic, opened fire with everything they had, saturating the area.

The enemy force remained under cover initially. Their return fire was accurate and delivered with cool deliberation. Nunez could only admire their combat skills.

It did little to ease the situation. Nunez, who had seen action in Africa and Grenada—where he had barely escaped capture during the American invasion—saw that he wasn't going to get much support from the Puerto Ricans. He was going to have to depend on his own men, of which there were only half a dozen.

Falling back, he gathered them around him, delivering the swiftest instructions in his career. "There are only a few men out there, but they know their business. We'll fall back to the base and defend that. At least we have the rest of our people there. Now get these PRISM idiots out of here before we lose the whole group."

"Looks LIKE they're pulling out," James called across the firing zone.

"Keep up the pressure," McCarter directed. "Maybe they'll lead us back to their base."

Enemy fire was still coming their way, but to a lesser degree as the PRISM rebels were drawn back into the forest. The light from the flare was starting to fade now, the shadows lengthening again as darkness slid back into the forest.

"T.J., you and Cal cut around to the far flank. Try to keep them in sight without showing yourselves. We'll follow, let them know we're still around. If we make enough noise, they'll concentrate on us, and it might give you time to pinpoint their base."

Hawkins and James slipped into the forest without a word, circling around to run almost parallel with the retreating PRISM force.

Manning and Encizo checked out the downed rebels. They were all dead, having been caught in a heavy cross fire. There was time to pick up additional weaponry and ammunition from them. Encizo found that one man had a number of fragmentation grenades clipped to his combat harness. The Cuban took them and passed them around.

"U.S. grenades," McCarter observed. "Kalashnikov rifles. These blokes don't give a damn where they get their gear from."

"The uniforms are Cuban supply," Encizo said, "still pointing to the connection we were given at the mission briefing."

"Move out, mates," McCarter said. "We might have a long walk ahead of us."

CONTACT WITH THE ENEMY came sooner than expected.

A roving scout belonging to Nunez's Cuban advisers almost walked into Gary Manning.

The burly Canadian had chosen to take the outer flank of McCarter's skirmish line. He was moving around the perimeter of a forest pool, where the brackish water gleamed dully in the moonlight, its surface covered by a green scum over which hovered masses of tiny flies. The far side of the pool was shielded by a thick tangle of twisted, intertwined foliage. As Manning drew level with the pool, he picked up the crackle of the foliage being disturbed by the passage of some animal as it came to drink. The Canadian saw the dark, four-legged creature emerge from the foliage and dip its head toward the water. The darkness partially cloaked the animal, making identification impossible.

The distraction might have been fatal. But Manning, while watching the drinking animal, hadn't abandoned his primary role, and the greater part of his attention was still on the forest that surrounded him. He picked up a fainter sound than the one previously caused by the thirsty animal.

This was the cautious but unmistakable sound of a human moving through the undergrowth. Manning knew it was human. No animal wore clothing that rustled gently. Nor did animals carry equipment that made soft, familiar sounds as metal touched metal.

Turning toward the source of the sound, Manning caught a glimpse of a uniformed figure detaching itself from the surrounding undergrowth. The camo-clad figure lunged forward and up, slashing at Manning with a thick-bladed knife. Moonlight glinted on the blade as it cut at the Canadian's midsection.

Manning sucked in his stomach, leaning away from the slash of the blade. He felt it cut his shirt as it passed. Then he made a quick sweep with the butt of the M-16, catching his attacker under the jaw. The wet sound of the stock cracking against the man's flesh was followed by the grunt of pain as he stumbled sideways.

He recovered quickly, making a backward slash with the knife even as he fell to his knees. Manning avoided it easily. He reversed the M-16, slamming it down across the man's back, directly between his shoulders. The man sprawled facedown in the dirt, the knife bouncing from his hand and landing in the pool with a splash. Closing in, Manning was surprised when the downed man flipped over on his back, kicking out and catching him on the hip. The blow halted Manning long enough for the man to gain his feet. He came at the Phoenix Force pro fast, his right leg sweeping around in a high kick that cracked against Manning's side, spinning him to his knees. A follow-up blow bounced off the big Canadian's chest, but laid him on his back.

Before Manning could react, the next kick spun the M-16 out of his hands. Rolling on his side, he avoided the next blow, twisting his head as he lashed out with his foot. He calculated right and slammed his heel against his adversary's knee, drawing a wrenching grunt from the man's throat.

A powerful sweep knocked the attacker's feet from under him, dumping him on his back.

Manning gathered his legs under him and threw his whole weight on the stunned figure, slamming the point of his elbow deep into the exposed throat. As the man began to choke, Manning hit him twice more, putting every ounce of his strength into the blows. The guy beneath him arched up off the ground, coughing up gouts of blood as he struggled to draw air in through his ruined windpipe. Pushing to his feet, Manning crossed to where his M-16 had fallen. He picked up the weapon and returned to where his attacker lay still and silent.

Kneeling beside the body, the Phoenix Force commando went through his pockets. Apart from a pack of cigarettes of Cuban manufacture and a lighter, the man carried little of interest except a folded manila envelope in one shirt pocket.

Manning took it, then got to his feet and moved back through the forest, ignoring the nagging ache in his ribs. He was alive, and that counted for a great deal.

NUNEZ REALIZED something was wrong as he led his group back to the base camp. It wasn't like Santos to vanish. The sergeant had been with him for a long time, and they had been through armed conflicts on more than one occasion. If Santos was missing, the reason for it would have to be serious.

As they reached camp, acknowledging the challenge from the perimeter guard, Nunez decided it was time to contact his superiors in Cuba. Matters had reached a point where he needed to involve the higher command. Let them make any further decisions as to the necessary response. If the plan was to go ahead, then Nunez had to have his position clarified. Security for his people was important. They were a long way from home, and though his force was made up of experienced soldiers, Nunez was well aware that he only had a small complement. He had been promised that once the initial takeover had been achieved, more men would be flown in immediately to supplement the Puerto Rican foothold.

It all sounded good in theory. Nunez knew that battles weren't won by theory. They were won through the sacrifice of the men on the ground, in the front line, where pain and suffering went hand in hand with death and spilled blood. Too many times the fighting men were sacrificed in the name of glory while the high command remained well behind the lines, directing the campaigns with little regard to the slaughter.

"Rivera, I need to talk to Colonel Calvado," Nunez announced as he entered the communications tent.

The Cuban radio operator now on duty glanced up, surprised. Whatever was inside his head stayed there as he operated the transmitter-receiver that would link them to Cuba via satellite. Communication silence had been ordered from the start. The risk of being overheard had been deemed unacceptable. If Nunez was ready to break that silence, then something bad had to have happened.

"If Calvado is not available, tell HQ to get him immediately," Nunez went on. "No excuses. I have to talk to him now."

The tent flap was thrown aside, and Sanchez, the PRISM commander, came inside. He was a humorless, heavyset man in his thirties, and he considered himself superior to Nunez, treating the Cuban with badly concealed disdain. The major didn't like him.

"What's going on, Nunez?" Sanchez demanded. "My men tell me half of their comrades have been killed. And you come running back here like a dog with its tail between its legs."

"Go away, Sanchez," Nunez said wearily. He had too much on his mind to allow himself to be bothered by this posturing moron. "I'm busy."

He turned away.

Sanchez grunted in anger, then reached out and laid a meaty hand on Nunez's shoulder, turning the Cuban to face him. "Don't walk away from me, you Cuban bastard!" he yelled.

Nunez actually smiled the moment before he slammed the hard edge of his hand against Sanchez's throat. The PRISM rebel reeled back, clutching his throat, gagging wildly, eyes bulging and streaming with tears.

"You were shouting again," Nunez said. "I've asked you not to."

"Major," Rivera said, "they're coming through"

Nunez took the headset.

"For God's sake, Nunez, what are you doing?"

The voice was that of Colonel Calvado, the commander of the Cuban special force.

"No choice, Colonel," Nunez said. "Things are starting to deteriorate here. Right now we're in a combat situation. I've already been in a firefight with some unknown force. I'm expecting them to show up here any minute. We've lost the helicopter bringing in backup weapons."

"What are you expecting me to say?" Calvado asked. "Give me your resignation and come home?"

Nunez chuckled. "Not this time, Colonel. The way things are going, I'll probably end up buried on this damn island. Do we carry on? Is the timetable the same?"

Calvado sighed. "The same. We're in this right up to the end, Nunez. No turning back now. Do what you have to. If I receive your signal on time, I'll have your reinforcements in the air immediately. And that is my word on the matter. No one else will give you that kind of promise.''

"Very well.''

"Are all your people ready?''

"Yes. I just hope we can carry this through. These PRISM rebels are not going to be much help.''

"Icing on the cake, Nunez,'' Calvado said. "I'm depending on our forces to do the bulk of the work.''

"Yes, Colonel.''

"We will wait for your signal,'' Calvado said. He paused for an instant. "Nunez, good luck.''

The connection went silent.

Nunez handed the headset back to Rivera.

He turned and went outside.

"Are the perimeters secure?'' he asked one of his men.

The Cuban nodded.

"I believe we will be having visitors soon. Be ready for them. And get some of those damn PRISM people up where I can see them. This is supposed to be their fight, after all.''

Nunez made his way across the camp. On the far side, beneath heavy camouflage nets, was their main helicopter, the one that would take them into the city in the hours before dawn, where they would join up with the other units and initiate the strikes that would herald the start of the PRISM attack.

"It might be a good idea to get this thing ready in case we have to use it sooner than we anticipated," he said to the chopper's crew.

He made his way back across the camp, his mind absorbed by a number of urgent requirements.

They all vanished from his conscious thoughts as there was a sudden uproar, the crackle of autofire and the boom of exploding grenades as their pursuers hit the base camp.

# CHAPTER THIRTEEN

*Pinar del Río Province, Cuba*

The province was dramatic, with its forested, mountainous landscape, hills and valleys, riddled with caves. Agriculture dominated the area, with tobacco being cultivated in parts of the region.

The life was paced, slow, the peasant culture still strong beyond the larger towns. Here the *guajiro*, the classic Cuban peasant, could still be found. Honest, hardworking people, they were the backbone of the country.

The village was small, the people friendly. Bolan stayed in the background, allowing Manuel Ramos to go about his business of arranging alternative transport for them.

The Executioner sat with Linda Ramos outside a white-painted café. They drank cups of rich coffee and ate a simple meal.

Pushing aside his empty plate, Bolan raised his eyes and met the steady, uncompromising gaze of Linda Ramos. Her deep brown eyes watched him as he reached for his coffee.

"Something bothering you?" he asked.

"Curiosity," she said. "I still wonder who you are. Why you are here in Cuba, involved in affairs that may not strictly be your problem. I have seen you walk into hostile gunfire. You have seen men die and you have taken some of those lives yourself. Now you sit calmly drinking coffee in a strange village where any man may turn out to be your enemy."

"Everything we do has an element of risk," Bolan said. "We're as safe here, for the time being, as anywhere else. As soon as Manuel has made his arrangements, we'll move on. These are good people. Real Cubans. If we asked them what they wanted out of life, they would say nothing more than a good crop each year. Enough food to eat and the chance to watch their children grow in safety. That's why I'm here. To try and make that happen. People are the same the world over. Only the faces and the language change."

"If it wasn't for the politicians, or the military, or the greedy, life would be better? Is that how you see it?"

Bolan smiled. "I'm not that naive, Linda. I understand that life is full of twists and turns. Nothing is ever as simple as it should be. But I do what I can to keep the balance. Or at least I try."

Manuel appeared, crossing the dusty, sunbaked village plaza. He slid onto the bench beside his sister. His expression was relaxed, but his eyes held a wary look that Bolan spotted directly.

"Trouble?" he asked.

"Perhaps," Manuel said. "No problem with the vehicle. I have made a deal. We get a small truck that will take us where we want. The man I did the deal with told me that there have been strangers in the village, men with guns who have been asking questions. This has been going on for a couple of weeks, so they were not looking for you, Mike. It seems they have been making the rounds. I believe it is to do with what we discovered. These people need to keep the pressure up while they make their plans, so they scour the countryside, looking for rebels, anti-Castro groups, anyone who might offer opposition. It will pay us to be extravigilant if these squads are still roaming around."

"It's time we moved on," Bolan said. "The sooner we leave this place the better for the people here. I don't want to place them in any danger."

Manuel stood. "We can go anytime."

Leaving money on the table, Bolan and Linda followed Manuel through the village to where an untidy frontage and workshop indicated the local garage. Derelict cars were strewed around the area and empty oil drums vied for space along with stacks of tires and vehicle parts.

Manuel called out, and a fat Cuban clad in stained coveralls appeared. He had a blackened, oily baseball cap on the back of his bald head and a thick cigar clamped between his teeth.

Bolan stayed to one side, allowing Manuel to complete the deal. He kept his eyes open and his ears tuned for any unusual sights or sounds.

The truck turned out to be of ancient Russian vintage, an ex-military vehicle converted to carry small cargo loads. Someone had repainted it during its colorful life. Now it was dirty and faded. But the engine had a healthy sound to it.

Manuel climbed behind the wheel, with Linda beside him and Bolan taking the passenger seat. Once they were inside and Manuel drove them out of the village, Bolan unzipped the backpack at his feet and took out his Beretta and Uzi.

The road ahead was narrow and dusty. On either side the lush Cuban countryside rolled away in shades of green, interspersed with vivid splashes of color.

"Tell me more about this man Salvano Cruz," Bolan said.

"Cruz is a very clever man," Manual replied. "He has great influence and moves in powerful circles. His friends are in the government and the military. He is very close to the people who control G-2. He has looked after them for many years. And he has the ear of Fidel Castro. Cruz is one of the main players in the Puerto Rico conspiracy. Along with other advisers, Cruz has persuaded Castro that the Puerto Rican plan is an opportunity for Cuba to regain its self-esteem."

"Does Cruz have ambitions beyond this conspiracy?" Bolan asked.

"Stepping into Castro's shoes?" Linda asked. "I believe he would jump at the chance."

"So couldn't this encouraging of Castro be a means to an end?" Bolan suggested. "Let's say Castro falls on his face, loses credibility. Wouldn't that be an opportunity for someone to step in and take over?"

"Castro is having an extremely hard time at the moment. His latest reforms are not producing what he expected. He has great support still, but people are not happy. They see other Caribbean nations developing, the people living better, conditions improving. Here at home Castro stubbornly refuses to let go. He digs in his heels and tries to keep things as they are. To his credit he has encouraged foreign investment, made tourism easier. But these things take too long. The people are impatient. They don't want to be old before the good times come. So Castro needs a victory, something to make the people forget their worries.

"In answer to your question, Mike, I would say yes. If Castro's invasion becomes a disaster, then even he will have a hard time talking the people around. A new leader, especially a modernist like

Cruz, would find it easier to bring public opinion around to his way of thinking.''

"Isn't that what you want," Bolan asked, "a new regime? Fresh ideas and leadership?''

Manuel gave a dry chuckle. "Yes and no. We do want Cuba to move into the real world, to get rid of the old ways, to embrace freedom. But not the way Cruz and his people want to do it. They would take us back to even blacker times than any under Fidel Castro.''

"Plunging Cuba into war over Puerto Rico is not the way, Mike," Linda said. "When we first met, we discussed this. Cuba in Puerto Rico would bring disaster. An armed response from America would follow. And once that happened, the rebel groups here would take up arms, each seeing the opportunity to become the party to liberate Cuba. The island would be torn apart by internal struggles.''

"Cuba would be destroyed," Manuel added. "Everything we have gained would be lost. Even what we have now, as bad as it is, would be lost. Nothing would get better. No one would win.''

"Not even Salvano Cruz? If he's as clever as you say, he must have anticipated things getting out of hand.'' Bolan watched the reaction.

"Cruz has many high-ranking politicians and military men in his pocket," Manuel said. "He would have the country's armed forces on his side. Believe me, Mike, he would use them. His justice would be hard and swift, and completely without mercy.''

''Damned if we do, damned if we don't,'' Bolan said softly. ''Hell of a way to run a country, Manuel Ramos.''

''Yes,'' Manuel agreed, ''but it's the only one we have.''

''Then Salvano has to be stopped for all our sakes,'' Bolan stated.

''Not so easy,'' Linda said. ''Cruz is well protected. Always surrounded by his bodyguards.''

''That's no guarantee of safety,'' Bolan replied. ''Get me to his place so I can have a look at the setup.''

*Casa Blanco, Residence of Salvano Cruz*

IT WAS NOON when Mack Bolan stood beside Manuel Ramos, looking down through the trees to the white house set amid lush gardens and lawns that appeared to have been manicured.

At the same time he was studying the sprawling mansion, he was counting the number of patrolling guards. Though their weapons weren't actually in sight, Bolan knew the men were armed. It showed in the way they moved, occasionally reaching up to pat a weapon back into position under their expensive jackets.

Though the day was bright, the light failed to penetrate the deep foliage under which Manuel Ramos had parked the truck.

"You said there were others involved. Do you have names?" Bolan asked quietly.

"I've seen Fuentes here. Colonel Lopez. Two government ministers. One from the military department. The other is a finance minister. Mike, I'm sure Cruz has Batiste down there. He is the one who was monitoring Cruz's trips out of the country. Batiste was going to bring us up-to-date with the details. I believe that is why Cruz kept him alive. To find out what Batiste knows. Cruz will be worried that Batiste may have identified the people he has been making deals with."

Bolan studied the layout again. The house stood about a quarter of a mile inland, and from his current position, looking out beyond the house and across the green canopy, he could see the hazy waters of the ocean. Right now it all looked serene, tropical lushness bordered by warm blue waters, with no threat of violence and unrest.

But all that could change so quickly.

It took only a spark to transform paradise into hell on earth.

Which was why Bolan was here.

"Look," Manuel said, his voice excited.

Bolan followed his finger.

A car had rolled out of the garage flanking the house and come to a stop at the front entrance. The men patrolling the grounds moved so that they could see the front of the building. Two of them flanked the car, guns now in open sight. The rear door was opened.

There was movement at the front door. Figures hovered, then moved into the daylight. First came another armed bodyguard, followed by three figures who walked directly to the car without pausing.

"The one in front is Lopez. It is unusual to see him out of uniform," Manuel said. "Behind him, in the cream suit, is Salvano Cruz." There was a moment's pause before Manuel spoke again, and this time there was a break in his voice. "The third man is Rico Jorges."

Bolan sensed the outrage in Manuel's tone, the taut bend of his body as he moved forward slightly.

"Easy, Manuel," Bolan advised. "What do you expect to do? Go charging down there and kill him with your bare hands? You'd be dead before you cleared the gate."

Linda, who had been sitting in the shade of the truck, pushed close to her brother, gripping his arm. "He's right, Manuel. Throwing away your life on a useless gesture will benefit no one."

Manuel seemed to shrink in height as he backed away. His eyes held a look of frustration. "It's hard to see him there, walking around alive and well. All I remember are my friends, beaten and murdered because of Jorges and Lopez."

"They'll pay for that," Bolan said.

"Do you think Batiste is still alive in that house?" Linda asked.

"There's only one way to find out," Bolan replied.

He was watching the car. With the three passengers seated in the rear, two of three armed bodyguards climbed into the front. A second vehicle moved into view, and four more armed guards climbed in. The second vehicle fell in behind the main car, and they both moved off along the curving driveway to the gates, which were opened. The vehicles rolled through and turned in the direction of the main road.

"Which way are they heading?" Bolan asked.

"Back toward Havana," Manuel replied.

The big American studied the departing cars, then glanced back at the house. He had Antonio Batiste to consider. If he was still alive, then Bolan felt an obligation to try to get him out.

"Manuel, I want you to tail that vehicle. Stay well behind but try to find out where it's going."

Manuel nodded and headed for the truck.

"No contact," Bolan warned. "Stay away from them. If they spot you, they'll kill you."

"How will we meet up?" Manuel asked.

"The old house," Linda said. "I will bring Mike there when he has done what he has to here."

Manuel started the truck and backed it slowly out of concealment. He turned it around and drove off along the narrow track that joined the road half a mile away. The truck wasn't capable of great speed, but that wouldn't matter on the curving, hilly roads that lay between this place and the city. He would be able to keep his quarry in sight from miles away.

"Will he be all right?" Linda asked.

"If he does what I told him," Bolan replied.

He unzipped his backpack, withdrew his combat harness and pulled it on. After clipping the waist belt, Bolan took the Desert Eagle from the hip holster and checked the magazine. The belt pouches held additional ammo clips for both the Desert Eagle and the Beretta 93-R. On the opposite side of the belt to the holstered handgun was a sheathed knife.

Linda watched his calm, methodical preparations with silent fascination.

Pulling out the Uzi, Bolan made certain that the reversible magazine setup was full. He slung the SMG from his shoulder by the black webbing strap.

There was no doubt in Linda's mind that this big American, even though he didn't show it in his cool manner, was making ready for war. It was the only way to describe his attitude, the unhurried, thorough way in which he readied himself and his array of weapons.

When he had completed his preparations, Bolan reached into the backpack and took out a spare handgun. It was a 9 mm Browning, brought along as a reserve weapon. He handed the gun to Linda, explaining how to use it.

"It's fully loaded and ready to fire. If you have to, don't hesitate. You won't get a second chance. Being dead is about as final as you can get. It'll be what the other guy will be thinking, too. Get your shot in first."

Linda took the gun, conscious of the weight, the cool feel of the metal under her fingers.

"It's there to defend yourself with," Bolan said gently.

"Worry about yourself, Mike. What will you do?"

"See if I can locate Batiste. Keep your eye on that place. I have a feeling when it's time to leave I'll be doing it in a hurry. Be ready to join me."

He slipped away from her, losing himself in the lush foliage, and started to work his way down to the grounds. If his calculations were right, then the armed presence had been considerably reduced now that six of the guards had left to escort Cruz and Lopez. There were only three men patrolling the grounds of the house as far as his observation had identified. The unknown quantity, as far as Bolan was concerned, was how many others were inside the house itself.

The Executioner didn't dwell on the subject. He concentrated on reaching the perimeter wall as quickly as possible without alerting the patrolling gunmen.

It took him almost thirty minutes. By the end of that time, Bolan was crouching in thick shrubbery on the inside of the perimeter wall. He had the three guards spotted, and they had eased their state of readiness visibly. Now that Cruz had left, they seemed to be less concerned. Not that it diminished the threat they presented. Armed men, trained to respond to intruders, would react with force if they detected Bolan. And any laxity would quickly be dismissed once they moved into combat mode.

The soldier hung his Uzi around his neck by its strap and pulled out his knife. He stayed under cover, eyes tracking the movement of the guard closest to his position.

Within minutes the patrolling sentry strolled by Bolan's hiding place. His autoweapon was slung from his shoulder, one hand on its muzzle, keeping the weapon from swaying as he walked.

Bolan had already checked the position of the other two guards. They were far enough away not to notice if he dealt with this one quickly enough. The alarm could easily be raised by an undue amount of movement that might attract someone's eye, or too much noise.

As the guard drew just ahead, Bolan moved out from cover. A powerful leg sweep knocked the man off his feet. He fell hard, unable to react quickly enough, slamming to the ground on his back. Before he could recover, Bolan had him by the throat, clamping a big hand over the guy's windpipe and restricting his intake of oxygen. There was a moment when the guard's eyes grew wide with surprise. An instant later the cold, hard blade of Bolan's knife pierced his heart.

Bolan dragged the inert figure into the undergrowth, then sheathed his knife. The Uzi on the man's shoulder yielded another 30-round magazine that the soldier tucked in an empty belt pouch.

He checked out the distance to the house. The garage, built on the side and set back from the frontage, would offer his best approach from where he was now. Time wasn't going to allow Bolan the freedom to scout around and locate something better.

He spent a few minutes trying to assess where the other guards might show. The trouble was that they didn't have a coordinated pattern of patrolling the grounds, which meant in actual terms that they might show up when he least expected it.

The Executioner was on his feet and sprinting across the smooth lawn when one of the guards *did* appear with warning. He moved into view on Bolan's right, having come from the rear of the house.

Bolan kept up his forward motion, but altered it by launching himself in a dive that took him below the anticipated trajectory of the guard's firing line. As he hit the lawn, going into a shoulder roll, he heard the rapid stutter of the sentry's Uzi. The harsh rattle of autofire would alert the rest of the household, but Bolan had no control over that. His main objective was staying ahead of the guard as the man advanced, still firing and trying to track in on Bolan's changed position.

The first spray of 9 mm tumblers hissed over Bolan. As he turned on his back, coming to a semi-sitting position, another volley threw slugs in a ragged line that chewed into the manicured lawn. Clods of dirt flew into the air.

By this time Bolan had brought his own weapon on-line, locking on to the guard's running figure. He pulled the trigger and sent a short, hot burst of slugs into his adversary's chest. The man went down on one knee, his own weapon forgotten as he concentrated on the raging pain in his chest. He paused for a moment, kneeling, head flopping forward to see the bloody patch spreading across the shirt. Then Bolan fired another burst, his shots catching the guy in the head, spinning him.

On his feet again, Bolan covered the ground and slammed against the wall of the house. He had already noted a window in that section of the wall. Aware of time slipping away, numbers falling with increasing speed, Bolan hit the window head-on, arms raised to protect his face. He landed inside feetfirst, the wood frame and glass exploding around him.

He was in a long passage that appeared to run the length of the house. At the far end, toward the rear, iron steps led into the basement. As Bolan scanned the corridor, an armed figure raced to the head of the steps and cut loose with an autoweapon.

Slugs chugged into the wall over Bolan's head, showering him with splintered plaster. The Executioner dropped to one knee, angling his Uzi in the direction of the advancing figure, and stitched the guy from waist to throat. The 9 mm slugs chewed into flesh and bone, driving the man against the wall and leaving a glistening smear of blood on the white surface.

A shadow fell across the floor at Bolan's feet. He turned, still down on his knee, and saw the third perimeter guard leaning in through the shattered window. The guy had time to register Bolan's presence before the stuttering Uzi sent a burst of slugs into his face, blowing him back in a splash of red.

Straightening, Bolan headed for the far end of the corridor. The presence of an armed man in the basement meant something to guard. He figured that could be a prisoner named Antonio Batiste.

He hit the steps at a run. At the bottom he saw a wooden door standing partway open. Bolan's foot kicked it wide, slamming it back against the wall. There was no response. About to move forward, the Executioner heard hurried footsteps in the corridor above him. He turned back, ejecting the used magazine for the full one taped to it, and by the time he had climbed the steps, the Uzi was cocked and ready again.

Bolan peered over the top step and saw three armed men heading his way. One of them spotted the Executioner and yelled a warning to his companions. All three swung their weapons into play, but the soldier triggered first.

Caught in the narrow confines of the passage, the trio was unable to escape the withering full-auto blast from the deadly Uzi. Bolan swept the muzzle back and forth, containing the volley. The three gunners were punched backward off their feet and driven to the floor. As the last one fell, the only sound in the corridor was the metallic tinkle of 9 mm shell casings from Bolan's Uzi rattling down the stairs around him.

Retracing his steps, and ramming a fresh magazine into the Uzi, Bolan stepped through the basement door and went looking for Batiste.

He found the Cuban at the far end of the basement, beyond the racks of fine wines and boxed foods. He was bound to a wooden chair beneath a small window that allowed shafts of sunlight to pierce the gloom.

Batiste raised his head as Bolan approached. He peered at the Executioner through watery eyes that were surrounded by swollen, discolored flesh. The whole of the Cuban's face was battered and bloody. His slack mouth revealed torn gums and broken teeth. His shirt was a mass of blood, and where it gaped open, Bolan could see that Batiste's chest and torso had been beaten, and burned with cigarette stubs. His shoeless feet and his hands were broken and pulped.

"Have you come to finally kill me?" Batiste asked. His words were forced, painfully slow because of his injuries, and even Bolan's basic understanding of Spanish allowed him to decipher their meaning.

"No. I have come to take you away from here," he replied, then added, "Do you understand English?"

Batiste stared at him, his vision still badly blurred. He was a little unsure what was happening, but he understood the gentle hand that cut away the ropes binding him to the chair.

"English?" he said finally. Bolan's question had pushed its way through his muddled thinking. "Yes. I understand."

There was no way the Cuban would be able to walk, Bolan saw. He caught hold of Batiste's tattered shirt, pulling him up out of the chair, and swung the man over his shoulder.

"Hang on as best you can," he said. "This could be a bumpy ride."

Bolan headed back across the cellar, the Uzi cradled in his hands. He went through the door and up the steps, passing the dead guards, and made his way along the passage. No one challenged him. Reaching the broken window he'd entered, Bolan stepped over the sill. He turned in the direction of the garage, hoping there was something inside he could use.

The small side door was ajar. Inside the expansive garage he found two cars. One was a small, two-seater sports model. The other was a silver Mercedes. Bolan crossed to the car and checked the doors. They were unlocked. He opened one of the rear doors and laid Batiste across the seat. Moving to the front, the soldier opened the driver's door and slid behind the wheel, dropping the Uzi on the leather seat beside him. The key was in the ignition, and the engine started smoothly.

Leaving the vehicle running, Bolan went to the door controls and pressed the button that raised the garage doors. He ran back to the vehicle, slid behind the wheel, dropped the car into gear and surged forward.

He was almost to the gate when he spotted movement in the side mirror.

Two of Salvano Cruz's armed guards were racing across the lawn to intercept him. The closer man raised his AK-74 and began to pump shots at the Mercedes.

Bolan felt the car shudder as a couple struck the bodywork. He jammed his foot on the gas pedal, and the car shot forward. The side window imploded, showering Batiste with fragments of glass. As the guards closed in on the car, by cutting across the grass at an angle, the Executioner saw that he was going to be forced to pass them. There was no other way out of the place. He reached for the Uzi lying beside him, then pressed the window button his door, lowering it.

Ignoring the bullets chewing at the bodywork of the car, Bolan slammed on the brakes and brought the vehicle to a rocking stop. He slipped the catch and kicked the door open, bringing the Uzi into play. His first blast caught the lead guard in the upper legs, pitching him facedown on the ground.

The second guard took time to aim. He triggered a single shot that burned through the flesh of Bolan's upper arm, the impact spinning him sideways in the driver's seat. Seeing his target react to the shot, the guard took his time to fire again, taking a couple of steps to the side in order to get a clearer shot.

The sharp crack of the handgun came from behind the guard. The bullet drilled between his shoulders, and as he began to turn, a second and third bullet struck him, driving him to his knees. His AK-74 slipped from numbing fingers.

Trying to ignore the bloody form of the man she had just shot, Linda Ramos ran to the side of the Mercedes.

"Mike!" she called.

Bolan slid across to the passenger side of the car.

"Get in and drive," he said. "We'll talk later."

Linda dropped Bolan's backpack on the floor of the car and slid behind the wheel, taking a quick look at the figure lying across the rear seat of the car.

"Batiste?" she asked.

Bolan nodded.

The woman closed her door, then swung the Mercedes down the driveway and out through the gate. Without reducing speed, she hauled the Mercedes onto the road and sped away from Salvano Cruz's estate.

Bolan had unzipped the backpack and extracted a small medical kit. He sensed Linda watching him from the corner of her eye as he pulled open the sealed pack. Giving a gasp of exasperation, she pulled the Mercedes to the side of the road and stopped.

"You will bleed to death before you can do anything," she said.

With steady fingers she rolled up his sleeve and tended the ragged flesh wound, finally wrapping a firm bandage around his arm. As she worked, she talked, the words tumbling out in a torrent.

"I have never killed a man before today. The worst thing I have done with a gun is to shoot at targets. It is different when you shoot at a man. No one ever told me what it would be like to take a life."

"It doesn't get easier the more times you do it," Bolan said. "Each time is like the first. I've done it too many times not to understand. You make your peace with yourself in the quiet times. It doesn't make it go away. It doesn't stop the nightmares. But it makes you thankful it was you who walked away and not the other guy."

Linda started the car and drove on.

"Is Batiste hurt badly?" she asked.

"They worked him over pretty hard. I didn't have time to check him out."

"Will he live?"

"I will live," came the answer from the rear seat. Antonio Batiste pushed himself to a sitting position, leaning back against the soft upholstery. "At least long enough to expose Cruz and his American partners."

Bolan twisted in his seat. "American? Then they are involved in this?"

Batiste nodded his head. "Oh, yes, my friend. I am afraid that a number of your countrymen are involved in this conspiracy."

"Do you feel strong enough to tell me what you know?" Bolan asked.

"In case I die before we reach safety?" Batiste said, then gave a mocking laugh at his own expense. "Yes, I will tell you."

THEY REACHED the outskirts of Havana in the late afternoon. Linda drove off the main road and along a narrow side road until she reached a small house that stood on its own in the middle of an overgrown lot. She pulled the Mercedes around to the rear of the building and switched off the engine.

"We used to live here many years ago," the woman explained, "when we were young. When our parents were still alive."

Bolan stepped out of the car, his Desert Eagle in his hand. He checked out the area. It was quiet, with only the sound of birds in the surrounding trees. He moved around the house, making sure the area was clear. Finally satisfied, he returned to the Mercedes and nodded to Linda.

"Looks clear enough," he said. "Maybe I should check the house."

"The house is safe, Mike," a familiar voice called.

Bolan turned to see Manuel Ramos standing on the small porch at the rear of the house.

"Manuel!" Linda stepped out of the car and ran to him. They embraced and held each other for a few moments.

"Mike brought Antonio Batiste from Cruz's house," she said.

"Is he hurt?"

Bolan nodded. "They gave him a hard time."

"May they rot in hell," Manuel cursed. "You see what we have to put up with, the monsters who hunt us down like animals. This is why we fight. To put an end to such things."

"Then help me find out what Batiste knows. If he can give me the information I need, maybe I can stop these people once and for all."

Manuel nodded.

He and Bolan carried Batiste inside the house and settled him on a bed. Linda joined them, carrying a small medical kit and a bowl of water.

"I will do what I can for him," she said. "But we should get him to a hospital as soon as possible."

"Cruz's people will be looking for him," Manuel argued, "and us."

"I can arrange for you all to be moved to a place of safety," Bolan said. "And there will be hospitalization for Batiste."

"America?" Manuel asked.

Bolan nodded.

The Cuban glanced at his sister. His shoulders stiffened slightly.

"I thought we'd cleared that point up," Bolan said. "Manuel, I'm not the enemy. America isn't your enemy."

Linda glanced up from where she sat on the edge of the bed. "Where else can we go, Manuel? Mike speaks the truth. After what has happened, how could we look on him as anything but a friend?"

"As usual, she is right. I find it hard to trust sometimes. When you are betrayed by your own kind, it makes you suspicious of everyone. We are in your hands, Mike."

"Where did Cruz go?" Bolan asked.

"He and Lopez were dropped off at a small airfield on the coast. They boarded a plane and took off immediately."

"Did you see which way they went?"

Manuel nodded. "Northeast."

"The Bahamas?" Linda asked.

"Yes," a hesitant voice interrupted.

Batiste had raised himself on one elbow.

"To meet their American partners?" Bolan asked.

Batiste nodded. He was weak and obviously in pain. He made no resistance when Linda gently laid him back on the bed.

"Three of them," Batiste said.

"How do you know this?" Manuel asked.

"Because I have seen them together," Batiste explained. "Do you remember when I was gone for a week? I went to Nassau. I waited because I knew Cruz would come. I had overheard him making arrangements with Lopez. I did not know which day, so I waited. For three days. I was almost ready to give up and return to Havana when Cruz finally showed up."

"But you never said anything about this," Manuel said, his tone close to accusing Batiste of betrayal.

"I had to be sure. How many times have you said yourself that we had to be certain of every fact before we could accuse anyone. And I was wary of telling anyone in case we were found out. I did not want to put all of us under such a responsibility."

"Sensible move, considering you had a traitor in your group," Bolan stated.

"You are right," Manuel said. "Antonio, who are these Americans?"

"I know only one of them. As I told Belasko, the others are strangers to me."

"But we must know who they are."

"Then maybe the photographs I took will be of help," Batiste suggested.

"You photographed them?" Linda said.

Batiste nodded. "I developed the film when I returned home."

"Have you shown them to anyone?" Bolan asked.

"No. I was going to bring them to Manuel, but then the call came for the meeting. I decided to wait until we had discussed our business, then tell Manuel and bring him to see them. You all know what happened."

"Wise move," Bolan said. "Under the circumstances, it was the best thing you could have done. Where are the photographs now?"

"In my apartment."

"Havana," Linda said, looking up from her work.

"We have to get them," Bolan stated. "Give me the address and where the photographs are."

"You'll never get near the place," Manuel told him. "Lopez will have his people all over the city, looking for all of us."

"That's the best time to go," Bolan said. "We'll be doing the exact opposite of what they're expecting. Could catch them off guard long enough to get what we want." He glanced across at Batiste. "You said you could identify one of the Americans."

Batiste nodded. "Lawrence Boyette. I have read about him in American news magazines, and he is known in Nassau. He owns property and runs a large motor cruiser."

"He's president of a large manufacturing corporation," Bolan said. "One of its main production facilities manufactures armament. And he has strong views on some U.S. government policies."

"You know this man?" Manuel asked.

"A little," Bolan replied. "He was a colonel in the USAF, back in the sixties, during the Cuban missile crisis."

"What is his link with Salvano Cruz?"

"That's what I intend to find out."

"Tell us what you want to do," Manuel said.

"I need to get back to the coast where I was dropped off. I have to get in touch with my contact to arrange transport for you."

"This is like running away," Manuel protested, "deserting in the middle of a fight."

"Manuel, there are times when a withdrawal is the only sensible thing. You'll be back. But right now you're all targets, liable to be killed on sight. You and Antonio are the only survivors of your group, and the information you have needs to be recorded.''

Linda touched his arm. ''We do understand, Mike.''

''Make Antonio as comfortable as you can. As soon as it's dark, we'll move out.''

# CHAPTER FOURTEEN

*Police Headquarters, Benedict County*

"I'm fine," Blancanales insisted. "But I'm not so sure about the others. I need Bear to come through on this. Benedict Base is out there somewhere. I need a location and I need it fast."

"We're running it down as fast as we can, Pol," Price said. "Aaron has penetrated the military network and he's digging. There's a lot to trawl through. It isn't easy because Benedict has been deactivated and seems to have been put on some kind of protected file."

"What about the tie-in between Dwyer and the other guys we tangled with?"

"It's there. Dwyer and Lester were both in Team Casper. So was Meecher, but only during the last year or so. He was a communications technician. The guy who set Casper up is a Colonel Ray Mc-Clain, a career Army man. He's been in almost every conflict since Vietnam, which was where Team Casper was born. From what we've learned, Casper has been around ever since. They've pulled some scary ops. A lot of the work they do seems to be in the shadows. Aaron is trying to pull any connections with the security agencies."

"CIA?"

"Could be. The kind of stuff Team Casper runs smells of Agency involvement."

"Anything else you can give me?"

"Hal pulled a few strings, so we're being fed data from NAVSTAR, which gives us a chance to check for any unusual movements around Cuba and Puerto Rico. So far, we haven't come up with anything useful." Price paused, then added, "For all we know, any hardware may have been shipped in before we came on the scene."

"Is there anything official supposed to be going on out there?"

"Not as far as we can find out. Benedict Base is off-line. And if anything is going on, it doesn't sanction the murder of private citizens or the killing of a military deserter."

"How about the other teams?"

"Phoenix Force is out of communication at the moment."

"Striker?"

"He asked for an extract some time ago, but not for himself. Some friends, as he put it. That's under way now. We hope he might have some update info for us."

"Hey, I just had a thought. Ask Bear if NAVSTAR can run a scan of the Benedict area. Maybe they can pinpoint the base for me."

"Good thought," Price said. "I'll get back to you."

"Sooner rather than later," Blancanales urged before saying goodbye and hanging up.

As Price put down the phone, she heard the elevator door swish open behind her, and Aaron Kurtzman rolled into the room. He had a sheaf of papers in one big hand.

"I don't know why I didn't think of this before," he said. "Trouble is we've been concentrating on Phoenix Force and Striker."

Price watched as he spread the papers on the conference table.

"NAVSTAR ran a scan for me across Benedict County, and damned if they didn't locate the base."

He glanced up and saw that Price was smiling.

"What?"

"Pol just suggested the same thing."

Kurtzman grunted an acknowledgment.

"So where is it?" Price asked.

He jabbed a finger at a point on the NAVSTAR printout. At first Price couldn't see a thing, then she made out the image in the center of the satellite scan.

"Takes a while to see past the landscape image," Kurtzman said. "But if you follow the lines here and here, you can make out the formation of the structure. The way it's built close to the ground makes it almost invisible from the air. The infrared scanners can read the wave patterns and highlight them." He pointed again. "Here. That's the exhaust duct that expels fumes from the power generators. There's no way to hide that from something like NAVSTAR."

"We have to get this to Pol right away."

"They should have a fax facility at Benedict PD. I'll get Carmen to access it."

"IT'S COMING through now," Blancanales said.

"The grid references are in place," Price explained. "Match it up to a map of the area, and you should end up with a pinpoint location."

"Okay. I'll be in touch when there's anything to report. Tell the team thanks."

Blancanales put down the telephone and reached for the fax sheet as it was disgorged from the machine.

Tom Craddock already had a map of the area spread across his desk. He scanned the fax, then marked off the coordinates. Working quickly, he penciled in the cross references.

"There," he said, tapping the map with the tip of his pencil.

"How long will it take to get there?" Blancanales asked.

"Around a half hour by chopper."

"And we're ready to go," Kris Landry said as she entered the office. "Right, Tom?"

"We?" Blancanales asked.

Craddock grinned. "Kris is the department pilot."

"And I suppose you have to hold the map for her?" Blancanales said.

"You don't need help?" Craddock asked as he shrugged into a black leather jacket.

Blancanales took the extra jacket Craddock passed him. Landry had brought along a selection of weapons from the PD's store. Craddock and his partner chose Franchi SPAS combat shotguns. The powerful autoweapons were effective man-stoppers. Considering that they could be working within the confines of the underground base, Blancanales saw the logic of the choice. He took one for himself. With the shotguns loaded and extra shells in belts around their waists, the next priority was their handguns. With these loaded and locked, they moved out of the office.

THE BENEDICT PD's helicopter was a black-and-white Hughes Cayuse. Blancanales was more than familiar with the speedy craft. He'd flown in them during the war and since.

Crossing the pavement to the chopper, Blancanales wondered what they might be up against once they reached the badlands around the base. The tone of the mission had been set by the violent reaction to Able Team's presence and the overt assassination attempt in the hospital. Something was happening at the base, and Lyons and Schwarz were out there.

Landry climbed into the pilot's seat, with Craddock alongside her. Swinging into the rear seat, Blancanales settled back as the Allison turboshaft engine began to turn over. Landry had a sure touch, and she coaxed power out of the unit quickly. The Able Team commando hardly felt a tremor as the Cayuse eased off the ground and lifted above the police building. Swinging the chopper about, Landry overflew Benedict and headed across country.

"THEY CAN'T KEEP US in here forever," Schwarz grumbled.

"Who says they can't?" Lyons asked. "There isn't a time limit. This bunch make their own rules. If they want to forget us and throw away the key, they'll do it."

"That really cheered me up," Schwarz said. "I get to spend the rest of my life locked up with you."

"Could be worse."

"Uh-uh. It couldn't be worse. Just promise me one thing. You won't start giving me funny looks."

Even Lyons had to smile at that.

They both glanced around as the locks on the cell door snapped back.

Lyons pushed to his feet, then stepped close to Schwarz.

"First opening, go for it," he whispered.

"You got it."

They stepped apart and watched the door swing open.

Two men in camouflage fatigues stood there. One carried a tray holding mugs and plates. He wore a Beretta 92-F in a military high-ride holster on his right hip. The second kept back, covering Lyons and Schwarz with his M-16.

"If it was up to me, you mothers could starve," the man carrying the tray muttered.

"With a personality like that, no wonder they got you delivering food," Lyons stated, his words directed at the tray carrier. "The only thing missing is the skirt."

The man turned to look at the Able Team commander, his face already coloring as he reacted.

"Eat shit!" he snapped, and threw the tray in Lyons's direction.

The big ex-cop had gauged the moment to perfection. As the man let go of the tray, Lyons dropped to the floor, sweeping his right leg around. He kicked the man's feet from under him, dropping him to the floor with a bone-jarring thump. The back of his skull impacted against the concrete floor with a crunch, and he jerked once then lay still. Rolling in close, Lyons snagged the 92-F from the man's holster and swept the muzzle around, laying it across the downed man's prone body.

The guard in the cell doorway pulled the muzzle of his M-16 away from Schwarz, tracking in on Lyons.

The Beretta cracked sharply as the Able Team leader triggered three shots into the guard's chest. The slugs pinned him to the door frame for a couple of seconds before gravity took over and the man pitched facefirst to the floor.

Schwarz hurried to him and took the M-16. He bent over the dead man and searched him, plucking an extra 30-round magazine for the M-16.

Lyons moved past him, checking the corridor. It was clear.

"The only way is up, pal," Lyons said.

Schwarz nodded.

They negotiated the hallway. Steps at the end led them to a closed steel door.

"Quick! They probably heard the shooting," Schwarz warned.

Lyons touched the catch, and the heavy door swung open on balanced rollers, revealing another corridor, longer than the one they had just maneuvered. It was brightly lit and silent.

As they traversed the corridor, Lyons took the lead, Schwarz keeping an eye on their rear. Boots clattered on metal steps, then a door burst open ahead of them and two armed men appeared. They wore civilian clothing, but the weapons they carried were M-16s.

The lead guy opened up while he was still on the move. The first shots took out a light fixture above Lyons's head, showering him with hot shards of glass. The second burst hammered into the white panels that lined the ceiling. The reason the muzzle had risen to that angle was due to the fact that Lyons had placed two 9 mm slugs in the shooter's chest, kicking him backward before pushing him to the floor.

Schwarz dropped to one knee, shouldering his M-16. He had a fraction of a second to make his shot and didn't waste it. His 5.56 mm slug caught the second newcomer in the head, blowing out of the back of his skull.

The electronics wizard flattened against the wall beside the open door. He scanned the stairway, which looked clear. Lyons had paused beside the downed men. He'd noticed that one of them wore a holstered 92-F. He ejected the magazine and slid it into his pocket.

"Set?" Lyons asked.

Schwarz nodded.

The big ex-cop took the stairs at a run, the Beretta tracking ahead of him. He was almost at the top when he caught movement. An armed figure lunged into view, and the stairwell echoed to the rattle of gunfire. Lyons pressed to the wall as the man he'd shot tumbled by him.

Somewhere an alarm began to wail.

Lyons was checking the way ahead. The corridor they faced had a set of double doors in the left wall, with frosted glass in the frames. Signs on either side warned that it was a security area. Shadowy outlines could be seen on the other side of the glass.

"Looks interesting," Schwarz said.

The shadows grew as figures moved toward the double doors. With a soft hiss the doors slid apart.

The first man out was Hiller, and he carried a Beretta handgun. The angry expression on his face turned to surprise as he was confronted by Carl Lyons.

The Able Team leader didn't waste time on talk. He slammed the barrel of his own 92-F down against Hiller's gun hand, and the Beretta spun from the man's grasp. Lyons's left fist slammed against Hiller's jaw, spinning him off-balance. The sergeant bounced off the door frame, clutching his bleeding face, and walked directly into Lyons's driving right. The hard steel of the Beretta crunched against Hiller's nose and mouth, and he stumbled to his knees, spilling blood across the floor. Lyons caught hold of him by the collar and hauled him back inside the room, where Schwarz had already covered those present with his M-16.

Lyons tapped the button to close the sliding doors. As they hissed shut, he turned to survey the operations center.

During the time Benedict Base had been up and running, the ops room had been heavy with electronic equipment. Now the wall panels were empty, with exposed cables drooping across the dead control consoles.

The overhead fluorescent lights threw their cold glow over smaller array of electronics now. There was only a single section that had been activated, with equipment that had been assembled by the people manning it.

Lyons counted six of them. Some were in uniform, others in plain clothing. He spotted the major who had talked to them on their arrival.

"Hand your weapons over before you make things worse for yourselves," the major said. "You don't realize what you're doing."

"I think you have this a little mixed up, Major," Lyons stated.

"Damn it, man, this is a military operation in progress."

"Cut the crap," Lyons said angrily. "We both know this is so off-the-wall it isn't real. This is no military operation. It's just a bunch of misfits try-ing to start a war of their own."

"You can't interfere now. It's already started."

"Then we stop it," Schwarz said.

"But you can't," the major insisted. "Don't you see? People are already committed, on the move. Planes are in the air, just waiting for the final com-mand to go ahead. Don't you realize there are armed men on their way right now? A plane will be touching down anytime. Are you boys going to fight off a whole assault team?"

"If we have to," Schwarz replied tautly.

"A pair of heroes, fighting with right on your side?"

"What's your excuse for pulling a sneak attack on Cuba?" Lyons asked. "Stemming the Red Menace?"

"Something like that. It's time this country got its pride back. There are too many sacks of shit in positions of power, backing away from what needs doing, letting dirt-poor countries make fools of us."

Lyons leaned forward, his eyes reflecting his contempt. "And you figure you and your gung-ho buddies are the ones to show us the way? To hell with anyone else. We're the ones who know? Bet-ter than the rest? Is that it, Major?"

The man rounded on him, his face dark with an-ger. "You're goddamn right it is, boy! And you'll see what I mean when we hit those Cuban peasants!''

His voice rose to a crescendo, his eyes staring at Lyons but not seeing him. The major's rhetoric had gotten the better of him. His common sense allowed itself to be overridden, too, and even as Lyons shook his head in disbelief the man snatched at the Beretta on his hip and aimed it at the Able Team leader.

Lyons put a single 9 mm slug right between the major's eyes. The force of the shot kicked the man backward. He lost his balance and slumped over the empty console he'd been standing in front of.

"What the hell did he do that for?" Lyons asked.

There was a rush of movement off to Lyons's right. Two of the men under Schwarz's M-16 decided the time was right to make their play, hoping that everyone would be too absorbed in the major's demise to react. They went for the autorifles laid across the desk in front of them.

Schwarz had been letting Lyons handle his part of the action. His attention was still focused on the others in the room, and while he couldn't cover them all in the same moment, his senses were at such a high level there was no way anyone could take advantage of him.

As the two men went for their weapons, sweeping them off the desk and on-line in a continuous movement, Schwarz dropped to a crouch, the M-16 angling around almost lazily. His finger stroked the trigger, and he laid two 3-round bursts into the pair within a heartbeat. They tumbled backward, chests erupting blood, arms thrown wide in a gesture of surrender that came seconds too late.

"All of you on the floor. Now!" Lyons crossed the room and disarmed the remaining three men as they stretched out, hands clasped behind their heads.

Lyons pulled Hiller to his feet and made him join his partners.

"Cut some of that loose wiring," he said to Schwarz. "We can use it to make sure these guys stay put."

As they completed the task, sound erupted from one of the radio receivers.

Lyons and Schwarz crossed to the set and listened in.

"Ground Control to Casper Air One. We have you on approach. Acknowledge my signal. Over."

"Ground Control from Casper Air One. Commencing run in. Monitor approach and advise. Over."

Schwarz glanced at one of the screens. He scanned the detail and looked across at Lyons. "Whoever he is, he's coming in for a landing."

His finger traced the green dot that was moving across the screen grid pattern. Even as Lyons watched, the dot drifted lower on the scale.

"They must have a team outside with a radar link to this setup," Schwarz said, "using instrument and visual to bring in that aircraft."

"The major's assault team," Lyons said, "for Cuba?"

"I guess so."

Lyons snatched up one of the discarded M-16s, checking the magazine as he headed for the door.

"Let's get out there and stop them from touching down. If they get the message they've been compromised, maybe they'll turn around and go home."

LANDRY HAD PUT DOWN the chopper a couple of miles short of the base in case spotters were out. Shouldering their weapons, they walked in through the empty desert. Blancanales found the going hard. His head was pounding, and he knew he wasn't over the effects of the concussion. Even so, there was no way he was going to allow his partners to be left on their own. He had to make some attempt to get them out.

They were close to the base when Blancanales, Craddock and Landry stretched out on a low hump overlooking the perimeter. Craddock scanned the area with a pair of binoculars he'd brought from the chopper.

"See anything?" Blancanales asked.

"Take a look over there," the cop said, handing over the glasses, "just beyond that clump of cactus about two hundred yards out and to the left."

Blancanales studied the section. It took him a while, but he eventually made out the blurry shape of a structure that rose no more than a few feet above ground level. He followed the line of the structure until it merged with the dusty earth and vanished.

"Looks like we're in the right place," Blancanales said.

"Where's the front door?" Landry asked.

"Does she always ask the awkward questions?" Craddock grinned. "Yeah, she does."

"Hey, smart boys," Landry said, "over there. I see something moving."

"I forgot to tell you she's got eyes like a hawk," Craddock said.

Blancanales checked out the section Landry had pinpointed and saw four men clustered around a bulky, olive drab piece of equipment. A few yards away from the men was a second piece of equipment, with a radar dish that was swiveling on a turntable. Blancanales studied the setup for a while.

"What is it?" Craddock asked.

"Looks like a mobile radar unit."

"What're they looking for?"

"I'm guessing an incoming aircraft. Once they pick it up, they'll be able to guide it in for a landing."

"A plan carrying what?" Landry asked.

"A military strike force," Blancanales guessed. "Specialists in covert ops. Ship them in here, wait for the word, then load them on a chopper for a fast run to Cuba and their targets."

"Targets? What damn targets?" Craddock asked.

"Could be anything from strategic installations to individual assassinations. I don't know."

Craddock rolled over to exchange glances with Landry. "And I was complaining we have a dull life."

Blancanales sat up and unslung his SPAS shotgun. He checked the weapon, then took a deep breath.

"That radar unit has to be put out of action," he said. "The problem is those four guys down there won't be agreeable to that."

Craddock nodded. "I hear what you're saying. Dammit, I didn't sign on just for the pension."

"Hell, me neither," Landry added.

"Spoken like a true daughter of Texas," Craddock said with a grin.

"Let's spread out and come at them from three directions. It should give us an even chance."

Landry looked up suddenly, scanning the heavens. "We'd better hustle," she suggested. "I have a notion that plane is on its way in."

They eased away from the hump, keeping low as they went their separate ways. The empty landscape didn't offer much in the way of cover.

Blancanales saw that their only advantage was the fact that the four men were absorbed in their task. He lost sight of Craddock and Landry within moments. The Benedict police officers knew their terrain well, blending with it and leaving little trace of their passing. Blancanales decided quickly that he seemed to be creating too much dust. He slowed his pace and tried to refrain from disturbing any more.

The sound of the approaching aircraft reached his ears. It was coming in from the north. He tried to spot it, but the sky was too clear and bright. It hurt his eyes and made his headache worse.

The distance closed all too quickly.

Blancanales found he was within range for the SPAS shotgun, and he figured that Craddock and Landry had to be in position by now.

The approaching aircraft was close, the sound of its engines unmistakable. Blancanales could make out its hazy shape. He pushed to his feet, raising the SPAS.

In the instant before Blancanales stood, one of the four men stiffened. He leaned forward, looking across to the base location. Abruptly he tapped one of his partners on the shoulder and said something. The second man followed his gaze.

Curious, Blancanales looked, too.

Despite the distance and the heat haze, he couldn't fail to recognize the belligerent stance and the rugged features of Carl Lyons.

Landry appeared to the right of Blancanales, as if from nowhere.

"This is the police!" she called out. "Put down your weapons and raise your hands!"

Somewhere close by, Tom Craddock muttered, "Oh, hell!"

One of the four men turned suddenly, a handgun in his fist. He snapped off a shot at Landry, and she jerked to one side as the bullet clipped her shoulder. The shotgun in her hands went off with a heavy crash, and the gunman was blown off his feet in a bloody mist.

After that, the whole world went to hell.

Blancanales and Craddock brought their weapons into play as a second man whirled to face them. They fired in concert, the combined blast from the two shotguns lifting the guy off his feet and dumping him in a lacerated mess on the ground.

An autopistol opened up, slugs gouging the earth close by Blancanales as the third member of the group joined in. He was an instant away from firing again when a 5.56 mm bullet from Lyons's borrowed M-16 cored its way in through the back of his head and dropped him instantly.

The surviving hostile had already committed himself to firing. There was no going back. He continued to pull the trigger, even though it was clearly too late. Blancanales twisted from the waist and triggered his shot, and the blast took the gunner full in the face.

CRADDOCK WENT TO CHECK Landry.

Blancanales picked up the handset, studying the monitor screen. He glanced over his shoulder. The aircraft was in clear sight now. It was a huge Hercules C-130H, the high-capacity workhorse of the military. Capable of carrying equipment and men, the Hercules could move heavy cargo over great distances.

"If that thing lands, we've got real problems," Lyons said, coming up behind Blancanales.

The Able Team commando reached across and cut the power switch on the unit. The rotating radar dish slowed and stopped; the monitor screen went blank.

Almost immediately the radio broke into activity.

"Ground Control from Casper One. Where is your signal? Repeat. Where is your signal?"

Blancanales keyed the transmit button.

"Ground Control just quit. This is a no-go area, Casper One. Turn around and go home."

The next voice coming through the speaker left no doubt as to the rank of its owner.

"What's going on down there? This is Captain Douglas Winslow. You'd better talk to me, mister."

"Then listen, Captain Winslow. Your mission is aborted. It's over. Benedict Base is closed. Your cover is blown, *mister,* so get the hell back to wherever you came from."

Blancanales broke contact. He glanced at Lyons and shrugged.

Gadgets Schwarz appeared, walking slowly across the dusty ground. He had a couple of LAW rockets under his arm.

"Maybe a demonstration will convince them," he suggested, handing one of the launchers to Lyons.

They waited as the Hercules made a low sweep across the perimeter, then fired the LAW rockets. The missiles detonated on contact with the ground, sending twin plumes of flame and smoke into the air.

The Hercules made a slow turn, gaining height. The small group on the ground watched as it completed a full turn and headed back the way it had come. None of them moved until the aircraft had vanished from their sight.

Blancanales crossed to where Craddock was binding Landry's shoulder with a strip torn from his shirt.

"You okay?" Blancanales asked.

Landry, pale faced, nodded. "This happens every day out here," she said.

"We'll get you inside," Blancanales told her. "Should be a med kit in there somewhere."

"THEY'VE GOT enough stuff in here for a siege," Schwarz said. He handed Craddock a medical kit, then joined Lyons and Blancanales at the activated console.

Blancanales had already made contact with Stony Man.

Brognola's voice came over the speaker. "Aaron will have a link in a few minutes," the big Fed was saying. "He'll access your computer and take a look at what they had."

"It looks like this was going to be used as a staging post for some kind of covert strike," Lyons said. "We've had a chance to check the place over. There are aerial photographs of Cuban military bases, airfields, supply centers, power stations." Lyons paused. "Hal, these guys really meant it."

"I guess they did."

"You figured it all out yet?"

"Not all of it," Brognola admitted. "We've got some of the main players. Lawrence Boyette is the one who funded PRISM and did the deal with a Cuban named Salvano Cruz to use his influence on Castro. He talked him into backing the PRISM coup prior to establishing Cuban control in Puerto Rico."

"All done through the back door?"

"Exactly. None of this has any kind of government sanction. It's just a bunch of people disillusioned with the way things are, then deciding to right imaginary wrongs. Trouble is we might never get all the names. These guys play it really close to their chests. That's why they pulled in McClain and his Team Casper. It was supposed to have been stood down. The members disbanded. But it looks like Boyette kept them under his wing. Kept former and current members on file. Probably funded them, as well."

"His own special-ops group, there to do his dirty work."

"*Dirty* is the buzzword. Looks like Boyette has been abusing every privilege he's ever earned. Using his influence and money to buy the people he needed. He just bypassed military regulations and built up his own cadre of officers and men within the system."

"Loyal to him and not the government?"

"Boyette and his cronies would argue it wasn't that way. As far as they see it, they're doing it for the nation. It happens, Carl. It's one of the risks within a democracy. You have to have trust, or the idea won't work.''

"But it leaves the system wide open to abuse, Hal. Look at this mess."

"What else is there? It works most of the time. But there are always those who want to go their own way, buck the system because they figure they have a better solution."

Price came on the line. "Aaron is ready for the uplink."

Blancanales nodded.

"Pol, let's get this under way," Kurtzman said.

He guided Blancanales through the linking procedure. When they had it completed, Kurtzman was able to access the data and draw the stored information into the Stony Man system.

Brognola came back on the line. "I'll have you guys out of there as soon as possible," he said. "Arrangements are being made now to have teams flown in. I've spoken to the Man, and he's sending in some Marine units to handle things there. It's going to take some untangling."

"What about the plane we scared off?" Lyons asked.

"That was picked up on its way back to a base in Georgia. The Marines were waiting when it landed. The plane was carrying a special unit under the command of an officer who is a very good friend of McClain."

"Talk about keeping it in the family," Blancanales said.

"I'll see you guys back at base," Brognola said. "I've got some interesting things to show you, information we got from those computer disks you picked up in Miami. It's all tying in with the feedback from the other teams."

"Sounds like fun," Schwarz murmured.

"What do you want?" Brognola asked. "A vacation?"

"Why not?" Schwarz said. "You forgetting what day it is tomorrow? Fourth of July. It's a national holiday, guys."

Lyons shook his head. He was about to make a reply when Brognola came back on.

"Talk to you later. We have an update on Puerto Rico." The line went dead.

The men of Able Team exchanged glances.

Puerto Rico meant Phoenix Force.

The front line.

# CHAPTER FIFTEEN

*Cordillera Central Area, Puerto Rico*

Conscious of their lesser numbers, Phoenix Force used surprise as the spearhead of their attack. Having made a swift recon of the rebel camp, assessing numbers as efficiently as possible under the conditions, the Stony Man team deployed around the perimeter, then went in hard and fast, aware that they needed to move quickly as the pale light of early dawn began to push the night shadows back into hiding.

Using the grenades they had liberated from the earlier encounter and the LAW rockets they were carrying, they launched a blistering assault on the PRISM base, gaining the advantage in the first thirty seconds.

Not that the assault went all their way.

Although the explosions created by the LAWs and the grenades filled the night with noise and destruction, taking out a number of the defenders, Major Nunez and his Cuban advisers responded quickly. Unlike their Puerto Rican protégés, the Cubans were experienced fighters. Hardened in a number of campaigns, both publicized and covert, they regrouped and fought back.

Encizo and James came in from the east side of camp, breaching a shallow barricade of timber and foliage behind which a half-dozen PRISM rebels put up token resistance. The rebels were armed with Kalashnikov assault rifles, and two of them manned a light machine gun.

James, his M-16 crackling with methodical precision, took out the first of the rebels to expose himself, his shot taking away the side of the man's face. As the screaming rebel tumbled back behind the barricade, his partner took one look at the bleeding wound and forgot why he was out in the forest. He threw down his assault rifle and turned to run. His action came too late to prevent a burst of fire from Encizo's M-16 that cut his legs from under him, ripped into his body, plunged him facedown on the forest floor.

Moments later James scrambled over the barricade, his M-16 spitting death as he took out two more of the rebels, ignoring the keen burn of a bullet scraping his left shoulder as it passed. Huddling on the other side of the barricade, James laid down a searing volley of fire that distracted the rebels, gaining time for Encizo to join him.

Rolling over the barricade, the little Cuban dropped to the ground, swiveling on one foot to trade shots with the machine gunner's loader as the rebel brought his assault rifle into play. Encizo's burst of 5.56 mm bullets, at close range, almost took off the rebel's head as the slugs shredded his neck. The dying man fell back, his blood spraying the face of his rebel partner. Pawing at his eyes, the machine gunner tried to turn his weapon on Encizo, but took a single 5.56 mm bullet through the brain as his reward.

Dragging the corpses aside, James grabbed the machine gun and lifted it bodily so that it now faced into the rebel camp. He waited until Encizo took up the belt to feed it in, then sent chopping bursts of gunfire across the camp, blowing holes in stacked supplies, cans of drinking water, and knocking the legs from under anyone who moved within his field of fire.

COMING IN from the west side of camp, McCarter, Manning and Hawkins met fierce resistance from the group of Cubans who had set up a defensive line in and around the radio tent and the helicopter behind them.

McCarter saw that the Cubans had dragged off the heavy camouflage net used to conceal the chopper. Men were scurrying around the aircraft, loading it with supplies. Others were completing the refueling.

"Try and keep that chopper from getting damaged," McCarter said to his teammates. "It could be useful."

The Cubans were responding by laying down a withering spread of autofire. McCarter dispersed his men with a sharp cut of his hand, and saw Manning and Hawkins melt from sight. He was able to concentrate on his own part of the battle now, knowing that they were capable of looking after themselves.

Both Manning and Hawkins had used up their LAWs during the opening moments of the strike. McCarter still carried his. Crouched behind the thick stump of a felled tree, the Briton unslung the compact weapon. He pulled the tabs, extending the launch tube, and swung the rocket over his shoulder. Scanning the camp area, McCarter located the radio tent, with its long, slender antennae. He steadied the LAW, sighting in on the tent, and depressed the trigger. He felt the tube quiver and heard the whoosh as the LAW fired. Seconds later the communications tent vaporized in a burst of flame and smoke. Men were flung in all directions by the force of the blast.

Throwing aside the spent LAW, McCarter pushed to his feet and advanced on the smoking wreckage, the M-16 in his hands spitting deadly fire.

TO THE FAR RIGHT of the Briton, Hawkins clashed with a pair of Cubans trying to outflank Phoenix Force's advance. The advisers came face-to-face with the Stony Man commando as he edged his way between close-standing trees.

Hawkins turned sideways, presenting a smaller target, and swept the muzzle of his M-16 around to cover the startled Cubans. In the space of a heartbeat, decisions were made and action taken.

The Phoenix Force warrior felt a slug sizzle by his face and gouge a chunk from the trunk of one of the trees. By that time, though, a volley from his M-16 had cut into the Cubans, turning living flesh into bloody tatters and depositing the corpses on the damp earth. Stepping over them, Hawkins moved on, trading shots with the hard-fighting Cubans and their less-than-competent rebel partners.

The detonation of McCarter's LAW rocket threw a brilliant light across the combat area. Hawkins, ducking to avoid being seen, almost stumbled over the prone figure of what he thought was a dead rebel. However, the Puerto Rican was far from deceased. He had gone to ground himself to avoid the sudden blast. Now he made a desperate lunge for the American intruder, his heavy, broad-bladed knife in his right hand.

Hawkins spotted the weapon in the brief moment before it cleaved his flesh. Twisting his supple body to the side, the Phoenix Force commando avoided the full cut of the blade but felt it slice a shallow gash along his left forearm. The sudden, sharp pain made him gasp, and also lash out in reflex. The barrel of his rifle clouted the rebel across the side of the face, opening a wound that bubbled with blood. The rebel fell back, unconscious if not dead.

Movement on his left made Hawkins turn, and he found himself confronted by a pair of Cubans. The uniformed invaders, clutching AK-74s, were wide-eyed from the blast, faces and clothing covered in dust and blood. One had a ragged tear across his cheek. As they made the face-to-face with Hawkins, the Cubans brought their weapons into play, the muzzles angling toward the Phoenix Force warrior.

Hawkins, counting off the seconds, advanced rather than retreated. He launched himself in a body slam that took the Cubans totally by surprise. Hawkins's body crashed into the pair, tucking and rolling to his knees, then twisted his body around, the M-16 following, and caught the Cubans in a double set of 3-round bursts. The line of slugs stitched his targets chest high as they pushed upright, driving them groundward in a bloody heap.

Back on his feet, Hawkins picked up his original course and pushed on toward the center of the camp, still firing as he advanced.

GARY MANNING FOUND he was closest to the parked helicopter as he skirted the fringes of the LAW blast. Smoke drifted across his path, momentarily obscuring the bulk of the chopper and the team hurrying to prepare it for takeoff.

There were four men, all carrying Kalashnikov assault rifles on shoulder slings. They called to one another as they worked, trying to ignore the chaos that had erupted around them.

Manning managed to get close before he was spotted. Having to duck and dive, trading shots with others in the camp area, the burly Canadian was unable to keep his eyes fixed exclusively on the chopper crew.

The Cuban who spotted Manning was able to unsling his weapon and track in almost to the point of firing before his target realized his predicament.

The moment he saw the AK aimed his way, Manning went to ground, hitting hard and rolling. His reaction was fast, but not fast enough to completely avoid the Cuban's shot. By a stroke of luck the gunner had his weapon set for single shots, so Manning's chances of escaping injury were higher. As he struck the ground, the big Canadian felt a solid blow that numbed his right leg. He flipped over, pulling his weapon with him, and returned fire, desperate not to hit the chopper. The burst from his M-16 caught the Cuban in the lower body, knocking him to his knees. The second burst tore away a portion of his skull.

Shouts of alarm went up as the chopper crew realized they were under attack. They instantly took up defensive positions, weapons coming on-line.

Manning, trying to ignore the aching pulse in his leg, pushed to one knee, tracking in with the M-16, taking out a second Cuban. The burst threw the man against the landing strut of the chopper. He sagged, his chest glistening where the 5.56 mm slugs had cleaved his flesh.

With increasing difficulty Manning swiveled the muzzle of the M-16 to line up the remaining Cubans. They were acting together, moving toward the Canadian, AKs dropping to pick up their target.

Manning fired a short burst, catching one gunner in the side.

The second Cuban uttered an angry yell and jerked his weapon into play. He was in the act of pulling the trigger when a burst of fire blew him off his feet.

The wounded Cuban, still able to wield his weapon, triggered a shot that missed Manning by inches before a further salvo drove him to the ground.

The big Canadian turned his head and saw McCarter and Hawkins approaching him.

"Lying down on the job again?" McCarter chided softly.

Manning shrugged. His leg was starting to hurt, and blood was oozing through the leg of his pants above the knee.

"Let's move, mates," McCarter said.

With Hawkins's help, the Briton hauled Manning to his feet. Supporting his weight, they moved him to the cover of the helicopter, sitting him down beneath the shadow of the fuselage.

"T.J., keep an eye on him," McCarter said.

The Phoenix Force leader ejected the spent magazine from his M-16 and snapped in a fresh one. Cocking the weapon, McCarter edged out from the shelter of the chopper and into the rebel camp.

JAMES AND ENCIZO pushed aside the machine gun as the weapon spit out its final rounds. Picking up their own weapons, they moved out across the campsite, scanning the area, seeking any further resistance.

They found none.

Silence, broken only by the moans of the wounded, descended on the rebel base.

Tendrils of smoke rose into the dawn sky from the smoldering ruins of the communications tent.

As James and Encizo moved across the area, disarming sullen Puerto Rican rebels, they met McCarter approaching from the other direction.

"Get these people rounded up and secured," he directed.

The Briton surveyed the scene of battle, his keen eyes searching the shambles of the camp.

"You looking for something?" Encizo asked.

"Maybe the sense to all this bloody nonsense," McCarter replied.

"The same as always," James said. "These poor sons of bitches are paying the price for someone's twisted ambitions. It usually comes down to that equation."

"Spare me the theory," Encizo said.

"Did I see some of our rebels taking off for the hills?" James asked.

McCarter nodded. "They threw down their guns and ran like their arses were on fire."

McCarter's description eased the tension a little, and a low chuckle escaped from James's lips.

"Cal, do a swap with T.J. I need you to check Gary over. Looks like he took a bullet in the leg. He's slowing down in his twilight years."

WITH THE SURVIVORS of the firefight gathered together and held under the guns of Hawkins and Encizo, James was able to tend to Manning's wound.

The slug had lodged in the Canadian's thigh, close to the main muscle group. James, the Phoenix Force medic, was unable to extract the bullet. He used the medical kit from the helicopter to clean the wound and give his teammate some painkillers. Luckily no major blood vessels had been ruptured. James was able to stop the bleeding and bind the wound.

While this was happening, McCarter climbed into the helicopter and checked it over. The aircraft was a Sikorsky Black Hawk, and the machine bore military markings. The Briton was curious as to where the rebels had gotten hold of it. Not that it was impossible. The way this mission was going, he wouldn't have been surprised at anything the opposition showed up with. Weapons and equipment appeared to be easily available to them.

Climbing into the cargo area, McCarter examined the goods already placed on board. The crates that had been loaded prior to Phoenix Force's attack on the camp contained weapons and ammunition. The arms were all of U.S. manufacture, and the boxes that held them were U.S. military.

Moving forward, the Phoenix Force leader discovered what looked like a large suitcase. He opened it and found a secure-satellite-uplink unit. Complete with its own collapsible satellite dish, the mobile unit could be linked to an orbiting satellite to secure direct communication.

Taking the case outside, McCarter fanned open the satellite dish. Switching on the unit, he keyed in the code that would link him with the U.S. orbiting COMSTAR system. Stony Man subscribed to this satellite, using a dummy company reference that linked the system to the Farm's own communications section. It was, as were all the other systems in use, monitored around the clock, so that if any of the Stony Man teams was able to make use of it, there was always someone around to pick up incoming transmissions.

Once McCarter got through to Stony Man, he asked to be connected with Brognola.

"I hate to ask, but where are you calling from?" the big Fed asked. His words came through with crystal clarity, almost as if he were standing beside McCarter.

"The Cordillera Central area. I need some backup here. Can you contact the Puerto Rican U.S. Navy base and get some people out here to take prisoners off our hands?"

"Give me your position," Brognola said. To someone close by him, he said, "Get me Barbara Price."

Price was on the phone in seconds. She listened as McCarter gave her an approximate relay of where they were.

"I'm on it," she said, and vanished from the line.

"What's the position out there?" Brognola asked.

"Cuban combat troops assisting PRISM. Looks like they've been training them, but not very well. The minute the firefight started, the rebels fell apart."

"There's more?"

"Bloody right," McCarter said. "The bunch out here isn't the whole of PRISM. I'd say these were a reserve force waiting to fly in by chopper to any position needing backup. They were waiting for extra weapons so they could pass them out. We took out the delivery."

"So where's the main force?" Brognola asked.

"I believe it's in San Juan. Gary got hold of some papers from one of the Cubans. They look like deployment orders. There are places in San Juan marked on a map—government buildings, radio and TV stations, the airport, main highway junctions. I think PRISM is concentrating on San Juan."

"So they're already in the city?"

"I'd say yes. And this being July 4, it's the ideal time to go for it. Everybody's out celebrating. Things are relaxed, and people are too busy to notice anything odd until it's too late."

"They still have to get their people to the right places," Brognola countered.

"I think we know how they're going to do it. We checked out the room of the PRISM guy who tried to kill Chavez and found a payment receipt that showed he'd rented a large warehouse on the outskirts of the city. We were going to check it out, but things got too hot. The paperwork we got from the Cuban had that warehouse down as a main deployment area. They've got a collection of public-utilities and transit vehicles parked there, such as buses and semitrailers. Maybe that's the way they're going to get their people into position— drive them there in public vehicles. No one would take a second look. They can drop them right on the doorstep and be in place before anyone can do a thing."

"What do you want from me?"

"Get the naval base on alert, but tell them to keep it low-key. Too much security could scare off any rebel attack before it happens. We want to catch these buggers red-handed."

"I'll do what I can. What's your next move?"

"As soon as reinforcements arrive, we're leaving in a borrowed chopper, heading straight to the warehouse. If I'm right, we'll catch the main PRISM force before it moves out."

"I'll hurry the Navy along. Anything you need?"

"Some weapons and fatigues. Running around the forest in leisure clothing isn't my idea of fun. We're making things up as we go along out here."

"I'll see to it. You guys okay?"

"One Canadian with a leg wound. I might leave him with the Navy. He won't like it, but he'll do what he's told."

"It's hell being in charge, isn't it?" Brognola said. "Take care."

# CHAPTER SIXTEEN

Gary Manning took the order to stay behind in stoic silence. It was obvious he hated the idea of missing out on the finale, but he was less than at his best, and he wouldn't have insisted on going along with the chance of placing his partners at risk.

The medic who flew in with the U.S. Marine Corps team took one look at the wound and confirmed what McCarter had suspected. Manning needed to be flown directly to the naval base hospital for an immediate operation.

The Marine lieutenant commanding the team, a tall, sandy-haired man in his early thirties named Dan Armus, had plainly been briefed about Phoenix Force's status. He deferred to McCarter when it came to procedure.

"Get these rebels back to the base," McCarter said. "Someone is going to want to question them."

"What about the Cubans, sir?" the lieutenant asked. "I mean, what's going to happen to them?"

"Good question," McCarter said. "I don't have an answer to that. It's out of my hands anyway. I believe you'll probably get your orders from Washington on that."

James joined McCarter. He was carrying a bundle of clothing, camo fatigues and boots the Marines had brought along, as well as weapons for Phoenix Force. He handed the gear to McCarter.

"These look about your size," James said.

McCarter stripped off his outer clothing and pulled on the fatigues. He pulled on a cap, aware that Armus was watching him closely.

"Something on your mind?" the Briton asked.

The Marine smiled. "Not the first time you've been in uniform," he said. "Looks right on you, sir."

"Quite an honor for a Brit to wear Marine Corps uniform," McCarter said, and meant it. He had great respect for the Marines.

Hawkins appeared. "We're ready to go," he said. "Chopper's loaded."

McCarter took the lieutenant's hand. "Thanks for the assist."

"You sure you don't want a few more of my men to go along with you?"

"The three you've given will do fine," McCarter replied. "I'll try to bring them back in the same condition they were in when you gave them."

"Good luck."

McCarter crossed the camp and climbed inside the waiting chopper.

One of the Marines seconded to Phoenix Force was a skilled helicopter pilot. Before the arrival of the Marine team, McCarter had planned to fly the chopper himself. On learning that there was a fully skilled pilot with the Marines, the Briton had stepped down. Impetuous he might be, but McCarter wasn't vain when it came to acknowledging the greater abilities of another.

As soon as they were in the air and on course, McCarter dropped into the seat beside the pilot, a taciturn Marine Corps sergeant named Ginty.

"The warehouse is situated on this side of San Juan," McCarter said. He showed Ginty the location, ringed on the map supplied by Lieutenant Armus.

Ginty studied the layout. "No problem, sir," he said. "How are we going to play this?"

"I'm banking on the fact that we're using their own helicopter," McCarter said. "It could get us in close before they realize something's wrong. Give us the chance to surprise them."

"Sounds good on paper, sir."

McCarter smiled at the sergeant. "I didn't say it was perfect. Any input is welcome."

"How about dropping off a couple of our squad at the rear of the place?" Ginty suggested. "Give us some support cover in case things get hot."

McCarter nodded. "Come in from the south side. Swing by the rear. If they don't have anyone out there on watch, we'll drop Carson and your boys. You'll have to come in low and slow. Can you pull that off?"

This time even Ginty cracked a grin. "Watch and weep, sir. Watch and weep."

McCarter went aft. He caught James's eye. "Carson" was the black warrior's cover name.

"When we reach the warehouse, Ginty is going to pull in around the rear of the place and come in low enough to drop off you and our two Marines. Soon as you touch down, move fast into position so you can give us cover fire if anything develops."

James nodded. He joined the two Marines and explained what was happening.

The Marines, both seasoned men, listened without comment.

"Any specifics, sir?" one of them asked when James finished. He was a lean, suntanned man with sharp, inquisitive eyes. His name, according to his uniform tag, was Landis.

"Stay alive, Landis," James said. "If these rebels want to play hard, taken 'em down."

"No prisoners, sir?" asked Carey, the second Marine.

"That's down to them, Carey."

"Aye, aye, sir."

They began to check their gear. Once they were on the ground, it would be too late.

James carried his 92-F, as well as an M-16 provided by the Marines Corps. The rifle was fitted with a 40 mm M-203 grenade launcher. On his webbing he carried extra ammunition, plus loads for the launcher. There was even a regulation bayonet in its sheath. Landis and Carey carried M-16s.

McCarter, Encizo and Hawkins were kitting up, as well.

The light was getting stronger now, showing a cloudless, empty sky. It had the makings of a hot day.

In more ways than one.

*PRISM Warehouse Facility, San Juan Outskirts*

"I STILL CANNOT raise them," the Cuban said over his shoulder.

The major in charge glanced up from his chart. He considered for a moment, then beckoned to Salazar.

"Is something wrong?" the PRISM leader asked.

Major Reynos shrugged. "It may be nothing," he said. "There appears to be a breakdown in communication with Nunez."

"Could it have something to do with the incidents that have been occurring?"

"Possibly," Reynos replied. "On the other hand, it could be nothing more than equipment failure."

"You should have allowed me to supply you with the American equipment we have obtained," Salazar said.

Reynos curled his lip. "You believe their equipment is better than ours?"

"To be honest, Major, yes."

Reynos dismissed the notion. "I have more on my mind right now. I suggest we hurry. Get everyone in the vehicles and ready to move."

"We have at least an hour before the deadline," Salazar protested.

"I would prefer to be overly cautious, under the circumstances. It may be necessary to bring the operation forward. In the event that something unexpected has happened to Nunez, we have to be prepared to go in alone."

"Without the others?" Salazar asked, his voice edged with concern.

"Jesus, we are the main force. Nunez and your people were always intended as a reserve force, ready to go to any area where they might be needed.

If they can't join us—and at the moment that is only a hypothetical possibility—then we will carry the full assault. We must also be ready to send the alert to Cuba ourselves. Not depend on Nunez."

"Meaning?"

"Meaning we will have to fight harder and be prepared to take heavier losses until the main force from Cuba arrives."

Salazar absorbed the information, his mind working overtime.

"Are you starting to have doubts?" Reynos asked. "This isn't the best time to be assessing your commitment to the cause."

"It has nothing to do with that, Major," Salazar said. "And my commitment to PRISM is as strong as ever."

"Go on."

"We know that there has been a breach in security. The man, Chavez, who infiltrated our group. The incidents here in San Juan. Now the lack of communication with Nunez. For all we know, there may be deeper penetration. Maybe our people in government, the radio and TV stations have been compromised. What about the PRISM people at the power stations? Those waiting outside the American naval base? What if they have all been taken captive? There will be no backup from them. We could be walking into a trap."

Reynos nodded. "Everything you say could be true, Jesus. On the other hand, if you are wrong, and everyone is in place waiting for our assault, do we betray them? Do we save our skins by dispersing quietly and leaving them to their fate? How do we resolve this dilemma?"

Salazar glanced around the large warehouse. The vehicles were ready, waiting for the PRISM rebels and the Cubans to climb on board. And the men themselves, Puerto Rican and Cuban, who had been working toward this day for a long time—they were waiting, too. This was to be an important event in their lives.

"Are you a gambler, Jesus?" Reynos asked quietly.

"A what?"

"A gambler. Willing to turn that last card. Win or lose, you have to turn it. If you don't, if you walk away and never find out, it will haunt you for the rest of your life."

"How can you compare what we are doing to the turn of a card?"

Reynos smiled. "Jesus, I have been a soldier all my adult life, and I can tell you one thing that is constant—every campaign, every assault and raid, they are all gambles. Prior information, planning, strategy. In the end none of them guarantee the final outcome. Only the men on the ground, facing the enemy, have the ability to win or lose. Each time a commander commits his people to battle, he does it knowing that he could be sending them to their deaths. That is the price you pay for leading. The decision is yours and yours alone. No one can make that choice for you.''

Salazar considered the Cuban's words and knew them to be true. He wanted, desired, a free Puerto Rico, a nation able to decide its own future, walk its own path devoid of outside pressure. He wanted Puerto Rico back in the hands of its people. That could only be achieved by struggle. That meant hardship and suffering. He might not even survive today. His death might be one among many. That didn't bother him. He had accepted long ago that he might die trying to free Puerto Rico. If that happened, so be it. And as Reynos said, there were no guarantees one way or the other.

Turning back to the Cuban, Salazar spread his hands. ''We go.''

Reynos signaled to the waiting groups. ''Let's get on board!''

GINTY SWUNG the helicopter over the main highway, which bore little traffic. He eased the controls, and the chopper began to descend.

''There she is, sir,'' he said.

McCarter followed his pointing finger. Below and to their left he saw the untidy complex of the industrial area. The large storage facility, with its block of warehouses, stood close to the main entrance to the site. A wide service road led to the highway heading into San Juan.

"There's no sign of any movement around the warehouse," Hawkins announced. He was studying the buildings with a pair of powerful field glasses, courtesy of the Marine Corps.

"I'll swing around and approach from the rear," Ginty said. "If you see anything that shouldn't be there, give a holler."

"I'm guessing they'll be keeping a low profile," McCarter said. "Probably brought all their people in during darkness. They wouldn't want anyone seeing anything suspicious, such as armed guards patrolling the warehouse. It would be a little difficult to explain that to the local cops."

Turning back to the rear of the chopper, the Briton signaled to Calvin James.

"You ready?" he asked.

James nodded.

"If we don't see any problems, we'll make a low-level approach from the rear. Be ready to go on my word. Sorry we can't take the time to put you down gently."

James rejoined his Marine partners at the chopper's side hatch, where Rafael Encizo stood ready to open it on McCarter's signal.

Ginty made a high-level sweep around to the rear of the warehouse.

After making a careful check, Hawkins gave McCarter the all-clear.

"Okay," the Briton said. "No outside patrols."

"No rear windows in the place," Hawkins added. "No security cameras in place, either. Brackets on the walls but nothing installed."

"Something to be said for cheapskate landlords," McCarter said. "Sergeant Ginty, let's do it. I've missed my breakfast because of this, and I'm starting to get impatient."

"Aye, aye, sir," Ginty acknowledged, and put the chopper into a downward curve.

*Inside the Warehouse*

"HELICOPTER APPROACHING," someone said.

Salazar listened and picked up the pulse of the chopper.

"Who?" he asked.

"Send someone outside to check," Reynos ordered. "It may be Nunez."

"It might also be the police. Or the military," Salazar said.

"Get those vehicles started," Reynos instructed. "Unlock the doors and let's be ready to move. One way or the other, there is no more time to waste."

The interior of the warehouse echoed to the sound of engines turning over and bursting into life. Clouds of diesel-exhaust fumes began to roll across the floor.

A PRISM rebel had slipped out of the small door set in the front wall of the warehouse. He was gone only for a few seconds.

"It's our helicopter," he said as he came back inside. "It's landing now."

"Get those damn doors open," Reynos ordered, "before we all choke on these stinking fumes."

Someone pressed the button that started the electric motors controlling the warehouse doors. They began to roll open along the rail set in the floor.

As they parted, the diesel fumes began to swirl about in oily clouds, pushed by the rotor wash from the chopper coming to rest on the concrete in front of the warehouse.

"Idiot of a pilot," Reynos cursed. "Doesn't he realize we have to drive out of here. He's blocking the damn way."

The moment he'd spoken, Reynos knew why the pilot had landed in front of the warehouse—because he knew what was inside the building.

And by parking the helicopter across the entrance, he was effectively preventing the rebel force from leaving the warehouse.

Which meant that Major Nunez wasn't on board the helicopter, nor were the PRISM rebels or the Cuban soldiers.

The only conclusion was that the helicopter was carrying a hostile group. Whether police or military, it made no difference. It meant the same thing.

Annoyingly it meant that Salazar had been right. But more importantly it meant the battle for Puerto Rico started here.

Now.

Reynos pulled his autopistol from its holster, then turned and signaled to his communications man. "Send the signal to Cuba! I want that backup force in the air now!"

McCARTER WAS the first one out of the helicopter. He exited the hatch before the skids touched the concrete, with Hawkins and Encizo close behind. They fanned out, conscious of the warehouse doors sliding ever wider. Clouds of diesel smoke were being sucked out the opening by the chopper's rotors, providing temporary cover for the Phoenix Force warriors. Unfortunately it did the same for the rebels inside the warehouse.

One of the rebels opened fire, slugs clanging off the front of the chopper. Others starred the canopy.

The roar of a revving engine filled the interior of the warehouse, and the bulky outline of a passenger bus became visible through the diesel smoke. The driver raced the vehicle out of the building, one side of the bus smashing against the still-opening doors, wrenching them off the tracks. Someone was leaning out the side door, firing an AK-74. The slugs went wide, chipping the concrete. The bus barreled forward, picking up speed.

Encizo, who found himself on the same side of the vehicle as the guy with the AK, lifted his M-16 and tracked in on the gunman. He triggered a couple of fast shots, picking off the shooter with ease. The guy gave a startled cry, fell from his perch and struck the concrete, rolling over and over.

The driver panicked and swung the wheel, taking the bus away from Encizo. The driver had lost some of his concentration and regained it too late to avoid the looming bulk of the helicopter. The still-rotating rotors clipped the aluminum roof of the vehicle, shearing the thin metal and shattering the windshield. The driver threw up his arms to protect himself from the shower of glass, forgetting the bus's line of travel. It slammed into the front of the chopper and came to a grinding halt.

As the bus hit the helicopter, McCarter thought about Sergeant Ginty. Was the man still inside?

He was relieved moments later when he spotted the Marine's familiar shape approaching him.

"Close one," McCarter yelled.

Ginty raised a thumb in acknowledgment.

Armed figures spilled from the stalled bus, immediately coming under the guns of Hawkins and Encizo, who traded fire with the PRISM-Cuban force. Three rebels went down, bodies riddled and bloody, sprawling on the concrete.

Observing the demise of their comrades, the others inside the bus moved to the rear of the vehicle, kicked open the emergency door and jumped to the ground, moving down either side of the bus. Yet others stayed inside, smashing out the windows so they could fire from the scant protection of the vehicle.

McCarter and Ginty separated as the rebels opened fire from the side windows, the slugs gouging bits of concrete from the floor.

The sergeant plucked a grenade from his webbing, pulling the pin with his teeth.

"Cover me," he yelled.

The Briton dropped to one knee, the M-16 to his shoulder. He began to punch out 3-round bursts, the 5.56 mm slugs driving the rebels back from the bus windows.

Ginty paused in midstride, turned on his heel and lobbed the grenade in the direction of the bus. It sailed in through one of the broken windows. Immediate panic erupted within the vehicle as the rebels pushed and fought to get clear.

The grenade detonated with an amplified blast, filling the interior with flame and smoke. The cries of the injured rose above the fading explosion. Glass-and-metal shards spewed across the interior of the warehouse.

More of the rebels appeared at the building's exit, some firing as they desperately tried to flee the scene.

McCarter and Ginty flattened themselves on the concrete and began to fire controlled bursts at the bunched rebels, while Encizo and Hawkins were doing the same on the far side of the bus.

JAMES AND THE MARINES were halfway along the length of the warehouse when they heard the sudden commotion coming from the front of the huge structure. Gunfire filled the air.

"Move it, guys," James said.

"Sir!" Landis called.

James glanced around and saw the Marine indicating a door set in the side of the warehouse wall. Landis tried the handle and found the door locked.

"We'll do it the hard way," James said. He set his M-16 on 3-round-burst mode and triggered into the door around the handle, the slugs chewing away at the thin metal. It took nearly a whole magazine before the shattered lock gave and the Phoenix Force warrior was able to haul the door open.

Landis and Carey breached the threshold, using the cover-and-maneuver procedure. James, replacing his spent magazine, followed.

The vast expanse of the warehouse was empty except for a collection of buses and semitrailers grouped near the main doors. The air around the vehicles was thick with diesel fumes from idling engines, and men were starting to exit the vehicles as the sound of gunfire increased.

"Looks like we arrived just in time," James stated.

"Yes, sir," Landis agreed.

"Shall we lend a hand?" James asked. There was no need to wait for an answer. "Pick your targets and fire at will."

James and the two Marines moved across the warehouse floor.

The smoke from the exhausts was starting to thin out now. As it dispersed, it showed the bunches of rebels exiting the parked vehicles. Someone was shouting orders, but not many rebels were taking any notice.

A number of the rebels caught sight of James and his partners approaching and grabbed for their weapons.

James triggered his M-16, as did the Marines, and the interior of the building rattled to the sound of their combined firepower.

The first blast took out a half-dozen rebels, spinning their punctured bodies along the sides of the buses before tumbling them to the floor.

Return fire found only empty air as James and the Marines spread apart, using the cover provided by the parked vehicles.

James, down on the floor, watched the movement of running feet. He waited until the rebels reached the rear of the bus before coming up on one knee. The moment they showed themselves, he triggered the M-16. His bursts found their targets, sending the enemy staggering back, bloody holes stitched across their chests and surprise etched on their faces.

Up on his feet again, James skirted the rear of the last vehicle and spotted a uniformed Cuban hunched over a radio transmitter-receiver. The man seemed to be in some conflict with another Cuban, obviously his superior. As the Phoenix Force warrior watched, the Cuban handling the radio gave in to his officer and reached for the radio's controls.

James ran forward, his M-16 tracking in on the pair.

The Cuban on his feet glanced around, saw James and stepped around to block the Phoenix Force commando from reaching the operator, grabbing for the AK-74 slung from his shoulder.

The M-16 spit out a single 3-round burst that caught the officer—Major Reynos—in the upper chest. The Cuban fell back, still attempting to bring his weapon into play. He collided with some empty fuel barrels and crashed to the floor. Rolling over with difficulty, Reynos tried to regain his feet, spitting blood and curses. He managed to get his feet under him before James fired again, this time a head burst that drove the Cuban facedown on the floor.

Turning back toward the radio, James punched a burst through a set, cutting off its transmission. He caught a glimpse of the Cuban operator sliding his fingers around an autopistol lying alongside the radio and turned the M-16 on him. The controlled burst drilled into the Cuban's chest and knocked him flat.

Caught by the unremitting fire from Landis and Carey, and that of James as he rejoined the battle, the main group of rebels and Cubans was driven toward the front of the warehouse.

Because of the bunching of the parked vehicles, the rebels were unable to disperse quickly as they exited the buses and trailers.

James and his partners had the advantage, being able to move along the rear of the vehicles with comparative ease, selecting their targets and preventing the rebels from gaining any advantage.

The possibility of freedom offered by the partly open warehouse doors proved to be just as hazardous for the rebels. Those who did break clear found themselves coming under the guns of McCarter and his people.

The occupants of the bus trying to break out of the warehouse had been reduced to a few walking wounded. The grenade Ginty had delivered had taken its toll. The badly wounded still lay inside next to the dead. The survivors who had scrambled out of the vehicle walked directly into the deadly firepower of the Phoenix Force team.

The resistance continued for some minutes, the rebels stubbornly refusing to yield. They exchanged fire with the Stony Man warriors, who closed in from both front and rear.

A light machine gun opened up from inside one of the parked buses, sending a stream of bullets through the open doors of the warehouse. The gunner was unable to select any targets because of his position inside the warehouse. It was a futile gesture that only resulted in the rebel force having to take cover themselves because they were in as much danger as anyone from the indiscriminate fire.

The machine gun fell silent shortly after Landis breached the bus and took out the gunner with a burst from his M-16.

A group of rebels boarded one of the other buses and opened fire, laying down a relentless stream of fire as the driver set the vehicle in motion, reversing it across the warehouse floor. When he reached midway, he braked. For long seconds he floored the gas pedal. With the engine at full throttle, the driver hit the gearshift and the bus lurched forward, heading for the front wall of the building. The rebels were trying to break out.

James found he was the closest to the moving vehicle. He realized what the rebels intended. Without a pause he sprinted forward, locking a high-explosive grenade into the M-203 launcher. As the bus loomed large in front of him, James raised the rifle and triggered the grenade launcher. The HE canister burst from the tube, curved across the warehouse and crashed through the windshield of the bus. Seconds later the grenade exploded with a loud detonation. Flame and smoke billowed from the shattered windows. The vehicle lurched, out of control. It swept past James and slammed into the rear of a semitrailer, coming to a grinding, swaying halt. Smoke gushed from the windows.

The bus crash seemed to break the resistance of the rebel force. Gunfire slackened, then stopped altogether.

McCarter quickly took control, not allowing the rebels any opportunity to regroup. After they threw down their weapons, he had them line up against a wall. His manner was brusque, his intentions plain for anyone to understand. It was a moment of extreme tension, one the Briton had experienced in the past. It needed to be handled swiftly, allowing the defeated to be controlled and removed from positions of strength.

Once he had the rebels disarmed and squatting in a silent, despondent group, McCarter assigned the majority of his team to stand guard over them.

"Ginty, check the radio in the chopper," he said. "If it's working, get in touch with your people. We need backup to take charge of this bunch."

The Marine nodded and headed for the chopper.

McCarter crossed to where James and Encizo were standing, their weapons trained on the defeated rebels.

"You know how many there are here?" Encizo asked. "Close to forty."

"I hate to think how many dead there are," James said.

"Probably a damn sight fewer than if this bloody rebellion had taken off," McCarter argued. "And a lot of those would have been civilians. They seem to be the ones who get hardest hit when these games get under way."

"Anybody picked out Jesus Salazar yet?" James asked.

Hawkins looked around. "He's over there. The guy with the shoulder wound. The way he's staring at us, I'm sure glad looks can't kill."

McCarter followed Hawkins's gaze and recognized Salazar from photographs. The rebel did have a sullen expression on his face, but the only thing McCarter recognized in the PRISM leader's eyes was utter defeat.

# CHAPTER SEVENTEEN

*Havana, Cuba*

Night closed around Mack Bolan like a protective shroud. The Executioner was back in Havana, prowling the shadows with the scent of death seeking him and trying to wrap him in its cold embrace.

Bolan knew he was pushing his luck to the limit. Salvano Cruz's lackeys, led by the predator called Lopez, were out in force. Their panic was almost tangible. Running scared as time slipped away, bringing their conspiracy ever closer, they scurried around in the shadows, seeking the ones they believed had information that might drag their treachery into the sunlight.

The ones they hunted were already out of the country.

Manuel and Linda Ramos and Antonio Batiste had left hours earlier, whisked away in a sleek combat helicopter piloted by Jack Grimaldi.

Grimaldi had touched down on the secluded beach just long enough to take his passengers on board, exchange a few words with Bolan and hand over fresh clothes and extra ammo. Then he was gone, taking the sleek black helicopter away from the island, skimming the waves so low he flew beneath any Cuban radar scans.

Before the chopper had vanished from sight, Bolan himself had moved on, merging with the darkness, returning to the car hidden in the dense undergrowth beyond the beach.

There he had stripped off his blacksuit and changed into civilian clothing—tan slacks and a bright shirt, and a brown leather jacket worn to conceal the Beretta's shoulder rig. Extra clips for the weapon went into his inside pocket.

The car was a nondescript Toyota, battered and streaked with dust. Manuel Ramos had used it to travel to the safehouse after ditching the truck. The Toyota was a backup vehicle, something hidden away for emergencies. The tank was full of gas, and there was a spare can in the trunk. Fuel was in short supply on the island, another of Castro's economic miracles gone wrong.

Easing the Toyota out of the underbrush, Bolan set off for the city. Havana lay about an hour's drive to the west. The soldier was heading for the section of the city known as Vedado, where Antonio Batiste had an apartment in one of the old converted mansions that dotted the area.

Back in the 1900s the area had been the home for wealthy Cubans and Americans. They had built their great houses on the wooded hills, overlooking the sprawl of Old Havana. In the fifties highrise buildings had gone up before the rot set in.

Bolan had been provided with a minutely detailed map of how to reach Vedado, with a description of the location of Batiste's particular building.

The Executioner drove steadily, not wanting to attract any undue attention. The Cuban roads outside the city were in bad condition, full of potholes and poorly lit. The only consolation was the fact they were little traveled, except for hitchhikers. Bolan ignored a number of pleas for a ride as he negotiated his way along the gloomy road. He had no intention of getting himself involved with any of the night travelers.

He approached the city limits with even greater caution, having been warned that the approach roads to Havana could be patrolled by Cuban motorcycle cops. These officers were in the habit of stopping vehicles at random. They were also keen to give traffic tickets for the simplest offense. Bolan couldn't afford to be challenged. He had no license or any documentation to prove he owned the Toyota.

It was close to nine-thirty when Bolan entered the outer limits of Havana. Soon after, he picked up the inner-city highway. He followed the map he'd been given, watching out for the poorly marked exits and picking up on the landmarks that had been added to assist him.

He was cruising through the La Rampa district, with its nightclubs and movie houses, looking for the avenue that would lead him to Batiste's place, when rain began to fall, sweeping in from the gulf. Within minutes it was a downpour, heavy sheets drifting across the rooftops and bouncing off the street. The Toyota's worn windshield wipers had to struggle to keep the window clear.

Turning off the main road, Bolan drove the small car up a hill, then took a right, ending up on the narrow avenue where Batiste's home stood. Through the rain-streaked windshield Bolan made out the dark bulk of the former mansion, standing off the road in its own ill-tended grounds. A low wall surrounded the large house.

Bolan drove by, stopping the Toyota some yards farther on. He sat checking the area. The street lighting was poor, leaving large areas in shadow. The rain added to the difficulty of spotting anyone else staking out the house.

The longer he waited, the more likely he might be tagged himself, Bolan decided. It wasn't his way to allow the enemy to dictate the action. He had to make the moves so that *he* was in control.

The soldier eased the Beretta from its holster, checked it and kept it in his hand as he opened the Toyota's door. The full force of the downpour struck as he climbed from the car and cut across the lawn toward the house. Discretion was the least of his worries this night. Bolan wanted in and out, with no delay.

Following Batiste's directions, the Executioner hit the steps leading to the front door, which was unlocked. The spacious lobby was a shadow of its former self. No longer the haunt of the rich, it served as nothing more than an entrance for the tenants who lived in the converted rooms.

Ahead of him lay the stairs. The once-rich carpet was faded, the pattern almost worn away by the tread of many feet over long years.

Bolan started up, keeping against the inner wall.

He noticed that there were damp footprints on the carpeting that led up to the next floor. More than one set. The house had had other visitors this night, and recently, because the rain had only been falling for the past ten minutes.

He reached the landing. Batiste's small apartment was to his Bolan's left, along a short passage, illuminated by a weak, dusty bulb.

Bolan wiped the rain from his face with a sleeve, pausing long enough to check that the damp footprints had hesitated on the same landing, then dispersed. Two sets had gone right, one to the left and along the corridor to Batiste's door, then farther along toward the dark end of the corridor, beyond the reach of the light cast by the overhead bulb.

The soldier moved along the side corridor. He had the key to Batiste's apartment in his pocket, and he palmed it in his left hand. Reaching the middle of the hallway, still moving, Bolan stretched up with his left hand and slapped it against the dangling bulb. It swung on its electric cord, throwing its yellow light into the dark recess at the end of the corridor.

The illumination was enough to outline the motionless figure of a stocky, bearded Cuban poised against the plaster wall. The man wore a rain-soaked coat and had a stubby submachine gun in his hands.

Exposed by Bolan's move, the Cuban lifted the subgun.

The Executioner had already brought the Beretta on-line, anticipating what might happen. He stroked the trigger and sent a 3-round burst chugging into the gunman's chest. The man fell back, brought up short by the wall behind him, and pitched facedown on the dusty carpet.

Moving to the apartment door, Bolan slid the key in the lock and turned it. He pushed open the door and slipped inside the dark room, hearing the thump of running feet as the Cuban's partners came to his assistance.

The first man ran by the door, but the second plunged straight through, his body outlined by the dim light behind him.

Bolan took him down with a single burst of 9 mm tumblers that chewed through his face and catapulted him across the hallway.

The surviving gunman stayed away from the door, opening up with a wild, sustained volley from his subgun. Slugs tore at the door frame, while others burned through the dark room and thudded into the far wall. Some of Batiste's possessions were shattered, dropping to the floor.

Bolan, on the far side of the room away from the gunfire, peered into the gloom. He was attempting to fine-balance two events: staying away from the hostile fire and gaining possession of the photographic evidence he had come for.

Batiste, anticipating that Cruz might send his people to search the apartment for any incriminating evidence, had devised an effectively simple hiding place for the photographs.

They had been placed in a thick envelope, sealed inside a plastic bag bound with tape, then concealed under one of the overlapping wooden boards on the outside wall of the house. Batiste had loosened the nails holding the end of the board in place, inserted the package, then resecured the board. The board he had selected was directly outside the window of the apartment's living room.

Exactly where Bolan was standing.

The gunfire had ceased abruptly. The soldier heard the metallic click of an ammo clip being snapped into place.

A floorboard creaked as the unseen gunman edged toward the door. The sound stopped, then continued.

Bolan eased open the window catch and slid the window open with his left hand. Leaning out, he counted off the boards until he reached the one described by Batiste. He slipped his fingers under the edge of the board and began to pry it away from the wall. The previously loosened nails came free smoothly. Bolan pushed his fingers beneath the board and felt the slick surface of the plastic wrapping. Getting a firm grip on the package, he eased it from its hiding place, then pulled back inside the room.

The gunman in the corridor fired off a heavy burst, raking the interior of the room, then lunged forward. The subgun in his hands swept back and forth, crisscrossing the apartment with bullets.

Bolan, flat on the floor, leveled the 93-R and placed two 3-round bursts into the guy's body. He crashed back over a low chair and sprawled in a bloody heap across the doorway.

The soldier slid the package into a pocket of his jacket and closed the zipper.

He paused by the downed gunmen and selected one of the autoweapons they had been carrying. Both were .45-caliber Ingrams. Stubby, squat weapons with an awesome rate of firepower, they could go through a full magazine in seconds. Bolan checked the dead gunmen, taking a couple of spare magazines for the Ingram. He snapped one of them in place, discarding the one that was partly spent.

He moved out of the apartment, heading down the corridor toward the stairs.

The front door burst open, and the crash of booted feet told Bolan his welcome was running out fast.

He peered over the rail of the stairs and saw a group of armed men starting toward the first step.

Bolan leaned over and raked the stairwell with a sustained burst, his blast catching the lead men. They tumbled back, bodies punctured and bleeding. Someone shouted orders, and there was hesitation. No one wanted to be the first up the stairs.

The Executioner used the delay to his advantage. He ran to the front of the house. Peering through the window, he saw that it was directly above the roof of the veranda fronting the building. Bolan took a couple of steps back, then launched himself at the window. He crashed through, shattering the frame, as well as the glass. The veranda roof lay six feet down. He landed and rolled, coming up against the low rail edging the roof section. On his feet Bolan ran to the far end of the veranda, checking the distance before swinging over the side and letting himself drop to the grass below. He landed on soft ground, breaking his fall.

Bolan crossed the lawn, angling to cut across the frontage of the next house to reach his parked car.

Behind him he heard the alarm raised as his pursuers realized he had made his break.

The rattle of autofire filled the night. Slugs chunked into the wet earth, kicking up muddy gouts, some of which slapped against the back of the soldier's legs.

He had almost reached the sidewalk when he saw a dark-coated figure detach itself from the shadows of a mass of shrubbery.

The man moved forward, quickening his pace as he confronted Bolan. Pale lamplight, hazed by the falling rain, glinted on the cold steel of the large autopistol in the man's hand. That same light broke across the newcomer's face.

Bolan took one look and knew the man instantly. It would have been hard not to have recognized the taut features and the cold eyes. The last time he had seen that face, it had been captured on videotape during the murders of Paul Chavez and Alan Moreland, the two FBI agents killed by the man posing as Michael Vasquez, but who was really Raul Fuentes.

"You should not have come back," Fuentes said, his voice raised above the sound of the rain.

Bolan didn't waste a second on words.

He threw himself below the muzzle of Fuentes's pistol, pushing the muzzle of the Ingram up at the Cuban and pulling the trigger. The subgun thundered its tune of death, expending the whole of the magazine into Raul Fuentes. He was driven back by the force of the blast, his lower body and chest reduced to bloody shreds by the stream of slugs. His single cry of protest was lost in the racket.

Bolan gathered his legs under him, hands busy removing the empty clip and replacing it with the spare from his jacket.

Bullets slapped at the earth behind him.

The Executioner whirled, returning fire. His coolness under attack unnerved the enemy gunners, and for a split second they were taken by surprise. That hesitation cost them dearly as Bolan raked the Ingram back and forth. He dropped two of them, wounding a third. The rest scattered, seeking cover from the American who seemed intent on destroying them all.

The moment the Cubans broke rank, Bolan turned and made for the parked Toyota. He was inside and firing up the engine before they realized he had gone. Only when the screech of tires on the wet street reached their ears did they know, and by then it was too late.

They rushed for their own parked vehicles, scrambling inside and roaring in pursuit. Reaching the bend in the road, they picked up speed as they hit the slope.

The lead driver picked up something in his headlights as he sped through the next curve in the road. He realized what it was too late and hit the brakes. The pursuit vehicle went into a skid on the wet road, the driver desperately attempting to correct the slide. All he succeeded in doing was to bring his car into a broadside collision with the Toyota Bolan had swung across the road, blocking the way.

Metal buckled and glass shattered. The locked vehicles spun in a half circle, barely coming to a rest before the second pursuit vehicle slammed into them. The driver tried to hang on to his steering wheel, but the rim snapped and he was thrown forward, the rigid column impaling him.

In the confusion and panic that followed, the final pursuit car slithered to a shuddering halt only feet from the tangled vehicles. The occupants piled out and ran to help their wounded comrades, dragging bleeding figures out of the wrecks.

One of the rescuers paused, looking around in alarm, nostrils flaring as he recognized a familiar odor.

Somewhere in among the tangle of locked vehicles, gasoline was gushing from a punctured tank. And elsewhere the barely audible sizzle of electrical wiring, overheating and burning off the outer covering, was lost amid the cacophony of other noises.

The man who had smelled the leading gas opened his mouth to yell a warning, which was lost in the sudden whoosh of flame that threw fiery tendrils out across the road, under the vehicles, seeking the raw source of the supply. And found it . . .

*Fourth of July, Nassau, Bahamas*

THEY WERE ALL GATHERED on the patio of the big house: Ray McClain, Salvano Cruz, Rico Jorges and Colonel Oswaldo Lopez.

Breakfast had been laid out in the room behind them, though no one had eaten much except Cruz. Despite the tension and the concern each of them felt, Cruz had retained his appetite. Even now, standing with the others, he held a plate in his hand.

"Glad to see someone's enjoying himself," Ray McClain observed.

"I see no point in starving myself," Cruz replied calmly. "However the day goes, we still need to eat."

Jorges turned away from the group. He stood by the low wall edging the patio and stared out across the ocean. The blue water looked smooth and calm beneath the clear sky, untroubled by the events of the previous night.

If only life remained as uncomplicated, Jorges thought.

His own thoughts were dark and confused. He trusted very few of the people around him, Lopez least of all. The colonel was a truly evil man, and Jorges knew how Lopez felt about him. Regardless of the fact that Jorges had fed important information to him, Lopez made it clear that he despised him. As far as the colonel was concerned, Jorges was a traitor to his own and not to be trusted. Jorges found himself trapped in a no-man's-land. He couldn't go back to his former life, and his future looked bleak with the people he associated with in the present. He had committed himself to Salvano Cruz. There was no way out of that. What troubled Jorges now was his future. How would he fit in to Cruz's plans?

If he did fit.

Left to Lopez, the only thing awaiting Jorges would be a bullet in the back of the head some dark night.

It was little wonder that Jorges had little appetite that morning.

Ray McClain turned as he heard someone enter the room. It was Boyette. Casually dressed as if he were on his way to the golf course, and showing little sign of his sixty-four years, Boyette crossed to the breakfast buffet. He took a plate and filled it with scrambled eggs, crisp bacon and mushrooms.

"Great morning, gentlemen," he said.

"If you say so," McClain remarked.

"This could be the best day of all our lives," Boyette added.

He became aware of the somber mood that existed.

"For a group embarking on something as important as our venture, you boys are looking decidedly sad."

"Maybe we have cause."

"Why? Because we haven't had feedback exactly on the minute?"

McClain nodded. "Something like that. No damn word from anyone, Lawrence. Not from Benedict. From Puerto Rico. Or from any of Cruz's people in Cuba."

For the first time a shadow of doubt flickered across Boyette's face.

"Nothing at all?" he asked.

McClain managed a mocking smile. "Is there something we haven't been told, Lawrence? A foul-up? Or haven't you been paying your telephone bill?"

Boyette put down his plate and turned to face the tight group of people. "I'm certain this isn't as bad as it sounds. We've put too much into this for it to fall apart now. There has to be a logical explanation."

McClain snorted in frustration. "I'll give you logic. It tells me we're sliding down the pan. This project is busting wide open."

"I think you're being hasty, Ray."

Salvano Cruz coughed gently, then stepped forward. "As Lawrence says, we have invested a great deal in this venture, all of us in our different ways. I for one do not intend to admit defeat just yet. There could be a simple explanation. A breakdown in communications. Even today, with high technology, making a simple telephone call can result in frustration. Remember, too, that in this part of the world, weather conditions can play havoc with transmissions."

McClain shook his head as he turned away. "Jesus, I'm in partnership with a bunch of morons," he muttered.

"I'm going to make a few calls," Boyette said, "and see if I can talk to some of our people. Give me half an hour, and I'll have news for you."

Boyette caught Cruz's eye. The Cuban followed him inside the house.

"I meant what I said, Salvano. This isn't over yet. The operation has only been under way for less than an hour. We have to expect this kind of delay. Military operations don't run to the minute. They never have and never will. Now don't you go soft on me."

Salvano drew a large Havana cigar from his shirt pocket. "I am going out there to smoke this. It is a beautiful day, and I will wait for you to come back and tell us all is well."

CRUZ WAS STILL smoking his cigar. The others were standing around in strained silence, and they turned when Boyette came back.

One look at his face and they all knew—even Cruz—that the day wasn't going to be theirs after all.

Boyette suddenly looked like an old man. He moved slowly, and his haggard expression said it all.

"Goddamn it all to hell," McClain swore. "I was right after all."

Boyette slumped into one of the patio chairs. "Bastards," he said softly. "Chicken-shit bastards."

"Don't tell me," McClain said. "No one will take your calls. All too busy. Out for the day. Out for the rest of your life. Is that the way it reads, Lawrence?"

For a moment defiance gleamed in Boyette's eyes again. He stared at McClain, angry because the man was mocking him, but more so because McClain was right.

"They won't talk to me. Not one of them. None of my Pentagon contacts." He gave a low chuckle. "Some of them have already gone. Been moved to other postings. I can't even get through to my own office. Do you believe that, Ray? My own office refuses to accept any calls from me. Of course the damn line is bugged. They think I don't know the signs."

Lopez moved to stand beside Cruz and bent to murmur something in his superior's ear. Lopez nodded quickly.

"Perhaps we should consider the possibility of—"

"Running out, Salvano?" Boyette snapped. "A while ago you were full of confidence."

"That was before. This is now."

"Fine," Boyette said. "Tell me, Salvano, where are you going to run to? Back to see Fidel? Ask his forgiveness? I don't think so."

"I have contingency plans," Cruz said, "money put aside in safe accounts. And I do have friends. I can bide my time."

"Fine," McClain snapped. "You cover your fucking ass, pal. Don't concern yourself with the rest of us."

"McClain, you came into this knowing exactly what you were doing. For you, this was simply another outing for your special-operations group. Only this time you were using it against your own people. You were offered money and the possibility of advancement. It was a calculated risk. Do not come to me expecting sympathy. If you wish for a shoulder to cry on, try Jorges. He will understand, being a traitor himself."

Jorges stepped forward, anger pushing away the bitterness he had been feeling for himself. "I gave up everything to help you, Cruz. I believed you were right for Cuba, the man to step in when Castro fell. I was obviously wrong. You are nothing. Just another little man with big ideas. If you fail, then Cuba has had a lucky escape."

"We will see," Cruz said with a sneer.

"I won't run," Jorges said. "I am going back to Cuba. If I make it, I will go to Castro and tell him everything. What happens after that, I don't care. I may be lucky. Castro might forgive me."

"He might, but I won't!"

They all turned at the new voice.

A tall figure, wearing a combat harness and fisting a Beretta 93-R, stood in the far corner of the patio.

Mack Bolan.

The Executioner had come to serve justice on the unholy alliance.

There was nowhere left for them run.

Jorges had already turned to face the intruder, his body chilling as Bolan's words reached him.

"Who sent you?" he asked.

"You'll meet them soon," Bolan replied.

The Beretta moved slightly, and Jorges looked death in the face. In the final moment of his life, he knew who had sent this man.

He clawed for the pistol stuck in his waistband, and the Beretta rapped out a 3-round burst. Jorges twisted violently as the 9 mm parabellum rounds punched into his skull.

"Son of a bitch..." Lawrence Boyette said.

Lopez thrust his hand beneath his jacket, reaching for the automatic pistol holstered there. At the same time he stepped in front of Salvano Cruz, protecting him.

As Jorges dropped to the patio, McClain turned and took three steps to the low wall edging the area. He was halfway over when Bolan's 93-R chugged a second time. The trio of 9 mm slugs caught him between the shoulders, burning deep into his body. McClain's breath blew out in a ragged gust. He felt himself being lifted over the wall and thrown headlong into empty space. He slammed facedown on the ground below, the impact stunning him. He lay coughing blood, his life ebbing away.

Turning from the waist and dropping into a crouch, Bolan swept the Beretta in a short arc.

A single shot from the autopistol in Lopez's hand hit a flowerpot to the soldier's right, only inches from his body. The impact blew shards of the hardened clay and clods of earth into the air.

Lopez cursed and adjusted his aim.

Bolan triggered another burst, laying 9 mm slugs in the chest of the Cuban terrormonger. Lopez gave a grunt, stumbling back. He made a final attempt to fire, and Bolan responded with a second burst that tore into his throat and lower jaw. Spraying blood, Lopez fell back against Cruz, his free hand clawing at the man's spotless shirt.

Cruz pushed him aside in panic, staring around, seeking a way of escape from the tall specter of death. There was no way out, except past the man with the gun.

"It must not end this way," Cruz said. He stared at Bolan. "Whatever you are being paid, I will give you ten times over."

"Jesus, don't beg," Boyette said, anger in his voice. "At least die like a man."

Cruz glanced at Boyette. There was a look of contempt in the older man's eyes.

As Cruz launched himself at the Executioner in a desperate attempt to live, Bolan passed the Beretta to his left hand and drew the big .44 Magnum Desert Eagle. He simply lifted it and fired, triggering two fast shots into Cruz, the solid impact of the powerful slugs knocking the Cuban backward, tearing gaping, bloody holes in his chest. The man slammed to the patio floor, his lean body twisted in agony, then going slack almost immediately.

Boyette stood with his hands raised to chest height, palms out. There was a look of resignation in his slack features as he faced the Executioner.

"I won't insult you by asking for anything," he said. "You've come to end it. No mistake there. I admire your forthright approach, son. Just give an old man a final request. Only a question."

"Go ahead."

"Are you who I think you are?"

Bolan remained silent.

"A man in my position covers a lot of ground over the years. Hears things. Remembers them, too."

Still silence.

"Few years back now. I remember the news reports. A place in Texas had you on trial. Boy, you had the whole damn country listening in. Mack Bolan. The Executioner, they called you. Almost tagged you that time. But you got clean away and vanished. Always made me wonder what you were doing."

"You figure I'm him?"

"Damn right I do. Hell, boy, I can't see why you figure what I tried to do is any different to what you deal. What the hell do you think my motives were? I was doing it for America, to make her stand proud again. Taking on the bad guys because the chicken shits in Washington wouldn't. Don't you see that?"

"All I see is a bitter old man willing to turn against the American flag because he wants to get his own way, prepared to compromise the country and drag it into a war it doesn't want or need."

"Shit, Bolan, all I was doing was trying to kick-start the country, get it on its feet and show it the way."

"And to hell with how many innocent people get dragged along behind?"

Boyette sighed. "Doesn't matter now. Just tell me. Was I right about you being Bolan?"

"Yeah."

"Well, I don't aim to stand trial and have people make a mockery of my values." His speech ended, Boyette drew a Browning Hi-Power from an ankle holster and in one fluid movement raised the pistol to his temple and fired.

It was over.

## Stony Man Farm

HAL BROGNOLA SAT across the table from Bolan. He closed the file in front of him and pushed it aside.

"This one gets about as tangled as they come," he said. "It's going to take some sorting out."

"That's for others," Bolan said quietly. "We cut out the cancer. All they have to do is smooth over the cracks."

A smile drew Brognola's lips into a curve. "Striker, don't go into politics. Life just isn't that simple. Not on the Hill."

Bolan leaned back in his seat, picking up his mug of coffee and eyeing Brognola over the rim. "Not my line of work. Too much back-stabbing. I like my enemies out in the open."

"You made certain of that," the big Fed remarked. "The decisions about Boyette and McClain were taken right out from under the President's nose."

"What about the other names?"

"The ones Meecher's girlfriend gave us? They linked up with the stuff we got from Batiste's photographs. Arkadian and Barret. They're both under arrest. It looks like they were in for the duration. Barret commanded a carrier, equipped with enough aircraft and armament to take out Cuba's airfields and radar. The feedback we got from Benedict Base had target locations for the whole of Cuba's defenses. Barret had Air Force clout enough to order up mainland-based bombers and fighters."

Brognola produced a cigar, which he unwrapped and started to chew on ferociously. "Dammit, Striker, it scares the hell out of me when I think how close we came."

"But the guys handled it, despite the lack of Intel. Proves one thing, Hal. In the field they're the best."

"Thank God," Brognola breathed.

"How are the casualties?"

"Both recovering. Both grumbling about being confined. Pol should be out in a day or so. That crack on the head caught up with him after the

Benedict Base operation. Looks like Gary is going to be out of action for a few weeks. Lucky for him they had a damn good doctor at the naval base."

"I'll drop in and see them later."

"They'll appreciate that."

"Hal, what about our Cuban friends?"

"Manuel and Linda Ramos? They gave us a great deal of information. So did Antonio Batiste. Right now they're at a secure location. When they're ready, they can make their own choices whether to go back or stay here."

Bolan stood, ready to leave. "Bottom line," he said. "Castro?"

"I wondered when you were going to ask."

"So?"

"The President made a call to him. It seems that Castro had already been made aware of how Cruz had betrayed him. That the whole Puerto Rican incident had been engineered in order to topple him. And the main players already dealt with. The President said he was dispatching a confidential file to Castro with all the relevant information."

"How did Castro take that?"

"From what the President told me, Castro tried to bluff it out at first, then accepted that both sides had been placed in difficult positions. It would appear it was agreed that both sides would honor the outcome without further recriminations."

"That was big of Castro," Bolan said.

"Not the first time he's tried a ploy and come out clean," Brognola said. "I doubt it'll be his last. Castro will do some in-house cleaning of his own. People will disappear. No questions will be asked."

"Status quo," Bolan said.

"Only for now," Brognola replied. "Wait until the dust settles. Then we'll see."

Bolan didn't reply to that one. He knew Brognola was right.

But for now he was content to let today alone. He needed to see the people that mattered to him. It was enough to carry on with.

**When all is lost, there
is always the future**

# JAMES AXLER

## DEATH LANDS ®

### Skydark

It's now generations after the firestorm that nearly consumed the earth, and fear spreads like wildfire when an army of mutants goes on the rampage. Ryan Cawdor must unite the baronies to defeat a charismatic and powerful mutant lord, or all will perish.

In the Deathlands, the future is just beginning.

**A new warrior breed blazes
a trail to an uncertain future.**

# JAMES AXLER

## DEATH LANDS®

## Bitter Fruit

In the nuclear-storm devastated Deathlands a warrior survivalist
deals with the serpent in a remote Garden of Eden.

Nature rules in the Deathlands, but man still destroys.

---

**Don't miss out on the action in these titles featuring THE EXECUTIONER® and STONY MAN™!**

## The Red Dragon Trilogy

| #64210 | FIRE LASH | $3.75 U.S. | ☐ |
| | | $4.25 CAN. | ☐ |
| #64211 | STEEL CLAWS | $3.75 U.S. | ☐ |
| | | $4.25 CAN. | ☐ |
| #64212 | RIDE THE BEAST | $3.75 U.S. | ☐ |
| | | $4.25 CAN. | ☐ |

## Stony Man™

| #61903 | NUCLEAR NIGHTMARE | $4.99 U.S. | ☐ |
| | | $5.50 CAN. | ☐ |
| #61904 | TERMS OF SURVIVAL | $4.99 U.S. | ☐ |
| | | $5.50 CAN. | ☐ |
| #61905 | SATAN'S THRUST | $4.99 U.S. | ☐ |
| | | $5.50 CAN. | ☐ |
| #61906 | SUNFLASH | $5.50 U.S. | ☐ |
| | | $6.50 CAN. | ☐ |
| #61907 | THE PERISHING GAME | $5.50 U.S. | ☐ |
| | | $6.50 CAN. | ☐ |

**(limited quantities available on certain titles)**

| | | |
|---|---|---|
| **TOTAL AMOUNT** | $ | |
| **POSTAGE & HANDLING** | $ | |
| ($1.00 for one book, 50¢ for each additional) | | |
| **APPLICABLE TAXES*** | $ | _____ |
| **TOTAL PAYABLE** | $ | _____ |
| (check or money order—please do not send cash) | | |

To order, complete this form and send it, along with a check or money order for the total above, payable to Gold Eagle Books, to: **In the U.S.:** 3010 Walden Avenue, P.O. Box 9077, Buffalo, NY 14269-9077; **In Canada:** P.O. Box 636, Fort Erie, Ontario, L2A 5X3.

Name:_____

Address:_____ City:_____

State/Prov.:_____ Zip/Postal Code: _____

*New York residents remit applicable sales taxes.
 Canadian residents remit applicable GST and provincial taxes.

**Humanity is headed for the bottom of the food chain and Remo smells something fishy.**

# THE Destroyer

## #106 White Water

### Created by
### WARREN MURPHY
### and RICHARD SAPIR

Fish are mysteriously disappearing from the coastal waters of the United States, and it's anybody's guess what the problem is. Red tide, pollution? But soon angry fingers point north, to Canada, and the two countries trade threats and insults, all signs of neighborliness gone.

Look for it in February wherever Gold Eagle books are sold.